PRAISE FOR *IN THE DIST*

Finalist for the Pulitzer Prize
Finalist for the PEN/Faulkner Award for Fiction
Winner of the Whiting Award
Winner of the Saroyan International Prize for Writing
Winner of the Prix Page America
Winner of the VCU Cabell First Novelist Award
Winner of the New American Voices Award
A Publishers Weekly *Top 10 Book of the Year*
A Lit Hub *Top 20 Book of the Decade*

"A gorgeously written novel that charts one man's growth from boyhood to mythic status as he journeys between continents and the extremes of the human condition."

—PULITZER PRIZE FINALIST CITATION

"Strange and transporting . . . A weirdness to which a reader willingly submits, because of the vigorous beauty of [Diaz's] words . . . *In the Distance* [is] an uncanny achievement: an original Western. . . . An affecting oddness is the great virtue of *In the Distance*, along with its wrenching evocations of its main character's loneliness and grief. And its ability to create lustrous mindscapes from wide-open spaces, from voids that are never empty."

—THE NEW YORK TIMES

"Though painstaking in its historical detail (without succumbing to the obsessive's need to show off), *In the Distance* has the feel of a very contemporary story, capturing as it does the struggle and the will at the heart of migration, along with the cruelties that inevitably surround it."

—LIT HUB, "THE 20 BEST NOVELS OF THE DECADE"

"A brilliant debut . . . This suspenseful novel is a potent depiction of loneliness, a memorable immigration narrative, and a canny reinvention of the old-school Western."

—PUBLISHERS WEEKLY, TOP 10 BOOKS OF 2017

"An episodic picaresque adventure, but the transitions are so smooth—and the prose is as un-broken as the horizon—that the past fades away like a dream. It's as if Herman Melville had navigated the American West, instead of the ocean."

—THE NATION

"Hernan Diaz explores two kinds of wilderness: the immensely taxing newness of the American West and the still-forming interiority of Håkan, a Swedish immigrant desperate to find a way back home. It's the second that makes the first feel new. He does this in language that can be plainspoken and wildly, even cosmically, evocative. Håkan's epic journey reminds us how the self is often hammered into existence by pain and longing. In the end the reader understands the country's twin potential for horror and hope."

—WHITING AWARD CITATION

"A page-turning adventure story that's also a profound meditation on solitude and companionship, foreignness and home; a bildungsroman in the grand nineteenth-century tradition that is also a fierce critique of the romanticized myths of the settlement of the American West. . . . One of the many delights of *In the Distance*, which was a finalist for this year's Pulitzer Prize in the United States, is the way the writing oscillates between the austere and the lyrical, the realistic and the dreamlike. The result is a singular and deeply affecting portrait of one man's life in a rapidly changing world, unlike any old-school or revisionist Western I've experienced."

—CARYS DAVIES, *THE GUARDIAN*

"As Diaz, who delights in playful language, lists, and stream-of-consciousness prose, reconstructs [the Hawk's] adventures, he evokes the multicultural nature of westward expansion, in which immigrants did the bulk of the hard labor and suffered the gravest dangers. . . . An ambitious and thoroughly realized work of revisionist historical fiction."

—*KIRKUS REVIEWS*, "13 FICTION DEBUTS & BREAKTHROUGHS THAT LIVE UP TO THE HYPE"

"A brilliant and fresh take on the old-school Western . . . Diaz cleverly updates an old-fashioned yarn, and his novel is rife with exquisite moments. . . . The book contains some of the finest landscape writing around."

—*PUBLISHERS WEEKLY*, STARRED REVIEW

"*In the Distance* did something new, subverting the Western genre and, in so doing, raising important questions about cultural attitudes made evident by assumptions we make about art, particularly toward guns and immigrants. It's also just a great story."

—*THE PARIS REVIEW*, STAFF'S FAVORITE BOOKS OF 2017

"[*In the Distance*] excels in creating a sense of disorientating foreignness. The result is richly drawn and something like *Huckleberry Finn* written by Cormac McCarthy: an adventure story as well as a meditation on the meaning of home."

—*THE SUNDAY TIMES*

"Stitched through with humor, this often-unpredictable novel will keep readers running along with every step of Håkan's odd escapades."

—*BOOKLIST*

"Diaz is bound to join ranks with Borges on the literary scene with this mythical personality, still at large in our consciousness long after we've put down the book."

—*BookPage*

"While set in the American West, this is no conventional Western, as it turns the genre's stereotypes upside down, taking place on a frontier as much mythic as real with a main character traveling east. In this world, American individualism becomes the isolation that is its shadow and the dream of freedom devolves into anarchic violence."

—*Library Journal*, STARRED REVIEW

"A Western about the conquest of being."

—MACHA SÉRY, *Le Monde*

"For someone not afraid to read a difficult but extremely rewarding literary work."

—FEMINIST PRESS, "THE BEST BOOKS OF 2017"

"A road movie without roads or plot or dialogue, a coming-of-age novel where loneliness would be the main character. This first novel was a Pulitzer finalist; we understand why."

—*Le Figaro*

"[An] extraordinary epic tale of a lone man's journey into the heart of the American frontier . . . Ultimately it is not [the protagonist's] quest to be reunited with his brother that impels the novel: it is a good old-fashioned yearning of the human spirit, and a beautifully commodious meditation on its absolute unknowability."

—*Financial Times*

"One of the best twelve books of 2020."

—*El País*

"The Western is a decidedly relentless genre that lends itself to great romantic frescoes. Proof of this is this masterful text by Hernan Diaz. With its beautiful writing, it is a harsh reflection, in a wild setting, on solitude and foreignness."

—*Rolling Stone* (FRANCE)

"Finalist for the 2018 Pulitzer Prize, this strange, sinister tale bewitches, making the Wild West of America as intense and otherworldly as any dark myth."

—*The Irish Times*

"Hernan Diaz's strange, absorbing novel *In the Distance* . . . upends the romance and mythology of America's Western experience and rugged individualism. . . . Diaz's take on the immigrant's experience strikes me as a modern story. It resonated most strongly when my mind went to the millions of people on the move around the world today."

—*Star Tribune*

"Diaz creates a landscape as brutal and majestic as the man who crosses it."

—*La Repubblica*

"[*In the Distance*] is the story of a young Swedish emigrant to the United States, some time in the middle of the nineteenth century, which begins as a vividly observed and emotionally nuanced Western, and evolves into a kind of epic of loneliness, as our protagonist wanders farther and farther into the desolate landscapes of the West, and comes dizzyingly close to a psychic point of no return. It's a hero's journey, or possibly a monster's journey—the ending recalls the austere beauty of the last scenes of *Frankenstein*—and one of the great pleasures of Diaz's singular book is to observe the complicated ways in which the hero and the monster coexist."

—*BOMB Magazine*

"A sensitively written, often harrowing odyssey through the desert—which will have made ten more year-end lists since breakfast."

—*Kenyon Review*

"Hernan Diaz's first novel dares to revisit, with talent, the founding myths of the United States. . . . The philosophical depth of *In the Distance* is remarkable. . . . Hernan Diaz offers a reflection about human nature, its nomadic drive, colonization, immigration, civilization, and diversity. . . . *In the Distance* is a historical novel that depicts a crucial era that still sheds a light on our present."

—*La Libre* (Belgium)

"[*In the Distance*] is well on its way to becoming a classic. For one thing, it was a dark horse Pulitzer Prize finalist. For another, it's wonderful, an update and subversion of the American Western that sees a young Swedish immigrant encountering good and very very bad in this strange American land, while on the hunt for his brother."

—Emily Temple, *Lit Hub*

"A powerful and singular novel . . . in which Hernan Diaz succeeds in the most difficult thing—creating a character that lingers in your mind. . . . The book, indeed, is anomalous, a meteorite in American literature."

—*Il Giornale*

"Hernan Diaz presents the dry carcass of all the imaginary of the West [and] questions a whole century of cinematic idealizations."

—*El País* (Catalan edition)

ALSO BY HERNAN DIAZ

Trust

IN THE DISTANCE

HERNAN DIAZ

RIVERHEAD BOOKS

2024

RIVERHEAD BOOKS
An imprint of Penguin Random House LLC
penguinrandomhouse.com

First published in trade paperback in the United States by Coffee House Press,
Minneapolis, Minnesota, in 2017

Copyright © 2017 by Hernan Diaz
First Riverhead trade paperback edition published March 2024

Riverhead trade paperback ISBN: 9780593850565

Printed in the United States of America
1st Printing

Hernan Diaz is available for select speaking engagements. To inquire about a
possible appearance, please contact Penguin Random House Speakers Bureau at
speakers@penguinrandomhouse.com or visit prhspeakers.com.

To Anne and Elsa

IN THE DISTANCE

The hole, a broken star on the ice, was the only interruption on the white plain merging into the white sky. No wind, no life, no sound.

A pair of hands came out of the water and groped for the edges of the angular hole. It took the searching fingers some time to climb up the thick inner walls of the opening, which resembled the cliffs of a miniature cañon, and find their way to the surface. Having reached over the edge, they hooked into the snow and pulled. A head emerged. The swimmer opened his eyes and looked ahead at the even, horizonless expanse. His long white hair and beard were threaded with straw-tinted strands. Nothing in him revealed agitation. If he was out of breath, the vapor of his exhalations was invisible in the uncolored background. He rested his elbows and chest on the shallow snow and turned around.

About a dozen chafed, bearded men in furs and oilskins looked at him from the deck of a schooner caught in the ice a few hundred feet away. One of them yelled something that reached him as an indistinct murmur. Laughs. The swimmer blew off a drop hanging from the tip of his nose. Against the rich, detailed reality of that exhalation (and the snow crunching under his elbows and the water lapping on the edge of the hole), the faint sounds from the boat seemed to be leaking from a dream. Ignoring the muffled cries from the crew and still holding on to the edge, he turned from the ship and faced, once again, the white void. His hands were the only living things he could see.

He pulled himself out of the hole, picked up the hatchet he had used to break the ice, and paused, naked, squinting at the bright, sunless sky. He looked like an old, strong Christ.

After wiping his brow with the back of his hand, he bent over and got his rifle. Only then did his colossal proportions, which the blank vastness had concealed, become apparent. The rifle seemed no larger than a toy carbine in his hand, and although he was holding it by the muzzle, the butt did not touch the ground. With the rifle as a measure, the hatchet over his shoulder revealed itself to be a full-fledged ax. He was as large as he could possibly be while still remaining human.

The naked man stared at the footprints he had left on his way to his ice bath and then followed them back to the ship.

A week earlier, against the advice of most of his crew and some outspoken passengers, the young and inexperienced captain of the Impeccable had steered into a strait where drifting slabs of ice, cemented by a snowstorm followed by a severe cold spell, had trapped the ship. Since it was early April and the storm had merely interrupted the thaw that had set in a few weeks before, the worst consequences of the situation were a strict rationing of provisions, a bored and annoyed crew, a few disgruntled prospectors, a deeply worried officer from the San Francisco Cooling Company, and the shattering of Captain Whistler's reputation. If spring would release the ship, it would also jeopardize its mission—the schooner was to pick up salmon and furs from Alaska, and then, hired by the Cooling Company, ice for San Francisco, the Sandwich Islands, and perhaps even China and Japan. Aside from the crew, the majority of the men on board were prospectors who had paid for their passage with their labor, blasting and hammering off big blocks from glaciers that were then carted back to the ship and stored in its hay-covered hold, poorly insulated with hides and tarps. Sailing back south through warming waters would decrease the bulk of their cargo. Someone had pointed out how peculiar it was to find an ice ship iced in. No one had laughed, and it was not mentioned again.

The naked swimmer would have been even taller had he not been so bowlegged. Stepping only on the outer edges of his soles, as if walking on sharp stones, leaning forward and swinging his shoulders for balance, he slowly made his way to the ship, the rifle slung across his back and the ax in his left hand, and in three agile moves, climbed the hull, reached the railing, and jumped on board.

The men, now silent, pretended to look away, but could not help staring at him from the corners of their eyes. Although his blanket was where he had left it, a few steps away, he remained in his place, looking out beyond the bulwarks, above everyone's head, as if he were alone and the water on his body were not slowly freezing. He was the only white-haired man on the boat. Withered yet muscular, his frame had achieved a strangely robust emaciation. Finally, he wrapped himself in his homespun, which covered his head in a monkish way, walked to the hatch, and disappeared below deck.

"So you say that wet duck is the Hawk?" one of the prospectors said and then spat overboard and laughed.

If the first laugh, when the tall swimmer was still out on the ice, had been a collective roar, this time it was a meek rumble. Only a few men shyly chuckled along while the majority pretended not to have heard the prospector's remark or seen him spit.

"Come on, Munro," one of his companions pleaded, gently pulling him by the arm.

"Why, he even walks like a duck," Munro insisted, shaking his friend's hand off. "Quack, quack, yellow duck! Quack, quack, yellow duck!" he chanted, waddling around, imitating the swimmer's peculiar gait.

Now only two of his companions snickered under their breath. The rest kept as far from the joker as possible. A few prospectors gathered by the dying fire some men had tried to keep going in the stern—initially Captain Whistler had forbidden fire on board, but once it seemed they would be stranded in the ice for a while, the humiliated skipper had little authority to enforce the ban. The older men were members of a party returning to the mines they had been compelled to abandon in September, when dirt started to turn into stone. The youngest one, the only man on board without a beard, couldn't have been more than fifteen. He planned to join another group of prospectors hoping to strike it rich farther up north. Alaska was new, and the rumors wild.

From the opposite end of the ship came excited cries. Munro was now holding a scrawny man by the neck and a bottle with his free hand.

"Mr. Bartlett here has kindly offered a round for everyone on board," announced Munro. Bartlett grimaced in pain. "From his own cellar."

Munro took a swig, released his victim, and passed the bottle around.

"Is it true?" the boy asked, turning back to his companions. "The stories. What they say about the Hawk. Are they true?"

"Which ones?" one of the prospectors asked back. "The one where he clubbed those brethren to death? Or the one with the black bear in the Sierra?"

"You mean the lion," a toothless man interjected. "It was a lion. Killed it with his bare hands."

A few steps away, a man in a tattered double-breasted coat who had been eavesdropping on their conversation said, "He was a chief once. In the Nations. That's where he got his name."

Gradually, the conversation caught the attention of the men on deck until most of them were gathered around the original group in the stern. They all had a story to tell.

"He was offered his own territory by the Union, like a state, with his own laws and all. Just to keep him away."

"He walks funny because they branded his feet."

"He has an army of cliff dwellers in the cañon country waiting for his return."

"He was betrayed by his gang and killed them all."

The tales multiplied, and soon there were several overlapping conversations, their volume increasing together with the boldness and oddity of the deeds narrated.

"Lies!" yelled Munro, approaching the group. He was drunk. "All lies! Look at him! Didn't you see him? The old coward. I'll take a flock of hawks any day. Like pigeons, I'll take them! Bang, bang, bang!" He shot all over the sky with an invisible rifle. "Anytime. Give me this, this, this gang leader, this, this, this, this chief. Anytime! All lies."

The hatch leading below deck opened with a creak. Everyone fell silent. Laboriously, the swimmer issued from it and, like a lame colossus, took a few burdensome steps toward the crowd. He was now wearing rawhide leggings, a threadbare blouse, and several layers of indeterminate wool wraps, covered by a coat made from the skins of lynxes and coyotes, beavers and bears, caribou and snakes, foxes and prairie dogs, coatis and pumas, and other unknown beasts. Here and there dangled a snout, a paw, a tail. The hollow head of a large mountain lion hung like a hood on his back. The variety of animals that had gone into this coat, as well as the different stages of decrepitude of the hides, gave an idea both of how long the garment had been in the making and of how widely its wearer had traveled. He held a log split down the middle in each hand.

"Yes," he said, looking at no one in particular. "Most of those things are lies."

Everyone quickly stepped away from the invisible line drawn between Munro and the man in the fur coat. Munro's hand hovered over his holster. He stood there with the stunned solemnity common to very drunk and very frightened men.

The massive man sighed. He seemed immensely tired.

Munro did not move. The swimmer sighed once again and suddenly, before anyone could even blink, clapped one log flat against the other with a deafening thunder. Munro dropped to the floor and curled up into a ball; the rest of the men either ducked or raised their forearms to their foreheads. As the clap swelled, echoed, and dissolved into the plain, everyone started to look around. Munro was still on the floor. Cautiously, he raised his head and got to his feet. Flushing and unable to take his eyes off his own boots, he disappeared behind his companions and then into a hidden recess of the ship.

The Titan remained holding the logs up in the air, as if they were still reverberating, and then made his way through the parting crowd to the agonizing fire. From his coat, he produced some rope yarn and tarred canvas. He threw the kindling stuff on the embers, followed by one log, and used the other to stir the coals before adding it to the flames, sending a whirlwind of sparks into the darkening sky. When the glowing vortex died down, the man warmed his hands over the fire. He shut his eyes, slightly leaning into it. He looked younger in the copper-colored light and seemed to be smiling contently—but it could also just have been the grimace that intense heat puts on everyone's face. The men started to clear away from him with their usual combination of reverence and fear.

"Stay by the fire," he said softly.

It was the first time he had addressed them. The men faltered and stopped in their tracks, as if weighing the equally frightening options of complying with the request and disobeying it.

"Most of those things are lies," the man repeated. "Not all. Most. My name," he said and sat down on a barrel. He rested his elbows on his knees and his forehead on his palms, took a deep breath, and then sat up, tired but regal. The prospectors and sailors remained in their places, heads down. Rolling a keg, the boy emerged from behind the throng. He placed it daringly close to the man and took a seat. The tall man might have nodded approvingly, but it was a fleeting and almost imperceptible gesture that could also have been a random tilt of his head.

"Håkan," the man said, staring into the fire, pronouncing the first vowel as a u that immediately bled into an o, and then into an a, not in a succession, but in a warp or a bend, so that for a moment all three sounds were a single one. "Håkan Söderström. I never needed my last name. Never used it. And nobody could say my first name. I couldn't speak English when I got here. People asked me my name. I answered them, Håkan," he said, placing his palm on his chest. "They asked, Hawk can? Hawk can what? What is it you can? By the time I could speak and explain, I was the Hawk."

Håkan seemed to be talking to the fire but did not mind others listening. The young boy was the only one sitting. Some remained in their places; others had stolen away and scattered toward the bow or gone below deck. Eventually, about half a dozen men approached the fire with casks, crates, and bundles to sit on. Håkan fell silent. Someone took out a cake of tobacco and a penknife, meticulously cut a quid from it, and, after examining the plug as if it were a gem, took it to his mouth. Meanwhile, the listeners gathered around Håkan, sitting on the edges of their improvised seats, ready to leap out, should the enormous man's mood take a hostile turn. One of the prospectors produced sour bread and salmon; someone else had potatoes and fish oil. The food was passed around. Håkan declined. The men seemed to settle in as they ate. Nobody spoke. The sky remained indistinguishable from the ground, but both had now grayed. Finally, after rearranging the fire, Håkan started to talk. Making long pauses, and sometimes in an almost inaudible voice, he would keep speaking till sunrise, always addressing the fire, as if his words had to be burned as soon as they were uttered. Sometimes, however, he seemed to be talking to the boy.

I.

Håkan Söderström was born on a farm north of Lake Tystnaden, in Sweden. The exhausted land his family worked belonged to a wealthy man they had never met, although he regularly collected his harvest through his estate manager. With crops failing year after year, the landlord had tightened his fist, forcing the Söderströms to subsist on mushrooms and berries they foraged for in the woods, and eels and pikes they caught in the lake (where Håkan, encouraged by his father, acquired a taste for ice baths). Most families in the region led similar lives, and within a few years, as their neighbors abandoned their homes, heading for Stockholm or farther south, the Söderströms became increasingly isolated, until they lost all contact with people—except for the manager, who came a few times a year to collect his dues. The youngest and eldest sons fell ill and died, leaving only Håkan and his brother Linus, four years his senior.

They lived like castaways. Days passed without a word being uttered in the house. The boys spent as much time as they could out in the woods or in the abandoned farmhouses, where Linus told Håkan story after story—adventures he claimed to have lived, accounts of exploits supposedly heard firsthand from their heroic protagonists, and narratives of remote places he somehow seemed to know in detail. Given their seclusion—and the fact that they did not know how to read—the source of all these tales could only have been Linus's prodigious imagination. Yet, however outlandish the stories, Håkan never doubted his brother's words. Perhaps because Linus always defended him unconditionally and never hesitated to take the blame and the blows for any

of his brother's small misdoings, Håkan trusted him without reserva-
tion. It is true that he most likely would have died without Linus, who
always made sure he had enough to eat, managed to keep the house
warm while their parents were away, and distracted him with stories
when food and fuel were scarce.

Everything changed when the mare became pregnant. During one of
his brief visits, the manager told Erik, Håkan's father, to make sure
everything went well—they had already lost too many horses to the
famine, and his master would welcome an addition to his dwindling
stable. Time went on, and the mare got abnormally big. Erik was not
surprised when she gave birth to twins. Perhaps for the first time in
his life, he decided to lie. Together with the boys, he cleared a spot in
the woods and built a hidden pen, to which he took one of the foals
as soon as it was weaned. A few weeks later, the manager came and
claimed its brother. Erik kept his colt hidden, making sure it grew
strong and healthy. When the time came, he sold it to a miller in a distant town where nobody knew him. The evening of his return, Erik
told his sons they were leaving for America in two days. The money
from the colt was enough for only two fares. And anyway, he was not
going to flee like a criminal. Their mother said nothing.

Håkan and Linus, who had never even seen a picture of a city,
hurried down to Gothenburg, hoping to spend a day or two there, but
they barely made it in time to get on their ship to Portsmouth. Once on
board, they divided up their money, in case something happened to one
of them. During this leg of the trip, Linus told Håkan everything about
the wonders that awaited them in America. They spoke no English,
so the name of the city they were headed for was an abstract talisman to
them: "Nujårk."

They arrived in Portsmouth much later than expected, and everyone was in a great hurry to get on the rowboats that took them to shore.

As soon as Håkan and Linus set foot on the wharf, they were sucked in by the current of people bustling up and down the main road. They walked side by side, almost jogging. Now and then, Linus turned to his brother to teach him something about the oddities around them. Both of them were trying to take it all in as they looked for their next ship, which was to leave that very afternoon. Merchants, incense, tattoos, wagons, fiddlers, steeples, sailors, sledgehammers, flags, steam, beggars, turbans, goats, mandolin, cranes, jugglers, baskets, sailmakers, billboards, harlots, smokestacks, whistles, organ, weavers, hookahs, peddlers, peppers, puppets, fistfight, cripples, feathers, conjuror, monkeys, soldiers, chestnuts, silk, dancers, cockatoo, preachers, hams, auctions, accordionist, dice, acrobats, belfries, carpets, fruit, clotheslines. Håkan looked to his right, and his brother was gone.

They had just passed a group of Chinese seamen having lunch, and Linus had told his brother some facts about their country and its traditions. They had kept walking, gaping and wide-eyed, looking at the scenes around them, and then Håkan had turned to Linus, but he was no longer there. He looked around, backtracked, walked from the curb to the wall, ran forward, and then back to their landing place. Their rowboat was gone. He returned to the spot where they had lost each other. He got on a crate, short-breathed and trembling, screamed his brother's name, and looked down at the torrent of people. A salty fizz on his tongue quickly became a numbing tingle that spread over his entire body. Barely able to steady his quaking knees, he rushed to the nearest pier and asked some sailors in a dinghy for Nujårk. The sailors did not understand. After many attempts, he tried "Amerika." They got that immediately but shook their heads. Håkan went pier by pier asking for Amerika. Finally, after several failures, someone said "America" back to him and pointed to a rowboat, and then to a ship anchored about three cable lengths off the shore. Håkan looked into the boat. Linus was not there. Perhaps he had already boarded the ship. A sailor offered Håkan his hand, and he got on.

As soon as they got to the ship, someone demanded and took his money and then showed him to a dark corner below deck where, among berths and chests and bundles and barrels, under swinging lanterns hanging from beams and ringbolts, loud clusters of emigrants tried to settle in and claim some small space of the cabbage- and stable-smelling steerage as their own for the long trip. He looked for Linus among the silhouettes distorted by the quivering light, making his way through screaming and sleeping babies, laughing and haggard women, and sturdy and weeping men. With increasing despair, he rushed back on deck, through waving crowds and busy sailors. The ship was clearing of visitors. The gangplank was removed. He shouted his brother's name. The anchor was lifted; the ship moved; the crowds cheered.

Eileen Brennan found him starved and feverish a few days after they had left, and she and her husband, James, a coal miner, cared for him as if he were one of their own children, gently forcing him to eat and nursing him back to health. He refused to speak.

After some time, Håkan finally left the steerage cabin but shied away from all company, spending his days scanning the horizon.

Although they had left England in the spring, and summer should now have settled in, it was getting colder every day. Weeks went by, and Håkan still refused to speak. Around the time Eileen gave him a shapeless cape she had sewn out of rags, they spotted land.

They steered into unusually brown waters and anchored in front of a pale, low city. Håkan looked at the faded pink and ochre buildings, searching in vain for the landmarks Linus had described to him. Rowboats packed with crates shuttled back and forth between the ship and the clay-colored shore. Nobody disembarked. Increasingly anxious,

Håkan asked an idle sailor if that was America. Those were the first words he uttered since shouting his brother's name in Portsmouth. The sailor said yes, that was America. Holding back his tears, Håkan asked if they were in New York. The sailor looked at Håkan's lips as he produced, again, that glob of molten sounds, "Nujårk?" While Håkan's frustration mounted, a smile on the seaman's face widened until it became a peal of laughter.

"New York? No! Not New York," the sailor said. "Buenos Aires." He laughed again, hitting his knee with one hand and shaking Håkan's shoulder with the other.

That evening, they sailed on.

Over dinner, Håkan tried to find out from the Irish couple where they were and how long it would take for them to get to New York. It took them a while to understand each other, but in the end, there was no room for doubt. Through signs and with the aid of a small piece of lead with which Eileen drew a rough map of the world, Håkan understood that they were an eternity away from New York—and getting farther from it every instant. He saw they were sailing to the end of the world, to get around Cape Horn, and then head up north. That was the first time he heard the word "California."

After they had braved the wild waters of Cape Horn, the weather got milder, and the passengers grew eager. Plans were made, prospects were discussed, partnerships and parties were created. Once he started to pay attention to the conversations, Håkan realized that most of the passengers discussed only one subject—gold.

They finally cast anchor in what seemed to be, strangely, a busy ghost harbor: it was full of half-sunken ships looted and abandoned by crews that had deserted for the goldfields. But the derelict vessels had been occupied by squatters and even converted to floating taverns and general stores out of which traders sold their overpriced goods to newly arrived prospectors. Skiffs, barges, and rafts went back and forth between these improvised establishments, ferrying customers and merchandise. Closer to the shore, several of the larger ships slowly foundered as their decaying frames were forced into the most whimsical positions by the tides. Intentionally or not, a few boats had run aground in the shallow waters and become lodgings and shops with scaffoldings, lean-tos, and even proper buildings attached to them, thus reaching dry land and extending into the city. Beyond the masts, there were large tan-colored tents pitched between smoke-grimed wooden houses—the city had either just sprung up or just partially collapsed.

It had been months since they had set sail, but when they docked in San Francisco, Håkan had aged years—the lanky boy had become a tall youth with a rugged face, weathered by the sun and the briny wind, and furrowed by a permanent squint full of both doubt and determination. He had studied the map Eileen, the Irishwoman, had traced in lead for him. Although it implied traversing a whole continent, he concluded that the quickest way to reunite with his brother would be by land.

2.

The Brennans insisted that Håkan join their prospecting expedition. He was going inland anyway, and they needed help carrying their equipment. They also hoped he would stay on and mine with them for a while—he would need money to get to New York, and they could use another man to stake their claim once they found gold. Their chances were good, they said, since James was a coal miner and understood rocks. Håkan agreed. Even if eager to set out as soon as possible, he understood he could not cross the continent without horses and provisions. There was no doubt in his mind that his brother had made it to New York—Linus was much too smart to get lost. And although they had never planned for a situation like this, New York was the only place where they could meet, simply because it was the only place in America they both were able to name. All Håkan had to do was get there. Then, Linus would find him.

As soon as they landed, the Brennans realized that their life savings were worthless. A harness in California was the price of a horse in Ireland; a loaf of bread that of a bushel of wheat. After selling all their possessions back home, they barely had enough for two old burros, a wheelbarrow, some basic supplies, and a flintlock musket. Ill-equipped and bitter, James led his family inland shortly after they had disembarked.

The little party would not have made it very far without Håkan, since one of the donkeys soon bloated up and died, after which he did most of the lugging. He even devised a yoke of sorts—made of leather, rope, and wood—so he could more easily pull the wheelbarrow uphill.

The children took turns riding in it. Several times a day, James would stop, read the dirt, and set off on his own, following a sign visible only to him. He would then pick at a rock or pan some mud, study the results while mumbling to himself, and then signal everyone to move on.

America did not make a deep impression on Håkan. Having heard so many of Linus's tales, he had come to expect a dreamlike, outlandish world. Even if he was unable to name the trees, did not recognize the songs of the birds, and found the dirt on barren stretches surprisingly red and blue, everything (plants, animals, rocks) came together in a reality that, although unfamiliar, belonged, at least, to the realm of the possible.

They moved in silence through the interminable sagebrush, whose monotony was interrupted, now and then, by small packs of dogs and busy, terrified rodents. James failed to shoot jackrabbits but seldom missed a sage hen. The children buzzed around the wheelbarrow and the burro, hunting for glittery pebbles they submitted for their father's consideration. They collected wood along the way for their cooking fire, by which Eileen nursed Håkan's hands and shoulders, severely blistered by the wheelbarrow's handles and the harness, and read from the Bible to the family before sleep. It was a tedious journey that tested their patience more than their courage.

After crossing a forest of giant trees (the only landscape bearing some relation to Linus's outrageous American vignettes), they found a hirsute, laconic trapper wrapped in a greased hunting frock, and, a few days later, their first mining camps. They walked by modest settlements, clusters of precarious tarp shelters and malformed log cabins with burlap roofing, guarded by hostile prospectors who never invited them to sit by the fire or share a cup of water. The small things they asked for (food for the children, a nail for the wheelbarrow) were offered to them at extravagant prices and could be paid for only in gold.

Håkan barely understood scattered fragments of these exchanges—occasional words and, at best, the general intention suggested by the surrounding circumstances. To him, English was still a mudslide of runny, slushy sounds that did not exist in his mother tongue—r, th, sh, and some particularly gelatinous vowels. Frawder thur prueless rare shur per thurst. Mirtler freckling thow. Gold freys yawder far cration. Crewl fry rackler friend thur. No shemling keal rearand for fear under shall an frick. Folger rich shermane furl hearst when pearsh thurlow larshes your morse claws. Clushes ream glown roven thurm shalter shirt. Earen railing hole shawn churl neaven warver this merle at molten rate. Clewd other joshter thuck croshing licks lurd and press rilough lard. Hinder plural shud regrout crool ashter grein. Rashen thist loger an fash remur thow rackling potion weer shust roomer gold loth an shermour fleesh. Raw war sheldens fractur shell crawls an row per sher. At first, the Brennans (especially Eileen) made an effort to keep Håkan informed of their plans, but eventually they gave up on him. Håkan followed them without attempting any questions. They were, for the most part, heading east, and that was enough for him.

Wanting to stay clear of the other diggers, James refused to follow the faint trail over the mountains. They tried to find their way through valleys and over low hills, but the wheelbarrow was too cumbersome for the terrain. They got into a country where there was no grass and water was scarce. The skin on Håkan's hands and shoulders (where he fitted the leather harness to pull the cart) was, for the most part, gone, and the exposed flesh glistened, pale pink, under the viscous honey-colored varnish of incipient infection. During a steep descent, the compresses in which Eileen had wrapped Håkan's hands slipped off, and the rough handles burned his blistered palms, tore off his scabs, and pierced his raw flesh with dozens of splinters, forcing him to let go. The wheelbarrow raced downhill with increasing speed, first rolling, then

tumbling and flipping on itself, and finally turning somersaults and pir-
ouetting with surprising grace until it smashed against a boulder, shattering beyond repair. Håkan lay on the rocks, almost unconscious from
the pain, unassisted by the Brennans, who, mesmerized by the catastro-
phe, stared at the path made by their belongings strewn down the hill.
Eventually, James came out of his stupor, rushed over to Håkan, and
started kicking him in the gut, yelling—a wordless scream, a deep howl.
Somehow, Eileen managed to contain her husband, and he collapsed on
the dirt, weeping and drooling.

"It is not your fault," she kept telling Håkan over and over again as
she picked him up and inspected his hands. "It is not your fault."

They collected their things, camped by a nearby stream, tried to
sleep by a feeble fire, and put off the discussion about their prospects
until the following morning.

Apparently, there was a town a few days away, but they did not
want to leave their effects behind. Håkan could not be sent for help,
and James seemed to refuse to leave him with his wife, children, and
property. The kind Irishman who had boarded in Portsmouth was
vanishing—since they had docked in San Francisco, he had darkened
with disappointment and was quickly being reduced to an angry and
distrustful shadow of his old self.

Deep in thought, James wandered down to the stream with his pan,
more out of habit than with a clear design, and submerged it absent-
mindedly in the water while murmuring to himself. When the pan
came out, he stared into it, transfixed, as if he were looking into a mirror without recognizing the face that was supposed to be his. Then, for
the second time in two days, he wept.

That was the first gold Håkan ever saw, and he found the minute
nuggets disappointingly pale. He thought quartz and even the mica scales
on any ordinary rock were more impressive than those opaque, spongy

crumbs. James, however, had no doubt. To make sure, he placed the pale yellow pea on a boulder and hammered it with a stone. It was soft and did not break. It was, beyond question, gold.

Tracing a line from the spot of his finding to the mountain, James started working with his pick on a flaky hillside off the riverbank. His family looked on. After a while, he stopped, spat on the rock, and rubbed it with his fingertips. Suddenly pale, panting and stumbling stiffly like a flightless bird, he went to his children, dragged them to the hillside, and seemed to explain to them what he had just found. With eyes shut, he pointed first to the sky, then to the ground, and finally to his heart, on which he tapped while repeating the same phrase over and over again. The only word Håkan understood was "father." The children were frightened by James's rapture, and Eileen finally had to step in when he grabbed the youngest one by the shoulders and delivered a possessed soliloquy whose ardor brought the boy to tears. James did not notice the effect his state had on his family. He never interrupted his vehement address to the rocks, the plains, and the heavens.

The following weeks resembled, in many ways, Håkan's life back in Sweden. He was mostly in charge of gathering and catching their food, for which he went on long excursions with the children, just as he used to do with his brother. It was plain James did not want him around the mine. He trusted Håkan only with menial, brawny tasks that kept him far from the actual extraction—moving boulders, shoveling dirt, and, eventually, digging a canal from the creek to the mine. Meanwhile, James worked alone with pick, chisel, and hammer, crawling into his holes and hunching over pebbles, which he spat on and rubbed against his shirt. He dug from dawn until well into the night, when his eyes got dry and bloodshot from laboring by the weak light of two flat-wick lamps. When the work of the day was done, he disappeared into the darkness, presumably to hide his gold, and then returned to camp to eat and then collapse by the fire.

Their living conditions deteriorated rapidly. Absorbed by work, James had never taken the time to build a proper shelter for his family—Håkan had tried to erect a precarious hut, but it was only good for the children to play in. Exposed to the elements, their clothes started to degrade, and under the tatters, their red skin bubbled with blisters. Eileen and the children, who were very fair, even developed white reptilian scabs on their lips, nostrils, and earlobes. Since James did not want to attract attention to his quarry by firing his musket, they could only supplement their dwindling provisions with small game—mostly sage hens, which, they soon discovered, were so unfamiliar with humans that the children could simply walk up to them and smash their heads with a club. Eileen cooked the birds in a thick bittersweet sauce made of a kind of huckleberry Håkan never found again in his travels. The children ran around with Håkan all day, dodging their mother's halfhearted attempts at schooling them. James, working uninterruptedly and hardly feeding himself, was becoming a gaunt specter, his eyes—at once distracted and focused, as if seeing the world through a dirty window and inspecting the grimy glass rather than looking through it—bulging in his haggard, angular visage. He lost at least three teeth in a matter of days.

Each night, he scurried away to his secret spot. Once, Håkan happened to be nearby and saw him remove a slab of stone that covered a hole and put the yields of the day inside. James stayed there for a while, crouching, peering into the pit. Then, he replaced the slab, covered it with sand and pebbles, pulled his trousers down, and defecated on it.

The trip to the nearby town could no longer be postponed. They needed basic supplies and, above all, tools to expand the operation— James was mostly concerned with getting lamps that would allow him to keep working through the night. After complex, secretive preparations, he decided it was time to leave. He gave Eileen and the children meticulous instructions that always came back to the same basic

command—no fire. He packed the burro lightly and ordered Håkan to
follow him.

Their journey was uneventful. They did not cross paths with anyone on the trail. Silence was seldom broken. The weak burro dragged
his feet behind them. James rarely took his hand off his chest, against
which, under his ragged blouse and fastened to a string tied around his
neck, hung a little canvas sack. On the third morning, they arrived.

The town was only one block long—an inn, a general store, and
about half a dozen houses with their blinds shut. The rough, skewed
constructions seemed to have been erected that morning (the smell of
sawdust, tar, and paint still lingered in the air) with the sole purpose of
being taken down at dusk. New but precarious, as if decrepitude had
been built into them, the houses seemed eager to become ruins. The
street had only one side—the plains began where the thresholds ended.

Tethered to posts along the street, a few emaciated horses twitched
under swarms of flies. Meanwhile, the men leaning against walls and door-
sills seemed immune to the insects, which were probably repelled by
the strong tobacco all of them were smoking. Like James and Håkan,
the bystanders were also in rags, and under the wide-brimmed hats,
their weather-beaten faces were bark and leather abstractions. Still, the
onlookers retained faint traces of civilization that life in the wilderness
had completely erased from the newcomers' countenance.

James and Håkan walked under the silent scrutiny of the smokers,
and that same silence followed them into the general store. The shopkeeper interrupted his conversation with an old man in a faded dragoon uniform. James nodded at them. They nodded back. He walked
around picking up kerosene lamps, tools, sacks of flour and sugar, blankets, charqui, powder, and other supplies he requested from behind the
counter with laconic grunts. When James was done, the shopkeeper
went through the items, pointing at each one softly with his index and

middle fingers, as if blessing them, and then presented his customer with a bill jotted down in lead. James barely looked at it. He walked to the back of the store, hid poorly behind some casks, turned his back to everyone, hunched over as if doing something obscene, looked behind his shoulder a couple of times, and then returned to the counter, on which he put down a few gold nuggets.

The shopkeeper must have had a well-trained eye, because he neither haggled nor examined the gold but swiftly put it away, thanking his customer. A boy around Håkan's age but half his size started dragging their things outside. The dragoon slipped out without saying good-bye.

While the burro was being loaded, James and Håkan went to the inn. Heads turned, several pairs of eyes looked up from froth-crowned mugs of ale, a dealing hand froze in midair, a light lingered too long in front of a cigar. The Irishman and the Swede also paused. Everyone stared at them. With the newcomers' first step toward the counter, the patrons came back to life.

The bartender nodded as they approached, and by the time they had reached the bar, two ales and a plate of dried meat were waiting for them. Håkan had never had liquor before and found the warm, bitter brew repulsive. He was too shy to ask for water and made the mistake of eating some of the charqui. James took a pull at his ale. Nobody looked at them, yet they were unmistakably the center of everyone's attention. James patted his chest, trying to conceal the pouch that kept showing through the tears in his tattered shirt. The bartender kept his mug full.

A door opened on the second floor, across the room from the counter. Only James's and Håkan's heads turned around and up. Fleetingly, Håkan saw a tall woman in a purple dress with silver scales. Above the corset, her bosom also sparkled with glitter. Her hair poured in waves of thick amber over her shoulders, and her lips were a red that was almost black. She tilted her head, looked at Håkan with an intensity that somehow came from her lips rather than her eyes, and vanished behind the doorjamb. As soon as she was gone, the shabby dragoon came out of the room, followed by a tidy fat man. The rotund fop hobbled down the staircase, following the dragoon, and headed straight for the two strangers. Despite being soaked in sweat, he was the only clean man in the place, the only one who was not caked with grime. An orange-blossom aura surrounded him. He wiped his brow with an immaculate handkerchief and folded it fastidiously before returning it to his chest pocket, after which he flattened his hair to one side with his hands and cleared his throat. All this was done with the utmost gravity. Then, as if a spring activating a hidden mechanism had been set off, he smiled, took a small bow, and, quite loudly, addressed the strangers. It seemed to be a formal speech. While talking, the fat man described an arc with his upturned hand, encompassing the whole bar or maybe even the entire desert beyond it, and then stretched out his other arm, as if accepting or offering an enormous gift, shut his eyes beatifically, and said, in conclusion, after a solemn pause, "Welcome to Clangston."

James nodded without ever looking up.

With the loud and affected friendliness that Håkan would later find in preachers and peddlers, the perfumed man asked a very long question and then widened his frame by fitting his thumbs into his waist-coat's armholes.

James grunted a brief response with a dryness that was either defiant or fearful.

The fat man behind the imperturbable smile nodded compassionately, as if dealing with a sick infant or a harmless idiot.

The dragoon, who had slithered to the darkest corner of the room, pressed down on one of his nostrils and cleanly shot out a plug of snot from the other. The fat man sighed, signaled in his direction with a soft hand, and apologized in a tired, somewhat maternal tone. Then he turned back to James and asked him another question, always smiling, always polite. James stared into his mug of ale. The fat man repeated the question. Only a few of the gamblers and drinkers could keep pretending to go on with their conversations. James swept the filthy counter with the edge of his hand a few times. With affected patience, the man pointed at the general store where they had bought their supplies and explained something in a condescending tone. Once done, he shrugged and looked at James, who, after a long pause, said, "No." The fat man shrugged again, folding his lower lip over the upper one, and then clapped his hands against each of his thighs, emitting a potent surge of orange blossom, and shook his head, as if resigned to accept some outlandish fancy as an irrefutable truth. He stood in silence for a while, assuming a contemplative air, and then arched his eyebrows and nodded, pretending that James's answer had finally sunk in and that he was genuinely at peace with it. The dragoon blew the other side of his nose. Nothing came out.

The bartender was about to top James off once more when the boy from the store peered into the bar and announced that the burro was ready. James produced a few coins from his trouser pocket, but the fat man, feigning grave offense, cried, "No, no, no, no, no, no," and interposed his starched sleeve between James and the bartender. He made a brief ceremonial statement, took a deep breath, and finally repeated, as his fingers crawled between the buttons of his waistcoat, "Welcome to Clangston."

Håkan and James went outside and inspected the ropes and straps fastening their goods to the burro. James started out slowly, without turning back, but Håkan lingered by the tethering posts. He looked around to make sure nobody was watching and then drank avidly from the trough by the fly-ridden horses, cupping the brown water in his hands. The men inside the bar laughed. Håkan turned around, startled and ashamed, but the door was just a black hole in the sunstruck façade. Then he remembered the woman and looked up. The window glistened impenetrably. He caught up with James, and together they made their way down the single street of Clangston.

They traveled back as fast as they could, stopping after dark and leaving again before daybreak. For long stretches, James had Håkan follow him backwards, sweeping the ground with a stick to dim and confuse their tracks. From time to time, James would suddenly stop and stare into the void, his index finger crossed over his lips and his hollowed hand to his ear, listening for pursuers. They ate charqui and biscuits (both of which James had to soak in water), and they never built a fire.

Although they had spent only a brief time in Clangston—and even if its short, shabby street could hardly be called a town, and its few filthy inhabitants had almost been eroded by the elements—Håkan was still astounded by the sight of James's rustic mine by the stream. The camp was just a heap of branches, some planks salvaged from the wrecked wheelbarrow, and garbage that could only have any value in that extreme isolation—all scattered around an ash pit. Eileen and the children, jumping for joy at their arrival, were shredded, swollen, pustulated creatures. Not just their clothes, but their very skin was ragged, and it hung off their flesh like worn gauze. They were gaunt yet bloated by the sun, and their small gray-blue eyes set in this contradictory frame shone with a feverish spark, all of which made their delight a frightening thing to witness. Håkan thought of the condemned forest creatures in his brother's tales.

Rather than improving their situation, the new supplies only deepened the void that separated the Brennans from the world. After setting up his new lamps, James was able to work around the clock. He became a demented skeleton, hammering away day and night, pausing only to sneak into the dark to hide his daily findings. Eileen and the children remained as lively as ever, but they were careful to stay clear of James, whose mistrustful fits of anger were becoming impossible to contain. When he was not digging the canal or lugging boulders, Håkan spent his time with the children, who also taught him some English—although the words he learned did not go far beyond their immediate environment and the modest demands of their games.

A few days passed. How many, Håkan could not tell—he was not even sure how long it had been since he had landed in San Francisco. In Sweden, back at the farm, they had neither calendars nor clocks, but work had both divided the days into regular segments and grouped them into constant cycles. At the mine, however, time seemed either to be frozen or to slip away—it was hard to tell which. James worked ceaselessly. Eileen invented chores for herself. The children roamed around. Each day resembled the last, and their lives remained unchanged until a speck of dust appeared on the horizon.

By the time Eileen alerted James, the speck had grown into an ochre smudge hovering on the skyline, and while James fetched his musket, it became a cloud shrouding six riders and a carriage. James looked at the approaching convoy while loading shot into the muzzle and fumbling with his powder flask. His wife asked him nervous questions. He ignored her and readied the flintlock. The children stood by their father, gaping at the horizon. Always staring ahead, James pushed them away from him. The horses approached at a slow walk. Gradually, the crunch of pebbles being ground under the steel tires, the chirp of springs and poorly oiled axles, and a jingle of bits, buckles, and spurs became audible. All eyes were on the carriage. It was a purple coach covered with shiny spots that reflected the midday sun. The four plumed horses driving it seemed to feel insulted by the heat. Nervous tassels dangled from the sides of the roof. As the carriage got closer, the shiny spots revealed themselves to be gilded volutes, flowers, laces, and wreaths that framed vividly painted scenes of men suffering the cruelest torments and of women forced in unspeakable ways, of villages in flames and heaps of rotting animals, of whippings and impalements, of beheadings and burning stakes, of pillories and gibbets, of agonized faces and spilling entrails. At the front of the contingent, Håkan saw the tidy fat man and the dragoon.

They stopped at a prudent distance but close enough to address James without screaming. Nobody dismounted. They all had guns at their belts, and one of them brought two burros in tow. James stood still. The children hugged Eileen's waist. The door and windows of the carriage remained shut. The heavy black velvet curtains swelled and collapsed, slowly, regularly, as if the coach were breathing.

The fat man patted his shiny gray lovingly and leaned over her neck, whispering something to her. He cleared his throat; the hidden spring activated his mechanical smile; and—after raising his hat to Eileen, who shyly curtsied back—he started delivering one of his long, smug speeches. He addressed Eileen for the most part, but he also had sanctimonious smiles and admonitory finger-wags for the children. Suddenly, he pretended to have discovered the mine and the canal and to be deeply impressed by them. A spirited oration ensued. Once done with his condescending panegyric, he feigned having a hard time extinguishing his enthusiasm, but when he had finally composed himself, he arranged his paper cuffs, rubbed his hands, and moved on to serious business. After a lengthy preamble, he laboriously detached his pommel bag and held it wide open. It was brimful with paper money. He made a dramatic pause, stressed by an emphatic adjustment of his waistcoat. James kept his eyes on him. The fat man wiped his brow with his handkerchief and uttered a few words with sacerdotal pomp. Then he motioned to the mine once again. This time, he seemed to refer to it with some disdain, and to conclude, he pointed again to the money with great satisfaction.

"No," said James with determination.

The fat man sighed stoically, like a doctor dealing with a super-stitious patient who refuses to accept what is best for him, then turned to Eileen and, resuming his patronizing tone, in a singsong manner, said something about the children.

James, trembling with fury, started screaming. He ordered his fam-ily to step back, and yelled at the convoy, brandishing his old musket. The fat man pretended to be scandalized by this outburst. James turned his wrath to the carriage. Håkan did not understand the words, but it was clear enough that James was asking who was in there and demand-ing he come out. Eventually, he gestured too vehemently toward the coach, which prompted the men to draw their guns. James paled. The dragoon rode in a slow curve, putting Eileen and the children directly in his line of fire. The fat man intervened with conciliatory phlegm, as if he were the only adult present. Again, he spoke with resignation about James's children. This time, he was brief. A moment of silence ensued, after which the fat man snapped his fingers, and the burros were led to James's side. The fat man tossed James the bag of money and explained that the burros were for Eileen and the children.

"Go," he concluded with surprising curtness. "Now."

James attempted a response.

"Now," he repeated.

James looked at the mine with quivering lips. He had the expression of an obsequious dog ordered to follow a command it did not under-stand. He glanced toward the secret hole where he hid his gold. Eileen put the children on one of the burros and went to get her stunned hus-band. Håkan started to pack whatever supplies were at hand.

"No. Not you," said the dragoon, nodding in Håkan's direction. His voice was surprisingly pleasant, "What's your name?"

"Håkan."

"What?"

"Håkan."

"Hawk?"

"Håkan."

"Hawk can what?"

"Håkan."

"Can what?"

Håkan remained silent.

"Get in the coach, Hawk."

Håkan looked around, confused. The Brennans were too busy and dumbstruck to mind him. He walked hesitantly to the coach and opened the door. Blinded by the midday sun, the interior seemed to him as vast as the night sky. It smelled of incense and burned sugar. He sat awkwardly on a mangy velvet seat, and, as shadows became visible in the dark, across from him, gradually, the tenuous yet gleaming outline of the woman with thick lips and amber hair took shape.

"You don't speak English. You don't understand. That's fine." The words spilled out of her full lips. That was all the woman said during their four-day journey to Clangston.

Håkan ate and slept with the men but rode with the woman in her dark, suffocating carriage. Toward the middle of the trip, she requested, both through gestures and by firmly guiding his body, that he recline his head on her lap. She caressed his hair and stroked the back of his neck for the next two days.

3.

Two men escorted Håkan through the empty barroom and led him upstairs to a room adjacent to the woman's. A bed, a barred window, a bucket of pine-smelling water. He was ordered to strip and wash. When his efforts were deemed too timid, one of the men grabbed a brush and scrubbed him down vigorously. The other man left the room, returned with two bundles, and threw a new suit of clothes on the bed and some rags to wipe up the soapy water on the floor. Then they both left, bolting the door behind them.

Håkan got into bed, his skin burning from the cold, the bristles, and the pine oil. Underneath the pain, he sensed the vastness of the plains weighing on his heart. But further down, in a part of himself new to him, he was, to his surprise, content and at peace. It felt good to be in bed, hurting, alone. And it felt good to slide into the deepest sadness he had experienced since losing Linus. His grief was indistinguishable from his ease—both had the same texture and temperature. Comfort and gloom, he realized, came from the combination of cold water and the scent of pine resin. He had not felt that tingling since his ice baths in the lake back in Sweden. And that smell. Håkan and Linus, following their father's lead, would crack a hole open on a safe spot (the ice had to be thin enough for the ax but thick enough to bear them), plunge into the lead-colored water, stay afloat with calm semicircular kicks, holding their breath for as long as possible to keep buoyant, and then climb out of the hole, imitating their father's relaxed indifference to the cold and suppressing their impulse to run to the shore, whose knuckle-shaped pebbles forced them to proceed swinging their arms like wire walkers, until they reached the pine tree under which they found their clothes safe from the snow that was netted in the intricate, angular weave of perennial needles.

The coarse sheets rubbed pleasantly against his skin. He wondered whether his brother had also spent months without sleeping in a bed. He tried to conceive the distance separating him from New York, where he knew Linus was waiting for him, but could think only of that infinite extension in terms of time—the countless days, the many seasons it would take him to cross the continent. For the first time, Håkan was almost glad to have been forced to go on this journey: after his long trip and all the unimaginable adventures that lay ahead, he would arrive a grown man, and, for once, surprise his brother with tales of his own.

A clinking of glasses and cutlery came from below, together with the voices of three or four men talking calmly. Håkan got up and inspected his new clothes. Because he had worn mended hand-me-downs all his life (clothes received from Linus, who had inherited them from their father, who, in turn, had got them from some unknown source), he unfolded the crisp trousers and shirt with reverence. Despite its stiffness, the fabric was soft and downy. He put the collarless shirt to his nose. It had a scent he had never smelled before, a scent he could describe only as new. He got dressed. The navy trousers did not quite reach his ankles, and the white sleeves ended about two inches before his wrists, but otherwise the clothes fit him perfectly. In his new outfit, he felt, with an intensity that not even the perpetual plains had yet managed to convey, that he was in America.

He placed his hand on the window. The sun-blasted desert vibrated on the glass. More clatter came from below. It was getting crowded. Individual voices were no longer discernible in the constant masculine rumble punctuated now and again by a burst of laughter or a fist hitting a table. The sun was setting discreetly, and it was impossible to tell at what point its last dull echoes were replaced by the moon's insufficient efforts. Downstairs, two men seemed to be having a mock argument— the entire room cheered and booed in turns, and the debate ended in general laughter. Håkan went back to bed. Someone started playing an instrument he had never heard before—the tickling legs of a happy insect. The patrons stomped along, and had they not been all men, Håkan would have sworn he heard the shuffling feet of twirling couples. The shadows in his room slowly shifted with the moon. He dozed off.

A scream beneath his window woke him up. A drunkard was flogging his horse, and with every lash, the man gave a woeful cry, as if he, rather than the mare, were the one getting whipped. The horse, snorting briefly with each blow, shone with blood and was visibly in pain, but took the beating with poignant dignity. Finally, the man collapsed, sobbing, and his friends took him and the beast away.

Only a few people remained in the bar. They talked quietly and sporadically. Perhaps they were playing a game of cards. The moon had rolled over to the other side of Clangston's single street and was now out of sight. Håkan urinated soundlessly into the pail with the pine-scented water. Four or five men left, and with that, the muted conversation downstairs ceased. Someone started sweeping, and glasses were put away. Then, a man coughed, and that was the last sound to come up from the bar. Håkan sat quietly on the bed, afraid of the rustling sound of his new clothes.

Nothing interrupted the mineral silence of the desert. In its complete stillness, the world seemed solid, as if made of one single dry block.

The sound of footsteps came up the stairs and toward Håkan's room. He stood up, more out of politeness than fear. The door opened. He recognized two of the men from the convoy. They told him to follow them down the corridor, to the threshold of a dark room. The men showed Håkan in and gently shut the door behind him.

The drowsy smell of incense, wilted flowers, and bubbling sugar saturated the air. The thick-lipped woman sat by the window. She turned the knob of a faint lamp, and her face and the room lit up with a trembling glow. She wet her glossy lips, slowly rubbed them together, and rearranged herself on a small skirted chair. Her makeup was heavier than usual, and there was more glitter on her cheekbones and her bosom. Coiling around her smooth neck, her amber hair poured down her chest and pooled on the finely embroidered corset. Still looking at Håkan, she cocked her head, and her left eye disappeared under a wave of hair.

The room was beclouded with ornaments and heavy brocade drapes. Wherever he looked, Håkan saw an ivory statuette or an old bibelot, a fading Gobelin or some gewgaw. Gleams of gold and hints of crimson came trembling out of the darkness, blurred by waves of gauze and chintz. Layers of curtains, festoons, and fringes smothered every window. There were silver-framed mirrors, knickknacks, and gilded books with brass clasps on little marquetry tables with spindle legs, and porcelain figurines, music boxes, and bronze busts on marble consoles. Diptychs, cameos, enamel eggs encrusted with jewels, and all other sorts of baubles were on dim display behind the beveled glass of convoluted cabinets. A case with a greening saber, dusty epaulets, ribboned medals, wax-sealed letters, frayed aiguillettes, and an embossed snuffbox occupied a place of honor.

The woman shut her eyes and nodded softly but gravely, indicating that Håkan should approach. He stood in front of her, embarrassed by his visible erection. When he tried to cover his crotch, she gently took his hands in hers, which were gemmed, cold, and unused. From a little side table, she picked up a pair of cuffs and secured them to Håkan's sleeves with expert care, fastening them with gold cuff links studded

with rubies. Håkan looked down, red-faced, pretending to be immune
to the woman's touch. Once done, she proceeded with a starched collar.
She pointed to the floor while raising her chin. Håkan bent his knees.
She repeated the gesture. Håkan kneeled. Frowning and pursing her
lips, she secured the collar to the shirt. Her hands touched the back of
his neck, and he felt ashamed of his goose skin. He pulled back timidly, but she held his head firmly and close to her breast, looking over
his shoulder while working. After attaching the collar, she moved on to
a silk cravat. Håkan could hear her breathe while she tied it and then
pierced it through with a golden pin crowned with a red stone. She
pushed him back with gentle firmness, looked him over, and took a
velvet jacket from a valet stand. She bent over and fitted it on Håkan,
slowly, ceremoniously, paying attention to how his body gradually filled
the fabric. Once again, the sleeves were too short, but the chest and
shoulders fit perfectly. She touched his arms, his ribs, and his back, as
if confirming that the jacket was indeed full of him, and then stood up
straight. Håkan was still kneeling. She caressed his hair and pulled his
head toward her, indicating he should rest it on her stomach. Håkan's
arms hung along his body. She took a small step back, without letting go
of Håkan's head, thus forcing it to slide down to her lap. The wilted flowers, now laced with sweat, became more intense. They both remained
in that position for a long time, hearing and feeling each other breathe.
Håkan's face was wet from the moist heat of his exhalations caught in
the laces and the velvet. At last, she let him go. The room got colder.
His hair was glued to his forehead. She took his hands and, with her
chin, signaled him to get up. They walked to a divan on the periphery
of the circle lit by the lantern, and, with a gesture, she asked him to lie
down. She undid his trousers, gathered her dress around her waist, and
mounted him. The sun was coming out. Håkan felt that he was gliding
upward, into a new, lonelier region. The woman looked down at him,

and, as dawn penciled dusty traces of light across the room, she shut her eyes, smiled, and opened her lips, revealing black, gleaming, toothless gums, streaked with bulging veins of pus, and poured her breath, heavy with the scent of burned sugar, over him with a moan.

Most mornings, between daybreak and sunrise, Håkan was escorted back to his room after spending some time with the woman. Their encounters were always silent (she communicated her wishes through subtle yet assertive gestures or by bending and molding his body) and without fail revolved around clothes—she dressed, undressed, and dressed him again in uniforms, blouses, tailcoats, sashes, breeches, gloves, pantaloons, knickers, and waistcoats, and decked him with numerous accessories. These fittings took up most of their time. She took meticulous care in getting Håkan into the clothes, following each limb as it filled each hole and then, as she had done the first night, clutching the sleeves, feeling the chest, grasping the legs, and pressing the back, confirming that the fabric that had been spectrally limp moments ago was now firm with living flesh. She then arranged a long series of details—studs, pins, spats, rings, and some final element, a small relic handled with reverence, which invariably came from one of the glass cabinets. When she had finished, she stepped back and examined the results without ever looking at Håkan's face, after which she modeled him into some ordinary yet precise position (usually, she had him stand in the middle of the room, looking straight ahead with his chin parallel to the floor, feet shoulder-width apart, with his hands at a very particular distance from his thighs), which she asked him to hold for a long time, until she signaled him to kneel down and rest his head on her lap. They remained that way until dawn. She did not always take him to the divan afterwards, but generally demanded to be pleasured in one way or another before releasing him.

Back in his room, Håkan washed his face with the pine-oil water
left over from his nightly scrubbings, trying to wipe out the impression of
burned sugar. It was lodged underneath his forehead and eyes, smeared
on his palate, and coated on the walls of his throat. Had the smell merely
rubbed off the woman or were his own gums now rotting, shedding
their teeth, and emanating that putrid perfume? He tapped on his inci-
sors and tried to wiggle his molars to make sure they were firm. Had he
known the word for it, he would have asked for a mirror.

Håkan spent his days staring out at the desert, hoping Linus would
feel his gaze through the osseous void. He looked at the plain until it
became vertical, a surface to be climbed rather than traversed, and he
wondered what he would find on the other side if he made it all the
way up and straddled the sepia wall stretching into the drained, dim
sky. No matter how hard he scanned the horizon, all he could see were
rippling mirages and the phosphorescent specks his exhausted eyes
made pop in and out of the emptiness. He pictured himself out there,
running, insect-like, in the distance. Even if he ever managed to escape
and somehow outdistance his mounted pursuers, how would he make
it all by himself through that vast barren expanse? All he knew was that
New York lay east and that he, therefore, had to follow the sunrise. But
the journey without help or supplies seemed impossible. He had stopped
trying to push out the bars from his window frame a long time ago.

There were three books in his room. He knew one of them was the
Bible and had devoutly put it under his pillow. He had never had the
chance to inspect a book at his leisure before. Several times a day, he went
through the other two from beginning to end, studying the indecipher-
able characters. The crowded yet orderly signs brought him a sense of
calm after staring at the blank expanse of the desert. He would choose
a letter and, with his finger, map the patterns its recurrence created on
the page.

The room trembled with heat when smitten by the sun. Håkan often fainted and sometimes, without knowing how long he had been unconscious, was woken by a hand slapping his face. He was taken to the outhouse twice a day, shortly after his meals, which were given to him in his room. Before dusk, the bathwater and a fresh change of clothes were brought in. The first patrons usually arrived at the bar as he finished scrubbing. And most nights, after the last customer had left, a guard unbolted his door and led him to the woman. On occasion, with no regularity, he was left alone, and he eventually understood that he would not be taken to the woman's room if dawn came before his guard. These were the only events that vaguely organized his existence, which took place in an elastic present that kept on stretching without the slightest distortion and without ever promising to snap.

4.

Summer came to an end. The ragged blankets they gave him were insufficient, but he was used to being cold. The landscape remained impervious to the freezing temperatures. Nothing changed. Looking through the window, Håkan imagined that it was cold only in his room and that if he were to stick his hand out, he would find it to be blazing hot, just like the day he arrived.

It was getting harder to get into his clothes. His feet dangled over the edge of the bed. Some of his guards started to look at him with apprehension.

Linus was all Håkan could think of. At times, he imagined him prospering in undefined yet extravagant ways; he pictured him working various indeterminate jobs, resolved to succeed spectacularly and rise to a prominent position, not out of ambition or greed but only to be easier to find when his young brother came looking for him. His triumph would be a beacon. Håkan would arrive in New York, and the name of Linus Söderström would be on everyone's lips. Any stranger would be able to direct him to his door. At other times, Håkan's fantasies were more restrained, and he saw his brother toiling and struggling, roaming the hostile streets of that gigantic city (which he still envisaged through Linus's whimsical descriptions), and returning every single evening, after the work of the day was done, to the port to ask the newly arrived passengers and seamen for his brother. In either case, Håkan was convinced that Linus would not fail to find him.

The warm weather returned, and Håkan felt that he had gone back in time one year.

On the first truly hot morning of that new summer, shortly after sunrise, one of Håkan's keepers came into his room to deliver a mauve suit he recognized from a few weeks ago, a pair of exaggeratedly buckled shoes he was often asked to wear, and a short top hat that was new to him. It was the first time they brought him clothes in the daytime. He was told to get dressed at once. Håkan was surprised to find himself smoothing out his shirt, pulling down his jacket by the lapels, brushing his sleeves, and tending to other small details in the exact same way in which the woman would go through his outfit after dressing him up. The guard, who had been waiting impatiently, took him down to the barroom and then out through the back door. Half a dozen armed men on horses clustered behind the dragoon and the tidy fat man. Right next to them, in the only patch of shade, stood the carriage, harnessed to its plumed and arrogant horses. He was shown into the cab. It was like diving into a vat of black syrup. The woman ignored him as he sat across from her. The door was shut; darkness took over. The coach set off in an unknown direction, rocking on its squeaking belts and springs, its velvet curtains bulging out and curving in like membranes.

It was nearly impossible to breathe in the overused, viscous air. Soaked in sweat under his velvet coat, Håkan shivered from the heat. Even in the complete blackness of the cabin, he could feel the woman actively not looking at him. He fell asleep.

Silence woke him. They had come to a stop. The door opened, and when his eyes adjusted to the razor-edged light, he saw he was being asked to step out. They had been traveling for at least half a day, but were he to judge from the landscape, they had not moved an inch—the same unbroken expanse of level ground, the same oppressive monotony. The coachman had dismounted to water the horses, which were

foaming with heat. The rest of the men stood in line relieving themselves, except for the fat man, who leaned into the carriage, presumably
offering the woman his services. Without ever sitting down, the men
ate soda crackers and black pudding. The woman remained unseen.
With their mouths still full, the riders got back on their horses, and the
driver returned to his seat. Håkan got into the carriage, hoping they
were headed east. Nothing else mattered to him.

It got cooler. The sun was probably setting. Suddenly, branches
started rattling against the coach on either side. The unvarying steppe
seemed to have come to an end. After a long, tortuous ride through
uneven terrain, the coach finally stopped. Once again, Håkan was shown
out. This time, the woman alighted after him, pulling down a black veil
that covered her eyes and brushed her chin.

The pale evening sunshine came streaming through the conical sum-
mits of spruces and firs, was sifted by the feathery leaves of junipers and
the white-green boughs of aspens, and lastly settled, like mist, on fox-
tails, moss, and lichen. These were the first plants Håkan had seen in a
long time, aside from the ever-present sagebrush. In a clearing at the foot
of a knoll stood a small village of six or seven houses that were, each in its
own way, angular versions of the forest surrounding them—the sturdiest
building was a log cabin; there were some flimsy shacks with clay mortar between timbers; others, like cubic rafts, combined coarse irregular
planks with tarpaulin, joined with hemp rope. In the center of the ham-
let, there was a heap of saplings and branches curled with dry leaves. It
looked like a pile of dead twigs waiting to be burned, but it was propped
up by pillars and planks. Underneath this shaggy shelter, a group of children, sitting on stumps, held their slates and books while staring at the
newcomers. By the makeshift school, one woman had stopped churning
butter, while another wiped her hands down on her apron, having just
taken a Dutch oven off the fire, and yet a third, in the back, slowly and

mechanically went on dyeing her yarn. All three women had their eyes fixed on the recently arrived group. Despite its precariousness, it was, as far as Håkan could see, a harmonious and prosperous colony. The hides neatly hung to dry around the small tannery, the patterns taking shape on the weaving loom, the smoke welling softly through the leaves from a clay stack, the healthy white pigs in their pen, the burlap sacks brimming with grain—everything spoke of the industriousness and purposeful order-liness of the settlers. The women and children conveyed a sense of calm decency. Håkan felt ashamed to be in his costume.

As usual, the fat man started to activate his inner mechanism (shirt bosom flattened, necktie straightened, hair swept, throat cleared), which resulted in a smile that could only emphasize the impatience it was supposed to conceal, and then proceeded with one of his pompous addresses. He had uttered only a few solemn words, which he seemed to pin into the air with his pinched thumb and forefinger, when the woman took a step forward and raised her palm without looking at him.

"Caleb," she ordered through her barely open mouth, glaring at the colonists from behind her veil.

Håkan realized that he had not heard birds in an eternity. Now, in the tense expectation that followed the woman's single word, the grove swelled with unknown songs.

The dyer stepped forward, drying her blue hands, and said that Caleb was not there.

"Well, I'll call him," the veiled woman responded, and then whis-pered something to the fat man, who, in turn, gave the dragoon a brief command.

The old soldier went behind the carriage and quickly reappeared with a wobbly leather sack. The lady pointed to the wood and tarp dwelling farthest from the school. The dragoon sauntered over to it, opened the bladder, poured its liquid all around the walls, lit a match, and threw it into one of the puddles he had just made. The air rippled, the ripples became blue waves, and the blue waves yellow flames. The women rushed to the children and removed them from the shrubby school building, which was now nothing but a pile of kindling the smallest spark from the neighboring fire would set alight. Following the veiled woman's directions, the dragoon led the settlers and their children to the log cabin, safely removed from the fire, and placed two sentinels at its door. The burning house, in the meantime, had become a smooth fiery sphere that seemed to spin in place, the crest of the flames curling over to reignite themselves from underneath in an ever-intensifying circle. Håkan looked around for water, walking back and forth with desperate eyes. He found a tub with clothes soaking in it, and started dragging it toward the fire, but was soon apprehended by one of the men, who brought him back to the woman. She smiled, as if touched by Håkan's despair and goodwill, and briefly caressed his cheek. The flames whistled in the air. Above the ball of fire, like a black mirror image of the blaze, spun a ball of smoke. A gust of wind turned the whistling into a roar and dissipated the smoke, which first coiled up and then was drawn out and twisted into ringlets, whirling in a succession of grim convolutions that finally dissolved in the darkening sky.

A group of riders smudged by the conflagration came galloping down the hill. The leader wrenched at his bridle and, with a furious pull, stopped the horse next to the woman. Both animal and man were breathing hard. With his index finger, he told his friends to spread out. Then he looked down at the woman.

"You came," she said with a smile, not unlike the one she had just given Håkan.

Caleb, who seemed to find each breath suffocating, curtly asked for the children. The woman nodded toward the log cabin. He dismounted and walked in short circles, his face disfigured by desperate thoughts, and then stopped to look at the woman with ireful eyes. Something like tenderness filtered through the woman's veil. After screwing up his mouth and his brow, Caleb managed to calm down and, in a tone that demanded all his might to pass as sensible and reasonable, started to explain himself. The woman remained silent, still wearing a gentle smile that did not correspond to Caleb's earnest plea, as if she were looking beyond him, into another time. With a supreme effort, Caleb changed his tone. In an attempt to match his cadence to her mien, he now seemed to be recalling pleasant memories or invoking a promising future. He even managed a smile himself. Then, out of nowhere, she produced a small ornate pocket pistol. Caleb stared at it with the expression of someone being shown a gigantic insect. He looked back up at the veil, and the woman shot him between the eyes. His head flung back, followed by the rest of his body.

From the log cabin came the screams of women and children. Caleb's men were quickly rounded up and disarmed by the dragoon and his party. Håkan could not look away from the shot man's face, already bleached by death. He was stunned by the suddenness with which the man had ceased to be. It had been like magic.

Next to Håkan, the veiled woman inhaled in short segments, as if able to take in only broken pieces of air. Her eyes were on the man she had destroyed. She took her trembling hand to her mouth, and soon her barely audible moans swelled into a wail, a long ululation interrupted only to breathe in those small, hacked-up portions of air that grief somehow managed to reconstitute within her so that they could then come out as a sustained utterance of despair. The children kept crying. The women kept screaming. They started to bang on the cabin door. After many unrelenting howls, the veiled woman's bawls became as broken as her breathing, so that each brief inhalation was followed by an equally brief cry. Finally, as if she had made a sudden

decision, she stopped. Still staring down at Caleb, the lady muttered a
few words to one of her men, who, in turn, signaled to two of his companions. Together, they carried the body away. Lowering her head and
burying the heels of her hands in her eye sockets, the woman regained
command of herself and the situation. She stood erect, taller than
before, and slowly rolled up the veil, fastened it to her hat, and opened
her eyes, inset with glowing rage.

"You!" she roared, pointing at the fat man. "Come here."

He approached and stood penitently a few steps away from her.
They faced each other in silence. The men who had taken the body
away were now piling up dry branches they had taken from the school's
roof. Unable to endure the silence, the fat man swept his hair, cleared
his throat, and started talking. With his first word, however, the woman
launched the most vicious assault Håkan had ever witnessed.

Gelatinous words of hate came spewing out of her rotten mouth.
Every care she had ever shown in hiding her gums disappeared. In
fact, the decayed black hole seemed to be displayed as the ultimate
insult and threat, more intimidating than the rumbling, slobbering,
malformed words that gushed out of it along with her dribble and
spit. She still held her gun and used it to point repeatedly at the corpse
and then at the fat man. The connection between both was the main
argument of her diatribe. She appeared oblivious to the fact that her
pointer was a gun, which made the weapon even more frightening—
as if once she remembered its true nature she would be obliged
to give it its true function. The women in the cabin had redoubled
their screaming and were ramming the door with some massive object.
The children kept crying. Taking a step forward and leaning over so
that her face was inches away from the fat man's, the woman covered
him in insults and saliva. Håkan understood the last words, under-
lined by the gun pointing at the rotund waistcoated chest—"your

fault." She ground her black gums at him and hissed. Rather than from the woman, the hiss seemed to come from the pair of shiny slugs in her mouth.

Caleb's body was placed on the disorderly pyre next to the ruins of the schoolhouse.

"Gently," the woman commanded and rolled down her veil. With a nod, she ordered the sentries to make the women stop their pounding. The children kept crying. With another movement of her chin, she directed the dragoon to light the pyre. All the men, the invaders and their victims, took off their hats. The fire caught on quickly. The crackling branches yielded, and the body suddenly sank into the flames, emitting a smell of sinister roast.

After a moment of silence, the woman, back in full possession of her usual coldness, turned once more to the fat man and gave him a brief order. With quivering lips, he attempted a response but, before a word was uttered, decided it was best to comply. He took off his coat, waistcoat, bosom plate, and shirt. All eyes were on him. The evening was bleeding out—some stars shone in the darkening blue. His shoes came off, and after them, his trousers. The woman showed her impatience. Hesitantly, he removed his underpants, and stood there, blubbery and milky, with only socks and garters on. Someone laughed. A barely visible gesture of the woman, and his clothes were thrown into the embers of the burning house. Another brief nod, and all the women and children were set free. Their husbands ran to meet them, but one woman remained alone with her child. She looked around, confused, and then, seeing the pyre, fell to her knees and wept. The veiled lady examined her with interest. All the Clangston men got on their horses, except for the fat man, who was left standing among the homesteaders while the dragoon led his gray away. The fat man's mouth bubbled with stuttering pleas. Håkan was told to follow the woman into the carriage.

They drove away with the convoy. The abandoned man's moans and sobs were soon inaudible.

The second night after their return, Håkan was summoned to the woman's room. She was sitting at a small table and pointed to the chair across from her. Håkan sat down, taking notice of a leather tool wrap. As she sometimes was inclined to do, she ignored him in a careful, studied way, looking impatient, as if his presence—which she had requested—were delaying someone else's arrival. Finally, after a long time, she untied the wrap and unrolled it on the table. It was divided into sections that contained scissors, tongs, flasks, clippers, small daggers, and other instruments Håkan did not recognize. The lady tapped her finger on the table. Håkan was confused. Irritated, she indicated that he was to place his hands on the table, which he did. She held down his left wrist against the table with a force that Håkan's docility did not merit, took the largest clippers out of their compartment, and applied them to his fingernails. His hands had softened during his captivity, but his nails remained as rough and angular as ever—some grew until they broke, others he trimmed with his teeth or the knife he was given for his meals. Once she was done with the clipping, the woman moved on to filing, and then to cutting and pushing up the cuticles with a flat, sharp-edged tool, which made Håkan wince and instinctively withdraw his hand. The woman clasped his wrist tighter and stabbed his hand with the tool. She did not break the skin, but her firmness made it plain that she would drive the whole instrument through his hand and pin it to the table if he offered further resistance. After the procedure was completed, she retouched and buffed his nails. From one of the flasks, she poured a greasy rose-scented unguent and rubbed it into Håkan's hands. Perhaps because the woman had never caressed his hands like that before, Håkan decided to speak to her for the very first time.

"I must go," he said.

She looked up from his hands with an expression that briefly acknowledged an event that, although extraordinary, did not surprise her. She smiled at him.

"I can't," she responded. "I can't let you go."

She put out the light and did something she had never done before—she kneeled down and placed her head on Håkan's lap, just like Håkan used to be asked to kneel and put his head on her lap, and then took one of his limp groomed hands and stroked her own hair with it, as if playing with a rag doll.

After those events, life sank back into its unaltered routine. Although unused to violence, Håkan started to hatch an escape plan that vaguely involved the blunt knife he used for his meals. He was encouraged by his own size, which an increasing number of his captors found intimidating. However, what happened a few nights later relieved Håkan from carrying out his half-formed designs.

It was during the quiet hour between the time the bar closed and the two guards came to take him to the woman that Håkan heard someone stealthily sliding the bolt of his door open. The cautious slowness of this operation was unusual, and even more remarkable was the fact that he had not heard, as he always did, two pairs of boots coming up the stairs. A whistling wind had whirled around Clangston all night, and now windows and walls rattled and creaked under its growing force. The bolt slowed down as it slid through the guides, clearly to prevent the click at the end of its trajectory. Silence. Håkan picked up a book, just to hold something solid.

The door opened, and there, badly scarred, scabbed, and still naked, stood the fat man. His left cheekbone had swollen to meet his inflamed eyebrow, submerging his eye in a mass of lustrous purple flesh. There were cuts, burns, and bruises all over his body, and his feet had been disfigured by the hot desert. He looked at Håkan with his single eye and smiled, revealing some newly broken teeth. Then, crossing his index finger over his cracked lips while softly shushing Håkan, he stood away from the door and pointed to the staircase.

"Go," he whispered.

Håkan looked at him, perplexed.

"Go," he repeated. "Go now. Go. Fast."

Håkan picked up his shoes, walked by the fat man, whose malicious grin had become a grotesque silent laugh, tiptoed down the stairs, across the bar, and through the door, briefly paused on the threshold, and, as soon as he set foot on the plain, ran.

5.

Dawn was an intuition, certain yet unseen, and Håkan ran toward it, his eyes fixed on the distant spot that, he was sure, would soon redden, showing him the straight line to his brother. The intense wind on his back was a good omen—an encouraging hand pushing him forward while also sweeping away his tracks.

With some luck, the lady would not call him that night, and his absence would not be noticed until late morning, perhaps even noon. But if the woman wanted him, the guards would soon be walking up the stairs to his room. After running for some time, Håkan looked back toward the town's feeble lights. To his surprise, Clangston had vanished. Now that it hit his face, Håkan realized that the wind was thick with sand. His vision first was limited to the nocturnal aura of boulders and shrubs perceivable only when these obstacles were a step or two away, and then it was reduced to nothing. Soon night itself was obliterated by the whirlpool of sand. The gale's force, together with the stinging dust it carried, made up a new element—something that, despite its roughness and dryness, was closer to water than earth and air. Håkan had to turn around to breathe. He kept on running, feeling safely cloaked by the storm, which plugged his ears with a roar. His face was shut up like a fist—even if the pelleted wind had allowed it, there was no point in keeping his eyes open in that double darkness. He took a tumble at almost every other step but welcomed each fall for the respite lying flat on the ground gave him from the harsh stream. Nevertheless, he would quickly get back on his feet and resume his blind race, panting through tight lips.

Morning never broke. The blackness just paled.

Tossed around by the wind, Håkan could no longer tell in which direction he was going. He only hoped that he had not been taken, in an extended circle, back to Clangston.

When the storm blew over, the midday sun shone right over Håkan's head, revealing a landscape identical to the stretch of desert he saw from his window. He kept his uncertain course. Soon, however, his own shadow started to stretch out ahead of him, and he made sure he was at all times preceded by it, firmly convinced that it would guide him east. No tracker could ever have been able to trace his steps after such a storm, but Håkan was still worried. How much progress had he made? Was he far enough from Clangston? Had he actually been walking away from his captors rather than back to them? He had no doubt that the woman would want him back at all costs and that she had sent out search parties as soon as the weather had allowed for it. How such parties were organized, he did not know, but even if she spread them out in every direction, he thought, the woman did not have enough men to comb the plains very closely. Håkan's hope was that his trajectory would fall in between two of the lines radiating from the hitching posts outside the bar. He wondered, however, how far he could make it without food or water. And should he be fortunate enough to find help, would not every settlement within walking distance from Clangston be under the woman's influence?

Night fell, and, unable to navigate in the dark, Håkan stopped. He lay down on the warm dirt, between two clusters of sagebrush. The desert, so quiet during the day, was now bustling with activity—animals growling, mating, eating, being eaten. Håkan was not concerned. Rodents, reptiles, and little dogs were all he had ever seen, and he assumed his size would intimidate these small creatures. He had not yet learned to fear snakes.

He woke up well before dawn, partly out of habit (he always got up in the middle of the night to be ready for his guards), but also because the ground had grown cold. The night sky had shifted. Håkan marveled at the concerted movement of the stars and now regretted never having asked his brother how those bright dots could travel across the heavens together, always keeping the distance that initially separated them from one another. Linus had explained other natural wonders to him. For instance, the fact that each day had its own sun. During its journey across the sky, the bright disc would burn out, sink, and melt on the horizon, pouring down the precipice at the end of the earth like wax. And just like a candle maker, god would reuse these drippings to make a new sun overnight. Night went on for as long as it took god to work on the new sun, which he lit up and released each morning. But the stars and their motion, Linus had neglected to explain.

As soon as the foregleam on the horizon showed him which way to go, he set out east.

Had it not been for the sage hens, he would have died in a matter of days. He clubbed or stoned a couple of birds every day and drank their blood. It made him even thirstier but kept him strong. The first few times, he would vomit as soon as he squeezed the warm syrup into his mouth, but he soon learned to control this reflex. His chin and his clothes, torn to rags during the sandstorm, were caked with coagulated spillovers. Eventually, Håkan realized that the brown hardened blood offered protection from the sun, so he started smearing it generously all over his arms, chest, neck, and face. The coating would become a runny paste with his sweat, and he constantly had to stop to daub and rearrange it. After a few days, however, there were enough layers, sunbaked and stuccoed by dust, to render further applications almost unnecessary. By then, Håkan had stopped smelling the mad odor of his coating.

He lost track of time. It seemed to him that he had been walking for an eternity when a feverish delirium took hold of him. He started to hear voices and hooves and had to turn around continually to swat away the imagined sounds. Sometimes he threw himself on the ground, believing the jingle of the black carriage was catching up with him. To mute these hallucinations, he started talking, mostly to Linus. Sometimes Linus responded. Gradually, Håkan's body became light and rigid. Walking was a constant miracle. The most difficult moment of each step was to put his foot down. He would look at his shoe, amazed to see it in mid-air, wondering how it got there and how it would ever manage to land. Then, on his next step, he would stare at his other foot with the same bewilderment. And each time his surprise was fresh, as if he were notic-ing his suspended foot for the first time. His gait became an odd bal-ancing act as he raised each foot increasingly higher and left it hanging for a short while, his arms slightly outstretched for balance, like a stiff monster. The sameness of the landscape only added to his derangement. He came in and out of consciousness and found himself in midstride, marching through a country identical to the one he had seen before his spell. It was impossible to know how much time had elapsed or how far he had traveled. Sometimes he thought he was walking in place.

One morning, he woke up shivering, embracing a dead dog. He could not remember catching it or breaking its neck.

He walked on until suddenly his foot failed to meet the ground—it kept dropping, slowly falling into a void revealed by the parting sand. The last thing he remembered was looking up at the sole that had remained on the surface.

6.

A fire warming his face. The stars above the flames. A damp cloth on his lips. The sun filtering through a canvas canopy. The taste of fever. The dreaded sound of carriage wheels. Dusk or dawn. Voices. The taste of honey. Eyeglasses. Linus smiling. A horse neighing. The smell of porridge and coffee. His own screams. Hemp rope around wrists and ankles. Linus telling him a story. A fire warming his face. Voices. A damp cloth on his lips. Eyeglasses. The taste of honey.

The blisters on his wrists woke him up, but he welcomed the burn underneath the rope as confirmation that he and his body finally had reconciled. He was lying in a covered wagon. The sun was a hot stain on the canvas. Two silhouettes on the driver's bench talked quietly. He could hear other men on horses or burros. Time flowed gently through him. Shapes, sounds, and textures were once again part of one single reality.

As his perception of his surroundings grew clearer, he realized that from the sides of the wagon came a wide array of chimes—quick shrill dings and slow low dongs. He turned his head and saw a crowded collection of jars hanging from every bow and bolt and fastened to the bed of the wagon. In them, suspended in a yellowish liquid, were lizards, rats, squirrels, cats, spiders, foxes, serpents, and other creatures. Some jars contained unborn animals, viscera, limbs, and heads. He stirred around but found himself firmly tied down. Lifting his head, he saw cages flapping with birds, baskets crawling with insects, and wicker trunks hissing with snakes. Håkan thought that his recovery had been just an illusion and that he was still trapped in one of his nightmares. He made a sound,

and one of the men in the front turned around. Håkan could see only
his outline against the bright sky. The man climbed into the back of the
wagon and leaned over Håkan, revealing the bespectacled face that had
hovered over him during his agony. The man smiled.

"You're back," he said.

Håkan tried to sit up, but the ropes kept him in place.

"I'm sorry," said the man, horrified as he remembered Håkan's bonds,
and swiftly proceeded to untie him.

As he worked on the ropes, he talked to Håkan in a soothing voice.
By the time he was done with his ankles, his speech had come to an
end. Håkan stared at him. The man asked him something. Silence. He
removed his eyeglasses and tried another question. Håkan looked into
his gray eyes—they were curious without being intrusive, compassion-
ate without being condescending. Like all the men Håkan had seen in
the wilderness, he was unshaven, but unlike all of them, he truly owned
the rich reddish beard that reached the uppermost button of his shirt.
His hair had been flattened and tamed by dirt, and it was easy to imagine that it would look wilder the cleaner it got. Here was a man who had
been improved by the plains. As his right eye started wandering off to
the side, he put his glasses back on.

"You don't speak English?" he asked.

"Little," replied Håkan.

The man asked him another question. It did not sound like English.
He tried again in a guttural, harsh language. Håkan looked at him, rub-
bing his raw wrists. Noticing this, the man apologized once more, and
mimicked a delirious, raving man, kicking and punching the air. Then
he pointed at Håkan, and touched his biceps with his index finger and
quickly withdrew it, as if the muscle had been white-hot.

"You're strong!" he said and laughed.

They were silent as the man inspected Håkan's blisters.

"Where are you from?" he asked, rearranging his glasses when he was done.

"Sweden."

The man was both gratified and troubled by this answer. Gently tugging at his beard and squinting, he seemed to reach into the past and finally said something that sounded very much like "My name is John Lorimer" in Swedish. Håkan lit up. Lorimer kept talking in a dream version of Håkan's mother tongue—a language that was and was not Swedish, that sometimes felt familiar but suddenly would become incomprehensible, that evoked home only to stress, immediately after, how remote its foreign sounds were. Later, Lorimer would explain that it was a hodgepodge of German and Dutch, patched together with English.

Laboriously, in his jargon of mixed tongues, Lorimer told Håkan that when they had spotted him walking stiffly with his arms outstretched in front of him, some thought that he was a devil. As they approached him and saw his dark skin, others believed he was an Indian. When they were close enough to see he was in fact covered in congealed blood, they were all convinced he was fatally wounded. Håkan did not seem to notice them, but when they tried to take him to the wagon to dress his injuries, he fought them fiercely, and it took three men to subdue him. Soon after that, he passed out and remained in a delirious haze for six days. Lorimer was baffled to find no significant wounds after washing away the dried blood.

In Swedish marbled with English, Håkan gave a brief account of his ordeals, beginning with the Clangston woman. He urged Lorimer to stay clear of her men and told him he would leave the convoy in the morning since his pursuers would not hesitate to murder everyone in the party to get him. All he needed was food and water, if they could spare some. Lorimer would have none of it. Håkan was to remain under their protection until he had fully recovered and they had made sure that he was

beyond the woman's reach. Their convoy was headed east anyway, at
least until reaching its next destination, the great salt lake of Saladillo,
after which Lorimer and his men would turn south. In the meantime,
Lorimer said, he would like to be taught Swedish. And anyway, he could
also use an assistant. Håkan looked at the heads in the jars with apparent concern. Lorimer laughed, told him not to be alarmed, and explained
that he had caught those creatures for the benefit of man.

With proper food, drink, and rest, Håkan made a swift recovery.
Soon he was out with the five men who assisted Lorimer in his labors
and escorted him for his protection. Håkan, in charge of their spare
horses and burros, rode next to Lorimer as often as he could, and they
taught each other their languages. Lorimer was a fast learner, and his
eagerness to practice Swedish came to the detriment of Håkan's English,
but after such a long time sloshing in the slippery sludge of foreign
sounds, Håkan welcomed the solid words of his mother tongue.

Originally from southeast Scotland, John Lorimer had traveled to
America with his family at the age of eleven. They had started a farm
in an unsettled land whose name Håkan could not retain. Mr. Lorimer
had wanted John to become a priest and had him recite entire books
of the Bible from memory and prepare biographical sermons delivered
to the family each Sunday before dawn. John, however, with his love
for all things wild, preferred terrestrial to celestial matters. By a nearby
thicket, the boy built a city of sorts (moats, ramparts, streets, stalls)
and populated it with beetles, frogs, and lizards. He covered the walled
structure every night and inspected it every morning, noting which creatures had vanished or died, which had moved from one compartment to
another, which were feared by the rest, and so on. He worked tirelessly
on his animal city until his father, suspicious of his long absences, followed him to the thicket, kicked the structure to the ground, stamped
its inhabitants flat, and flogged him with a switch made from the branch

of a nearby tree. It had been—he remembered the branch clearly and later had learned its name—a yellow birch. While whipping him, his father whispered that he would have to atone for his blasphemous pride—God, and God only, had the power to create a world; any other attempt was an arrogant insult to His work. A few years later, John was sent to university to study theology, but soon botany and zoology (disciplines Håkan at first found perplexing) had displaced divinity. Shortly after that, he traveled to Holland to study under one of Europe's leading botanists, Carl Ludwig Blume, whose name Håkan would afterwards remember for being amusingly fitting for his profession. Having completed his studies, John returned to America with the intention of classifying species of the West that had never been described or named. In the course of his investigations, Lorimer had come up with a theory for which, he said, his father, now long dead, would not have lashed him with a birch switch but crushed him under an oak beam. Over the course of the following weeks, in broken Swedish, and with the aid of his jarred specimens, new animals they caught along the way, and the ancient creatures they found crystallized in rocks, Lorimer would patiently explain his theory to his mostly silent but quite obviously baffled new friend. His purpose, he said, was to go back in time and reveal the origin of man.

Knowing that Håkan had experience with sage hens, Lorimer suggested that they start there. He asked Håkan to kill one by wringing its neck and then pluck it. Sitting in the narrow shade of the wagon, Lorimer cut into the bird with a small sharp blade and opened it up like a book. He showed Håkan its broken spine and explained why that fracture (as opposed to a broken wing or leg) had killed it. They followed the vertebral column to the brain, and Lorimer told his friend that everything we do, from breathing to walking, from thinking to defecating, is governed by that cord traversing our upper body. Håkan was profoundly moved by this revelation and knew it to be true without requiring further evidence. He could not say why this utterly new notion regarding organs he had never heard named before was correct, but watching the open bird on the ground, he had no doubt. Håkan had never looked at an animal that way. It seemed so clean, simple, and orderly—that he happened to be ignorant of the laws governing that harmonious system was unimportant. He asked Lorimer a great number of questions and ventured a few theories of his own.

Lorimer appreciated his new student's ardor, and as the weeks passed, that first lesson was followed by many others—conducted mostly in English since neither of them knew the anatomical terms in Swedish. Soon Håkan was dissecting all sorts of animals by himself. In his big, gentle hands, the scalpel delicately skated over the small gem-like organs, and he proved to have an extremely refined intuition concerning their function and their relationship to one another. After a few dozen dissections, he had mastered the rudiments of the mechanics of bones, understood the workings of muscular filaments and springs, had a basic grasp of the architecture of the heart, had mapped the main blood vessels, and was able to identify the ducts and sacks of the digestive tract. His infallible confidence with surgical instruments and the clarity with which he perceived, in one single glance, the internal organization of a body led him to discover (discreetly guided by Lorimer) an astounding fact—all animal life was, in essence, the same. And once and again, Lorimer concluded his demonstrations of this truth by drawing Håkan's attention to the spine and the brain.

Their small caravan moved on, leaving a trail of slashed birds, dogs, reptiles, and rodents.

During their lessons, Lorimer often reminded his student that his remarkable talent with the scalpel would amount to nothing if the knife was not held by a loving hand guided by a truth-seeking eye. The study of nature is a barren enterprise if stones, plants, and animals become frozen under the magnifying glass, Lorimer said. A naturalist should look at the world with warm affection, if not ardent love. The life the scalpel has ended ought to be honored by a caring, devoted appreciation for that creature's unrepeatable individuality, and for the fact that, at the same time, strange as this may seem, this life stands for the entire natural kingdom. Examined with attention, the dissected hare illuminates the parts and properties of all other animals and, by extension, their environment. The hare, like a blade of grass or a piece of coal, is not simply a small fraction of the whole but contains the whole within itself. This makes us all one. If anything, because we are all made of the same stuff. Our flesh is the debris of dead stars, and this is also true of the apple and its tree, of each hair on the spider's legs, and of the rock rusting on planet Mars. Each minuscule being has spokes radiating out to all of creation. Some of the raindrops falling on the potato plants in your farm back in Sweden were once in a tiger's bladder. From one living thing, the properties of any other may be predicted. Looking at any particle with sufficient care, and following the chain that links all things together, we can arrive at the universe—the correspondences are there, if the eye is skillful enough to detect them. The guts of the anatomized hare faithfully render the picture of the entire world. And because that hare is everything, it is also us. Having understood and experienced this marvelous congruity, man can no longer examine his surroundings merely as a surface scattered with alien objects and creatures related to him only by their usefulness. The carpenter who can only devise tabletops while walking through the forest, the poet who can only remember his own private sorrows while looking at the falling snow, the naturalist who can only attach a label to every leaf and a pin to every insect—all of them are debasing nature by turning it into a storehouse, a symbol, or a fact. Knowing nature, Lorimer would often say, means learning how to be. And to achieve this, we must listen to the constant sermon of things. Our highest task is to make out the words to better partake in the ecstasy of existence.

Håkan had been converted.

The landscape that had seemed so featureless to Håkan was now an expanding enigma he was eager to decipher, but there was little time left after tending to the business of staying alive. When they were not replenishing their supplies of water and firewood, hunting for food, or scouting for potential threats, Lorimer collected and organized his specimens. In the evenings, he would sit around the fire with the men and write in his notebook while they smoked and told stories (and on these occasions he always wore a tenuous, kind grin—whether his smile was brought out by the men's talk or by his own writing, Håkan could never figure out). In the few spare moments their busy life on the plains afforded them, Lorimer tried to teach his friend how to read, but Håkan found it almost impossible to recognize which letters faced forward and which back, and the characters in the words often seemed to move of their own accord. His practical knowledge, however, grew at an astounding rate, and soon Lorimer deemed him ready to hear the full extent of his theory. This required, Lorimer said, a basic knowledge of anatomy, but also an unprejudiced mind. He believed Håkan to have acquired both.

"You have seen for yourself how all life is connected, how everything is in everything, and how each single thing radiates to the whole," Lorimer told Håkan. "All present beings are tied to one another. But this is also true through time. Every natural event flows forth from something else, which flows forth from something else, and so on—a net of tributary veins, rivulets, and torrents rushing away from the headwaters. It follows that each living thing logs within itself the traces and records of all its ancestors. In the course of time, however, minor modifications are introduced, small adjustments and improvements. Where and how this process will end, nobody will ever know, since nothing in nature is ever final—all ends are ephemeral because they are pregnant with new beginnings. But one question we may be able to answer: What was the first source? What was the principle of life? Whence do we come?"

Lorimer left Håkan with the question unanswered for a few days, giving his young student room to think of these matters on his own.

Saladillo was not far away. The desert had become even drier. All plants and visible animal life had disappeared. The dirt was rock-hard, and the lack of dust gave the landscape a final stillness. There was something angular and sharp in that flatness.

They always bivouacked immediately before sundown to make the most of the daylight. Any place was as good as any other. They simply dismounted and sat down. Their tracker was careful to leave his saddle pointing forward to have some immediate reference when he woke up in the blank expanse. Food, water, and fuel were consumed sparingly. They wrapped themselves in homespuns and hides to make up for the small fire they let die out once dinner was cooked. It was during one of these fireless nights, as they were lying in their furs looking up at the stars, that Lorimer revealed his discovery to Håkan.

God did not create man. He created something that became man. If we could only go back in time far enough, millions of ages, our ancestors would start to lose their human features. Little by little, they would look less like men and more like beasts. And if we went all the way back to the dawn of days, we would discover that the creature that fathered us all did not even resemble any animal we have ever seen. We would find Adam, our forefathers' forefather, to be a passive, translucent gelatin, a blob of marrow bobbing in the otherwise barren ocean.

The history of the transformation from viscous sponge to man, Lorimer said, could be read in the spine. Reminding Håkan of some of his fossils carved into yellow stone, Lorimer explained that in remote times, the spine was a flexible duct made of cartilage. It was only after centuries upon centuries that this rubbery tube wrapping the marrow would ossify, hardening into the dorsal spine, as we know it today. But this cartilage was not just a conduit or a sheath for the marrow. It was, itself, fossilized marrow. And the marrow, in turn, was a projection of the brain. Brain, marrow, and spine were the same substance at different stages. And if all our limbs stemmed from and were subordinated to the spine, it followed that our entire body was a projection of the brain. The brain came first. And, quoting a South American naturalist whose name Håkan could not retain, Lorimer inferred that this principle could be applied to natural history as well. All species, in their inexhaustible varieties, sprung from one single source—a simple cerebral ganglion. All beings are simply dilations of this organ, of this primeval intelligent matter that contained in itself all the possibilities of future life forms. The qualities of each species are determined by how long they have been in the making or at what point, down the stream of time, they deviated from the original source. We had progressed from a shapeless intelligent being that was our remote but direct ancestor. A bodiless brain. Over the course of many millions of years, this thinking ganglion forged for itself the material structures that would become its frame and its instruments—in other words, the brain generated its own body. It was almost as if the cerebrum had thought and willed the rest of its anatomy into existence. At this point, Lorimer reminded Håkan of how, from the embryos in different stages he had shown him, it could be deduced that the skull itself goes through the progressive stages that define the development of the human species—from membrane to cartilage to bone. The skull, then, is the most primitive rigid formation. It developed as a box encasing the brain to shield it from a hostile environment. The spine resulted from the skull (whose structure is roughly replicated in each vertebra), and from this central column, particular appendages would stem out, members that later would become limbs, necessary to ensure the brain's survival. From this, a most significant revelation followed. Because he is the supreme intellectual creature, man has to be, necessarily, the very first form of life to have appeared and developed from that original thinking substance—the oldest being on the planet, still growing, through all the anteceding ages, from that earliest of all seeds. The inescapable and stunning conclusion of this was that human intelligence, in some form, must have preceded all organic matter on Earth.

This was the great discovery Lorimer had made traveling the plains and collecting his specimens, and now he was determined to find the final piece of evidence necessary to support it. All signs suggested that the intelligent proto-organism of which men are the most direct descendants first came to life in water (more specifically in salt water), where it would have vegetated like a thinking shell-less mollusk. Exploring the bottom of the ocean for proof of its existence was, of course, not a possibility. But luckily enough, there were some seabeds one could walk on. One such sea floor was the great salt lake of Saladillo. Formerly a landlocked sea, Saladillo had dried out millions of years ago, and given the inaccessible location and the extreme conditions of this salt flat, Lorimer expected it to be untouched by man. If confirmation of the existence of this first creature, this disembodied brain, could be found anywhere, it would be in Saladillo.

Silence followed Lorimer's discourse. What Håkan had just been told seemed to him as remote as the stars above—so distant from any idea ever taught to him, so removed from any thought that he could have come up with himself, that it would have defied even his brother's imagination. Linus's wildest tales were tame compared to Lorimer's narrative, and everything in Håkan's mind compelled him to dismiss what he had just heard. His limited knowledge of the Bible, his common sense, and, above all, his own humanity made it impossible for him to believe that his seniors, no matter how removed, had been animals. Had he understood Lorimer's rudimentary Swedish correctly? Even more outrageous and insulting was the notion of that primordial snot. Had he not been created in god's image? What, then, was god? And if this process was, as Lorimer claimed, still in motion, what would men become in the distant future? Would those faraway descendants regard his own bones as the carcass of some primitive beast?

And yet, despite his profound misgivings, Håkan felt his own past (with all that he thought he knew, with his father's few firm words, with the minister's unquestioned doctrine, and even with his brother's lovely stories) dissolve into the night and fade in the presence of the impressive and awful history he had just heard.

7.

The light was suffocating. They were gagged, stuffed, choked with whiteness. Through tears and fluttering eyelids they could barely make out the plain—as level and as blinding as a frozen lake. Despite the thumping heat, Håkan's first reflex was to look down to make sure they were standing on thick enough ice. On the frosted flats, a raised beehive pattern, each cell about four feet at its widest point, extended in every direction as far as the eye could reach. The design was surprisingly regular, and the lines of salt, protruding an inch or two, collapsed with a crunch under the wagon wheels but were often strong enough to resist the weight of their steps. The horizon was a noose.

Lorimer led his party farther into the glaring expanse. Just as James Brennan would stop at every turn to pick up a pebble or pan some dust in search of gold, Lorimer constantly paused to gather up crumbs of salt, inspect them carefully, and finally toss them away, growing more somber with each discarded sample. He dismounted so often that eventually he decided to walk, and he kneeled down so frequently that in the end he just proceeded on all fours. His men, still on their horses, looked at him, disconcerted. There was no talking. Even though they did not stop to rest at any point, by the time they camped for the night they had not advanced more than six miles, according to their disgruntled tracker's estimation. Lorimer, sullen after his unsuccessful first day at the salt lake, refused dinner and went to work in the wagon. Later that night, the men huddled around the small fire (wood had become a major concern) while the naturalist remained in the outskirts of the circle of light, a solitary bulk. Håkan could not quite follow the words whispered over the tin mugs, but their bitterness was plain. As the fire died out, it was agreed that posting a lookout was an unnecessary precaution in that wasteland.

The following few days were no different. The men advanced at a snail's pace through the salt flats, walking ahead of Lorimer, who, magnifying glass in hand, squatted over every flake and crawled across miles of salt looking for traces of his primeval being. The sky was as hard and deserted as the land. The men were wrapped in fabric, leaving only a slit open for the eyes—sometimes, exhausted by the whiteness, they even covered this opening and, knowing there were no obstacles for miles around, followed the blurred ghosts of their companions, still visible through the threads. They barely spoke. The alkali dust hardened and cracked their lips and made their noses bleed. Most of their food (biscuits, charqui) was salted, which gave Håkan the impression that he was being devoured by the desert with each bite he took. They were running out of water.

One morning, before dawn, they woke up and found that Lorimer was gone. They looked around in the twilight, using their hands as visors, as if somehow that would help them penetrate the shadows. Someone tripped on a rope tautly stretched toward the horizon. They walked along it. A few hundred feet later they found Lorimer crouching at the end of the rope and following with his eyes the straight line it traced over the salt. Ignoring them, he walked up and down, holding a half-full jar with some markings, stopping here and there and placing it horizontally on the rope while studying its contents. In the end, he looked up, smiling for the first time in days, and told everyone to get ready to ride at the swiftest pace possible while still sparing the horses. They were going farther into the salt field. After a moment of silence, the tracker spoke up. No one was sure how wide Saladillo was, he said, and there was no guarantee they could traverse it before exhausting their provisions and animals. They had to go back at once, since they had almost reached the point of no return. Following the tracker's speech, the rest of the men, usually shy and respectful of Lorimer's authority, started voicing their concerns and threatened to turn around and abandon their employer. In a stern voice Håkan had never heard him use before, Lorimer reminded his men of their obligations, which they would have to fulfill to be paid in full. He also told them they would not get far without the supplies in the wagon, which they would have to steal from him, together with horses and burros. The penalty for this offense, as they knew, was death by hanging. There was a pause. Then, more calmly, he asked for their trust and assured them he was not leading them to their death. He knew how to obtain enough water to cross Saladillo. Moments later, the resentful party set out.

Lorimer rode next to Håkan and confided to him, in their private jargon, that his approach to the expedition had been mistaken all along. Under such harsh conditions, with his limited scientific equipment, it would be impossible to find the minuscule shards of evidence he was looking for. Remainders of tissue in a salt desert blasted by the sun? Impossible. Water. He needed water. Vestiges of the primitive life form could only have been preserved in a liquid environment.

"Have you noticed we have been walking downhill?" he asked.

Håkan stirred in his saddle and looked around, confused, at the white barrens.

"It is a slight decline, of course. But it's there," Lorimer said. "I suspected we were on a tenuous slope and confirmed it this morning with that rope I was toying with when you found me. I tied it to a stick one foot above ground and walked away, holding it taut. About seventy paces away, I tied the rope to a second, slightly longer stick. I confirmed the rope was straight with the makeshift level I made with that jar. And wouldn't you believe it, here the rope is about three inches higher. The descent is hardly noticeable in this void, but it's there. And I'm sure that the incline indicates that this is a basin. I am convinced that if we keep walking downhill, we will reach the deepest point of this seabed and find water in the clogged drain in the middle of this white desert."

They pushed on. The uninterrupted beehive pattern on the salt made the plain even more oppressive. Despite its terrors, a uniform expanse could be calming. Håkan knew this well—he had often forgotten himself and become nothing with the void around him, and those oblivious moments were the only mercy the desert had shown him. But there was something asphyxiating about those regular cells. It was impossible not to count them, not to look for patterns within patterns, not to compare the thickness of the lines, not to look for the largest or the smallest cell in sight, not to search for the most regular shape, not to guess how long it would take to reach a certain cell, not to calculate how many cells there were to the horizon. All those lines and the numbing games they forced the mind to play were perverse reminders of the vastness they were challenging. How calming Håkan found the endless night sky after those long, gridded days! The firmament was certainly greater than the desert, but at least it did not tease him with lines and cells that brought the unfulfilled promise of an ending. Night also offered a respite from the inflexible whiteness, which was the color of their thirst—and thirst was everything. After a violent incident, their water supply had to be guarded with guns at all times. As they traveled on, even if the heat was as intense as ever, Håkan found that nobody sweated any longer. His urine was orange and its discharge painful. Two men suffered from hallucinations. Håkan now understood the human body well enough to know that they would die in a matter of days.

The dot on the horizon was not a hallucination because they could all see it. One of the tracker's men gave hoarse cries. Another one laughed.

The dot became a wagon. No animals. The wagon became a wreck. Surrounding the whitened remains of the wagon, the bleached bones of oxen. In the bed of the wagon, the skeletons of three children and their parents. One of the men started to cry. He bawled and twisted his face into a grimace of grief, but no tears came out. He grabbed an ox's tibia and tried to club Lorimer with it. Håkan was the only one to step in and stop him. The rest of the men had a murderous look about them but were too exhausted to attempt a coordinated mutiny. Once he had recovered from the shock of the failed attack, Lorimer started dismantling the old cart. In a barely audible murmur, he told his men to help him get as many planks as they could. Nobody moved.

"You want water? Get planks!" Lorimer roared.

They took the abandoned wagon apart, working around the bodies, which they left untouched. After removing the hood of their own wagon to make room for the longer planks, they loaded all the wood and got ready to leave.

"Sadly," Lorimer whispered to Håkan as they set off once again, "I think these bodies are a good sign."

And he was right. Shortly thereafter, they saw clouds on the ground. It looked like the end of the world, as if the flats had suddenly broken off and from that point there were only sky in every direction—even down.

"Water," the tracker said.

The crazed men galloped toward the reflection of the sky. Lorimer tried in vain to stop them. He and Håkan kept their moderate pace. When they got to the reservoir, all the men were lying on the ground, panting, by pools of their own vomit. One of them got up, retching. Lorimer mouthed something, but his voice did not come out. He tried again.

"Brine pools," he said.

"You promised water," the tracker whispered.

"Yes," responded Lorimer. "Build a fire with the planks."

The men on the scorching ground looked at him as if unable to make out his words, but after overcoming their own bewilderment, they got to work. The white flats outshone the flames, reducing them to a mere convulsion in the air. While the men labored, Lorimer filled the bottom of their largest stockpot with brine and placed a small empty pot in the center, keeping it in place with a rock. Then, he covered the stockpot with a waxed cotton cloth, tied it to the rim, and deposited a stone at the center, weighing the fabric down and creating an inverted cone. The whole contraption was put on the fire. Soon the brine was boiling. Lorimer adjusted the waxed cloth. The men gaped at the invisible flames. When a rattle replaced the bubbling sound, Lorimer asked Håkan to help him get the stockpot down. They uncovered it, and, to everyone's surprise, the smaller pot at the center, which was empty when they covered the stockpot, was now full of water.

"Drinking water," Lorimer announced as he poured it into one of their empty barrels. The tracker, skeptical, tasted a ladleful. He looked up at his companions and nodded. They all looked at the naturalist in awe.

As he got everything ready to repeat the procedure, he explained to Håkan the general principle behind what he had done—evaporation, the weight of the salt, condensation. He also explained that the dead family told him that the brine pools had to be near—quite apparently they had all died more or less at the same time, most likely stricken by the same malady. He guessed they had all had the brine, and after vomiting, the already dehydrated emigrants did not stand a chance.

The sun was setting. They boiled several batches throughout the night and replenished their reserves. The blazing fire was an additional joy. They were almost happy.

The following morning, Lorimer was knee-deep in the brine pool. The poisonous spirits in the basin were the distillation of the plains and the skies around and above it—colorless and impassively hostile to life. The naturalist had a tube about three feet long with a glass lid on the bottom and handles at the top, which was open. By submerging the windowed end of the cylinder and looking into it, he could see under water. And this he did all day long. On occasions, he dove in to retrieve some specimen. He tossed most pebbles back into the water, but every now and then he found a sample worthy of further examination and placed it at the edge of the pool. Around midmorning, there was a line of identical (at least to Håkan's eyes) white pebbles on the shore. The men had erected a few sunshades with some poles and tarpaulin, which they shared with some of the horses and donkeys. At first, they followed Lorimer's movements with curiosity, but as soon as they realized how monotonous his work was, they tilted their hats down to their noses and dozed off. Håkan offered to help, but Lorimer told him, in a distracted and distant tone, that he had no time to explain what he needed. By noon, the combination of water, salt, and sun had burned and lacerated Lorimer almost beyond recognition. His quivering lips had bloated to monstrous proportions. He found it increasingly difficult to control his tremors, and the ripples around his underwater viewing tube were becoming small waves.

That night, shaking in his furs, he begged Håkan, sobbing, not to let them take him away.

"This will pass. It's the sun," he said, shivering. "Please. I'll be fine. Never again will I come back here. If we leave. In my life. Promise me. I have. Nothing. I have. Just sunstroke. I have. Tell them. Money. I have. Nothing. Please. Please."

He cried himself to sleep.

Lorimer did not really wake up. By dawn, when mumbles started to seep out from his dreams, fever had turned him into its languid puppet. Håkan did not oppose the tracker's order to put him in the wagon and leave.

8.

A new layer of desolation came over that already destitute land. The lifeless flatland, with its ever-multiplying cells, stayed the same. The sun remained, as always, piercing and pervasive, sharp and blunt. There was only one change in that unyielding monotony—Håkan's loneliness, the only thing with depth in that flat and flattening world. With Lorimer fading among his crates and jars, Håkan felt a void almost as profound as the emptiness that overtook him during the crossing of the Atlantic Ocean. He missed Lorimer in the same way (if not with the same intensity) that he missed Linus. Both had protected him, deemed him deserving of their attention, and even seen in him qualities worth fostering. But the main virtue his brother and the naturalist shared was their ability to endow the world with meaning. The stars, the seasons, the forest—Linus had stories about them all, and through these stories life was contained, becoming something that could be examined and understood. Just as the ocean had swelled when Linus was not there to dam its immensity with his words, now, since Lorimer's illness, the desert had violently expanded to an endless blank. Without his friend's theories, Håkan's smallness was as vast as the expanse ahead.

The tracker was taking them back the way they had come. He suspected there was a cutoff, but they were nearly out of food and could not afford to get lost. Their rations had been cut to half a cup of cornmeal porridge and a biscuit for both breakfast and dinner. A few days into the trip, one of the men came into the wagon where Håkan was nursing Lorimer. He went straight for the wicker cages with the birds,

picked two of them up, and turned around to leave. Håkan grabbed him
by the wrist and ordered him, with a gesture, to put the cages down.
The man complied, but with his freed hand produced a single-barrel
pistol and put the barrel to Håkan's chest. Håkan's reaction (which later,
upon reflection, amazed him) was to tighten his grip on the man's wrist
rather than to let go of it. The man cocked his gun. Håkan released him.
That night, the men roasted the birds. Håkan had cornmeal. As they
moved along, they stewed Lorimer's snakes and broiled his cats. The
dogs were spared.

Illness had so reduced Lorimer that the movement of his sleeping
chest was almost imperceptible. His eyes were snuffed out deep in their
sockets; his lips had withdrawn from his teeth; his skin clung to his jaws
and cheekbones. The face was becoming a skull. Following the treatment he himself had received when rescued, Håkan fortified Lorimer's
water with honey. He tried to feed him mashed cornmeal, but the gruel
only lay on his tongue and dripped down his chin. The same day the salt
field first became dotted with dirt, Lorimer looked at Håkan, not with
that delirious gaze that seemed to go through him, but with eyes that,
despite being unnaturally dilated, were full of intention.

"Did we leave?" he barely managed to ask.

"I am sorry," responded Håkan.

Lorimer shut his eyes and, after gathering some strength, opened
them and tried to smile. Håkan gave him water to drink from a soaked-
up rag. His friend nodded with gratitude and slipped back into sleep.

During one of his occasional spells of consciousness, Lorimer was
able to give Håkan some basic instructions regarding his own cure. He
urged him to give him water at all times and even force it into him when
unconscious. Under his direction, Håkan prepared an unguent with
vinegar, agave, desiccated Spanish flies, and lavender oil, and applied it
to his blisters and pustules. He also asked him to add some salt and a

few drops of a particular tonic to his honey water. Should he get deliri-ous and restless, Håkan was to give him three drops of a tincture con-taining opium and other sedatives—under no circumstances should Lorimer get agitated and sweat.

As veins of red dust started to run across the white ground, Håkan found walking increasingly difficult. He had outgrown the shoes he had taken from Clangston, and the pain was crippling. With one of Lorimer's scalpels, he cut off the toe caps. His toes, dissociated from the rest of his feet, stuck out and protruded over the soles like blind albino worms. Gradually, the salt flats were reduced to crystal ripples on the dirt. Some scorched bushes started dotting the skyline. The abstract terri-tory became a landscape once again. The first sage grouse they spotted seemed to Håkan as fabulous as a flying toy.

Although still weak, under his own treatment administered by Håkan, Lorimer's moments of awareness became more frequent, until he fully regained consciousness. Håkan's first concern was Lorimer's animals. He wanted to tell his friend he had been unable to protect them before Lorimer noticed that they were all gone. Stammering and held back by fear, Håkan told the naturalist what had happened. Lorimer laughed feebly through his nostrils.

"Eaten. Good. Good." He laughed again. "A much more dignified end than the fate they would have met with me."

Lorimer conferred with the tracker, who, together with the other men, asked to be relieved of his obligations after delivering him safely to Fort Squibb, a week or two north and slightly east of there. This strong-hold had become a thriving trading post for trappers and emigrants, and there Lorimer would find rest, supplies, fresh horses, and maybe even a whole new party, should he want one. They shook hands on it.

Slowly, the plains regained their brown, red, and purple features. Håkan would not have been surprised if suddenly they had found themselves by James Brennan's gold mine or back in Clangston. Little by little, Lorimer started venturing out of the wagon and eventually got back on his horse for part of the day. After one of those rides, Håkan helped him dismount, and they ended up standing face-to-face. The naturalist looked at his friend, bewildered.

"Have you outgrown me?" he asked. "Could you possibly have grown taller than I over the last few weeks? Come here."

He measured Håkan, shaking his head in disbelief.

"How old are you again?"

"I don't know."

"Roughly."

"I don't know."

Lorimer proceeded to write down the dimensions of his skull, the extension of his spine, and the length and girth of his limbs, while shaking his head. After his disappointment in Saladillo and his illness, Lorimer's disposition to be astonished and delighted at every turn had become somewhat dulled, and he no longer rose with an impassioned tone to the highest flights of eloquence. But some of his former fervor resurfaced as he looked up at his young friend. After studying his notes and making a few calculations, he told Håkan he had never seen or even read anything like it. Håkan's growth rate was without precedent. He reminded Håkan that life is a struggle against the downward pull of gravity—life is an ascending force that moves every plant and beast away from the dirt (and the same can be said about a creature's moral evolution, by which it moves away from its primordial instincts toward a higher awareness). Every worm, crawling out of the opaque puddle of nonexistence and up the millennial coil of mutations, is an upright, cognizant species in the making. Was Håkan, reaching up beyond the rest of us, an example of what humans might become?

The convoy traveled on over the uneventful plains. After having nursed Lorimer and handled his tonics, Håkan could now detect a faint medicinal scent in the verdigris sagebrush. Otherwise, the desert, as unchanging as ever, seemed to defy the very idea that they once had left it. Lorimer spent most of the day writing, often leaning his notebook against the pommel of his saddle. The tracker and the rest of the men escorted him with cold formality, from afar.

One afternoon, they sighted a plume of smoke sketched on the sky. Two men, most likely moved by boredom rather than by bravery, volunteered to ride ahead and make a reconnaissance. Those who stayed behind inspected their powder horns and loaded their rifles. Nobody spoke, but it was apparent—from the way they fondled their guns, stirred in their saddles, and wore the arrogant look of untested courage—that they longed for some sort of confrontation. When the two scouts, who had left galloping, returned at a leisurely trot, the tracker and his men did not hide their disappointment.

"Just Indians," one of the scouts said and had some water.

"Dying," the other one added, reaching for his companion's canteen.

Håkan understood that the Indians had some hides and old horses they could easily take and trade at Fort Squibb. The rest of the men approved. A kind of worried severity took over Lorimer's face, and though he never said a word, he plainly disagreed with the party's intentions. The naturalist made sure to ride at the front of the convoy and seemed eager to be the first to reach the Indians. As they approached the camp, they found that the few lodges that had withstood the flames had been burned down to black bones. Hanging from these shapeless structures and a few broken poles stuck in the dirt, torn skins, hides, and patches of leather sagged in the breezeless air. Not a soul in sight. Strewn amid the ruins, chunks of dried meat, gourds, painted hides, tools of different sorts, and other objects broken beyond recognition. Some sickly ponies stared at the ground. A few dogs, ears angular with attention, looked at the strangers. The fire that had almost entirely consumed the largest tent and the shelters around it was dying under the weight of its own smoke. That bubbling black stream covered the back half of the camp and then rose in a concave wave whose crest dissolved into the sky. The dogs came out to meet the riders, some growling, others with welcoming yelps, most with cool curiosity.

"They were here," said one of the scouts, puzzled.

The tracker and the others stopped at the edge of the decimated camp and readied their weapons while pointlessly scanning for hideouts in the naked wasteland. Lorimer rode into the smoke. Håkan followed him. They covered their faces with their shirts as the smoke got thicker. The sun was reduced to a prickly twilight. In a whisper, Lorimer told his friend to stop and held up his hand for silence. They were wrapped and rewrapped by a thick, grainy whirlpool. They could have almost grabbed fistfuls of ashes from the air. The world ended right after their horses' ears. They dismounted, and Håkan followed the naturalist into the heart of the smoke cloud. Muffled coughs came from below. They both stared at the ground, but their feet were hardly visible. Lorimer stopped, bent over, and picked up a bundle. It was a small child, its face completely wrapped in a damp cloth, like a little mummy. Håkan squatted and discovered that the smoke hovered a foot or two above ground. Lying in the dirt, almost crushed by this low black ceiling, there were over a dozen bodies. The smoke seemed to rest on their backs. All faces were covered in rags. A hand feebly clutched Håkan's ankle, giving him a jolt.

"Get the children first," said Lorimer.

One by one, they pulled everyone out into the fresh air. They were badly wounded and barely conscious. One of the men produced a knife but was too weak to use it. As Lorimer started to inspect their wounds, the tracker and two other men rode over after having made it around the smoke cloud.

"Sneaky bastards," he said. "Crawled and hid under the smoke. I thought they had worked some Indian magic and vanished."

Lorimer did not bother to look up. He was busy tending to the wounded.

"We're loading the wagon with the hides. We'll split the ponies," added the tracker.

"The wagon and the ponies stay. Take the rest and leave."

The tracker was astounded. Was Lorimer staying? A heated discussion over the ponies ensued. Soon they were both screaming. Håkan could not make out the words, but the argument ended with Lorimer getting some gold coins from his saddle satchel and sending the men off. Fuming, the tracker took the money, turned around, and told the men to pack up their loot and leave the ponies. Before going back to the wounded, Lorimer faced Håkan.

"Most of these people will die without my help," he said. "I will stay. Fort Squibb is only a few days from here. Go with them."

"I will stay."

"Go."

"I will help."

Lorimer nodded and asked him to tie off a tourniquet on a man's leg. How all those badly wounded people had managed to hide under the smoke was a mystery. Fractured skulls, splintered bones, chests and limbs crushed by gunshots, entrails barely held in place by shaking hands. Curiously, most of the children were conscious and more or less untroubled by the smoke. As the sooty cloud dissipated, a few relatively unscathed adults started looking around, as if they had suddenly woken up in a new, unknown land.

They were all lean. There was nothing consistent about their attire—leather robes, ponchos, trousers, loincloths, blouses, sandals, boots, bare feet, headbands, hats, kerchiefs. Underneath the gore, they were all extremely clean, unlike all the white men and women Håkan had seen since arriving in California. Up to that moment, all the faces Håkan had encountered in the desert had been vandalized by the elements—shredded skin under which the flesh glistened like a disgustingly opulent fruit that, in time, inevitably acquired the texture and color of rotten wood. But these faces revealed no struggle with their surroundings. Håkan thought that Lorimer's face aspired to become one of those faces.

Håkan realized now that he had always thought that these vast territories were empty—that he had believed they were inhabited only during the short period of time during which travelers were passing through them, and that, like the ocean in the wake of a ship, solitude closed up after the riders. He further understood that all those travelers, himself included, were, in fact, intruders.

The man who had wielded his knife tried to attack Lorimer again but was struck down by pain. His left foot was backwards—his heel where the toes should have been, the skin twisted into a black spiral, torn at the ankle, revealing bone and tendon. There was room for awe and curiosity in Håkan's horror. Lorimer held the furious man's head and wiped his beaded brow.

"We are friends," Lorimer said.

The man stared up, still enraged. Lorimer took his gun out of the holster, showed it to the man, holding it by the barrel with his thumb and index finger, like a filthy animal, and tossed it aside.

"Friends," Lorimer repeated.

His fury yielded to confusion, but the man seemed to understand that they meant no harm. Lorimer asked Håkan to fetch his instruments, drugs, and salves from the wagon. As a first measure, they administered the sedative tincture to those who were in excruciating pain or needed to be operated on. Among those who made a quick recovery was an old man with short, very precisely trimmed white hair—an exception among his long-haired companions. Lorimer's work would have proved impossible without his help. Nobody dared to oppose his advice or his commands. If not the leader of the community, the short-haired man was an uncontested authority, and the more drastic treatments, such as amputations, could never have been carried out without his endorsement. This man also turned out to be an excellent physician with a subtle understanding of the human frame, and he had saved invaluable resources from the plunder—a local anesthetic made with crushed herbs and mushrooms, some ashes with miraculous healing properties, and other soothing unguents and poultices. He and Lorimer discussed each case through gestures. Håkan watched and learned.

In addition to his salves and his medical talent, the short-haired man made two contributions that altered Lorimer's understanding of surgical procedures and greatly influenced Håkan's future. When the naturalist was about to perform his first operation, the short-haired man grabbed his hand before the scalpel broke the skin. Gently, he led Lorimer to a pot of water boiling over a fire. In it were the man's own instruments. Through signs, he asked Lorimer to submerge his scalpel in the boiling water. Lorimer was confused but in the end did as he was told. The short-haired man hummed a melody while the instruments boiled away. After a while, he took them out with a pair of wooden tongs, making sure they never touched the parts that would be in contact with the patient. The second thing he did was wash his hands. For this, he used a strong alcoholic beverage he had salvaged from the raid. In some cases, he used the same liquid to clean the wounds. Before each operation, these two procedures—instrument boiling and hand washing—were repeated. In time, an amazed Lorimer had to conclude that the incredibly low number of infections must have been related to the man's rituals.

"Our learned scholars in our marbled academies have failed to understand what this wise man has gathered from his observation of nature—that the putrefaction that flowers in a wound and the diseases that bloom in an open injury can be nipped in the bud. The very seed of these maladies can be boiled and wiped away before it takes root in the flesh."

Håkan's memory of what followed that first operation was obscured by thick smudges of blood, but behind the crimson-black swirls, his recollections had the surgical precision of a picture painted with a single-hair brush. Until sunset, they extracted pellets buried in the deepest fibers of the flesh, fitted the serrated edges of broken bones into one another, reset viscera and stitched abdomens shut, cauterized wounds with white-hot irons, sawed off arms and feet, and sewed flaps of skin around muscle and fat and bone into rounded stumps. As he became absorbed by the work, Håkan discovered a form of impassive care completely new to him. His detachment, he felt, was the only proper approach to tending to the wounded. Anything else, beginning with compassion and commiseration, could only degrade the sufferers' pain by likening it to a merely imaginary agony. And he had learned that pity was insatiable—a false virtue that always craved more suffering to show how limitless and magnificent it could be. This sense of responsibility exposed a fundamental disagreement with Lorimer's doctrines. The naturalist claimed that all life was the same and, ultimately, one. We come from other bodies and are destined to become other bodies. In a universe made of universes, he would often say, rank becomes meaningless. But Håkan now sensed the sanctity of the human body and considered every glimpse underneath the skin a profanation. These were not prairie hens.

When it got too dark to continue operating and ministering to the wounded, Lorimer walked up to one of the burros with his rifle, composedly took aim at its head, and shot it dead. Two men with minor injuries helped him butcher the animal. The weak were given warm blood to drink. The healthier ones chose their own cuts—once the tongue, liver, and pancreas had been carved out and eaten, they broke the thighbones and sucked out the marrow. After grilling some ribs and salting the remaining edible pieces, Lorimer boiled the burro's head and later fed the broth to the feeblest. Two women baked a serpentine kind of bread. They rolled a long cylinder of dough and then twisted it in a spiral around a stick, which was placed at an angle on an X made of two other sticks over some embers. The dough spiral was turned at regular intervals, and finally the stick was removed from the center. The coiled bread was passed around, and each person broke off a ring of the spiral, charred on the outside and doughy on the inside.

That night, once their sedated patients had drifted away, the short-haired man and Lorimer shared a calumet. Compelled by the naturalist, who did not want to offend their host, Håkan also took a few puffs. Raspberries, urine, and wet down. He coughed discreetly through his nose and felt his stomach squeeze up against his uvula.

Lorimer wanted to know if the attackers had been white men. He tried to communicate through pantomime and by drawing scenes with coal. The short-haired man, focused on rearranging the contents of the pipe bowl, barely paid attention. Lorimer tried to stage a reenactment using Håkan and the impassive old man as actors. After a series of increasingly intense and abstract attempts, the short-haired man got up, put his fingertips on Lorimer's cheek, and said, "Wooste." Then he walked over to Håkan and, with a gesture that encompassed the Swede's whole body, repeated that same word—"Wooste." He pointed at both of them and said, one more time, "Wooste." Finally, he took Lorimer's arm, held it like a rifle, pointed it at the wounded lying in shadows, and fired. "Wooste."

As the days went by, the few men and women who had sustained minor injuries started cleaning up and rebuilding the camp. With the help of bone needles and catgut, they turned rags into quilts and quilts into tents. The children were also hard at work at their own camp, a smaller reproduction of the real one, made of leather scraps and fabric shreds. Perhaps because the miniature emphasized the vastness of the surroundings, it seemed denser, heavier with actuality than the real thing. Several times a day, the children asked Håkan to walk around the toy tents, and everyone, including the adults, was endlessly amused to see the massive man further amplified as he strolled through the scale models.

Eventually, it became clear that about a third of the wounded would die. Their lacerations were iridescent with gangrene, and their brains had been utterly consumed by infection and fever. The short-haired man readied them for their departure by meticulously washing them, brushing their hair, and anointing them with lilac-scented oil. Whenever their wounds allowed for it, he dressed and bedecked them with the few valuables their plunderers had dismissed—painted pebbles, feathers, and carved bones (that these spoils had been left behind confirmed that the pillagers had been white men—wooste). Those strong enough to stand on their feet prayed for the dying in shifts. In an almost inaudible hum, they sang what sounded like a lullaby. It was a remarkable song, not only for its great beauty (its softness had to do with touch—a tingling air—more than with hearing) but mainly because of its length and composition. It had no refrain. No part of the melody (or, as far as Håkan could tell, the lyrics) was ever repeated. It flowed forward in an ever-changing rivulet. And they sang it all day in groups of three or four, in perfect unison, never missing a note, a beat, or a word. When one

shift concluded, another group would take over without the slightest interruption or transition. Each and every time, regardless of the
group, they sang with astonishing precision without any visible signal
to mark the changes, as if their mouths were governed by a single mind
(Håkan thought of flocks or schools where hundreds of birds or fish
abruptly change direction, eddying to and fro at the exact same time
without any forewarning). If the song was circular, the curve was long
and subtle enough to make repetitions impossible to perceive. Whether
it was a never-ending song or a melody made up by immeasurably long
choruses, Håkan could barely conceive how such a feat of memory could
be possible. It occurred to him that the singers made the song up as they
went along and that they shared some sort of code—for instance, a certain sound of a certain length could only be followed by one specific
note of a specific duration (a similar procedure would apply to words),
so that the melody and the poem were entirely condensed in the ker-
nel of the first note and word. But this system could hardly account for
the richness and complexity of the lullaby, and if it did, the set of rules
would be as hard to memorize as an endless song.

Their first patient died. He had been increasingly disfigured by infection, until an acute inflammation of his neck and head had strangled him
to death. After closing the man's eyes, the naturalist looked around the
camp and then at his disciple with visible concern.

"I hope they understand we did our best," he muttered.

The reaction to the young man's death was surprising, but not
because his friends and family were angered by the outcome of the
treatment. There was no rage; there were no plaintive cries; there were
not even tears. Håkan was astounded to see that their response was
remarkably similar to how people mourned in Sweden. He recalled his
youngest brother's death clearly. His parents and the few distant neighbors attending the funeral had displayed the same austere grief as the

people now walking around this dead young man, pretending not to see him. Their stern faces seemed to imply that their sorrow transcended the realm of known feelings and, therefore, that familiar expressions of pain were no longer of any use. Rather than being clouded with tears, their eyes were hardened in defiance, and their quiet anger kept them from looking at each other. The short-haired man undressed the corpse. Those who happened to be around shared whatever suited them. The body was put on a canvas stretcher and carried out into the sunset. No funeral procession—only the short-haired man and his companion carrying the stretcher. Those who stayed behind seemed to have forgotten the dead man as soon as he was taken away. They returned to their chores, chatting casually. Their eyes had softened.

After making sure his patients could be left unsupervised for a few moments, Lorimer set out to follow the stretcher-bearers, keeping a respectful distance. Håkan joined him. They walked for about three miles through the stubborn desert. Dust. Sagebrush. Sky. Every now and again, the rumor of the stretcher-bearers' conversation. The sun set without pomp—it just got dark. The pewter moonlight was little more than a scent in the night. Suddenly, in a spot that resembled any other, the stretcher-bearers stopped, unloaded the body, rolled up the stretcher, and, without ceremony of any kind, turned around and walked away. They stopped when they reached Lorimer and Håkan and offered them some charqui and glazed cactus pulp, the first sweet the travelers had tasted in months. After the long process of chewing their rubbery victuals, they stared at each other, as if hoping someone would start a conversation. The short-haired man looked up at the waning moon. Håkan and Lorimer looked up as well. The man with the rolled-up stretcher did not. The short-haired man said something that Håkan would have translated as "all right, then," and started walking back to the encampment, followed by his companion. Lorimer gave Håkan a nod, and they walked over to the corpse. Håkan had never seen any-thing as dead as that mutilated body abandoned between the night and the desert. Corrupting, there, forsaken, becoming, already, nothing.

"And thy corpse shall be meat unto all fowls of the air, and unto the beasts of the earth, and no man shall frighten them away—to think that this is one of God's most terrible curses. But consider it carefully. No sepulchre. No cremation. No obsequies. Becoming meat for some-one else's teeth," said Lorimer with some of his past passion. "Can you imagine? Can you imagine what a relief? Will we ever dare to look at a body without the shroud of superstition, naked, like it truly is? Matter, and nothing more. Preoccupied with the perpetuity of our departed souls, we have forgotten that, on the contrary, it is our carcasses and our flesh that make us immortal. I am fairly confident they didn't bury him so that his transmigration into bird and beast would be swifter. Never mind memorials, relics, mausoleums, and other vain preservations from corruption and oblivion. What greater tribute than to be feasted upon by one's fellow creatures? What monument could be nobler than the breathing tomb of a coyote or the soaring urn of a vulture? What pres-ervation more dependable? What resurrection more literal? This is true religion—knowing there is a bond among all living things. Having understood this, there is nothing to mourn, because even though noth-ing can ever be retained, nothing is ever lost. Can you imagine?" Lorimer asked again. "The relief. The freedom."

Four more people died over the next few days, and each of them was ferried out into the desert at dusk.

The survivors healed. The never-ending lullaby stopped. Even if mangled and mutilated, all of the convalescents were conscious, and if they were in great pain, they were strong enough to conceal it. Among the maimed was the man who had tried to knife Lorimer. From his ankle, that vortex of bone and tendons and flesh, the infection had crept up his calf, and his leg had been amputated at the knee. As soon as he regained some of his vigor, he called Lorimer to his side. With great difficulty and a sour grimace of pain, he sat up. After catching his breath, he delivered a grave speech, brief but heartfelt. When he had finished, he took a leather tote bag and poured out its contents. On his palms were about two dozen teeth, perfectly extracted from the root, some grayed, some yellowed, all dull and gigantic. One of them was as long as the entire palm of his hand.

"Terrible lizards," said Lorimer with abstracted fascination. "Extinct reptiles. Dragon-like creatures blotted out of existence, vanished from the surface of the earth shortly after the dawn of time."

Some of the teeth were broken or jagged, but the man made sure to point out that there were a few large ones in perfect condition. He looked at Lorimer and with a solemn word offered him his treasure. Lorimer declined. The man insisted with great vehemence. The scene was repeated a few times until the naturalist understood that rejecting the gift was not only a great offense but also detrimental to his patient's health—the argument had consumed most of his strength. He took the teeth, and the man lay back down, physically and morally relieved. A woman next to him requested Lorimer's attention and produced a pouch of her own. She had fewer teeth and only one, displayed with great pride, was unmarred. Once again, Lorimer, who had cured a bullet wound to her abdomen, was asked to accept the treasure. One by one, each of the patients called Lorimer and, with a short ceremonial speech, gave him a handful of dragon teeth. Nobody was as rich (in either quantity or quality) as the first man with the amputated leg. As he made his way down the improvised ward, Lorimer had to start putting the offerings into the bowl of his hat. That heap of ivory shards no longer looked like teeth but rather like some unrecorded mollusk or ammunition for a weapon yet to be invented.

"What better form of currency?" Lorimer thought out loud as they walked back to the wagon. "Because they can't be manufactured (these long-gone creatures can't be bred), and because their stock is extremely limited, these teeth will never lose their value. Same principle behind gold or diamonds. But these are so much worthier. And they remind us of how all living beings, quite like goods, are valuable, precisely because they are interchangeable." He looked through the dagger-like bones. "The perfect standard."

Life at the camp gradually went back to normal. The wounded were out of danger, and all tents and huts were in good repair. The reverence everyone had shown Lorimer and Håkan dissipated, and eventually the foreigners were simply ignored. The only exception to the general indifference was Antim, the amputee warrior—who had made an extraordinary recovery and become strong enough to ride his horse. He was fanatically devoted to Lorimer and assisted him in every possible way. They spent a great deal of time together, and the naturalist, with his accustomed ease, quickly learned the rudiments of Antim's language.

Håkan's days were consumed, for the most part, by his eagerness to set out east. With each day, he felt the distance separating him from Linus increase. Additionally, since he had helped Lorimer with the wounded, he had developed a feeling of urgency entirely new to him. Up to that moment, his longing for his brother was intertwined and often confused with fear—he missed Linus, yes, but he also missed his protection. Now, however, Håkan did not fear for himself, but for his brother. He had the pressing sense that it was Linus who needed him; that he was the one who had to come to his older brother's rescue (this concern, Håkan realized, had developed together with his medical skills). But Håkan knew the desert well enough to understand that he could not venture out without provisions and animals. He could only hope that his friend would decide to leave soon—and that he would be headed east. Finally, one afternoon, Lorimer told Håkan that it was time to move on.

"I am going back to Saladillo. Antim has offered to help."

Håkan felt his blood thinning. He breathed in and looked around the plains for something to hold on to. Lorimer put a hand on his shoulder.

"Don't worry, my dear friend," he said. "You will be on your way to New York on a horse with all the necessary supplies. Antim, who feels indebted to you as well, will give you one of his ponies, and I will furnish you with all you need for your journey."

"Please don't go back to the flats."

"I must. I know you understand that."

Håkan could only look down.

"When we left Saladillo, I thought the chance to find the primeval being had been forever lost. How would I ever be able to return to that desolate land? And now Antim tells me that he can take me back there, that he will help me get to the alkali ponds. How can I refuse? I need to find the creature—the only living thing that deserves the name of creature, because it was the only organism ever truly created. The rest of us are only increasingly distorted reproductions of that foundational organism. You understand what such discovery would mean. How can I refuse?"

Håkan was given a pony and one of Lorimer's burros supplied with necessaries. The naturalist advised him to make a detour before proceeding east. Heading north for about a fortnight, Håkan would eventually come to a river (which would be badly needed by then), and a few days later, a major emigrant trail—even if he strayed off course, it would be impossible to miss that line stretching from coast to coast. Then, all he had to do was travel against the current of settlers, and in a few months' time, he would reach the Atlantic. Even if his provisions ran out and his animals fell ill, the emigrants would resupply him, and should he run out of money, he could work for a spell (although that would take him west for a while, those caravans were slow) and then resume his journey. The constant flow of pioneers made this the safest route. And, Lorimer added, smiling, the thick stream of emigrants going the opposite way with their wagons and oxen and furniture and horses and goods and women and livestock would even create the illusion that it was the world that moved while Håkan remained in place.

The morning they parted, the naturalist gave his friend some gold, a wad of bills of different denominations, and a polished tin case.

"The tools of your trade," Lorimer said as Håkan opened the case. It contained vials, bottles, scalpels, needles, suture, clamps, saws, scissors, and other surgical instruments. "Oh, I almost forgot," Lorimer added while searching his pockets. "You are a hopeless navigator. Do you have other talents? Unquestionably. But never mind telling left from right—I am shocked you know up from down! So here you are," he said, presenting Håkan with a silver compass. "Blume, my teacher, gave it to me, and now it's yours."

Their last moments together were spent over the dial, with Lorimer explaining to his friend how to find north.

9.

On the pony and next to his small burro, Håkan looked like a colossus. His attire increased the eccentricity of his figure. By the time he left the camp, he found it almost impossible to move without ripping his outgrown clothes. As a farewell gift, the women had mended and adjusted his shirt and trousers by keeping the original fabric and structure of the garments and grafting in additional material—offcuts from their tents, snippets from old quilts, patches they had woven whenever the scraps were too small. The result was a somewhat shapeless but cool and comfortable outfit whose provenance was impossible to determine—the European peasant, the Californian trapper, and the itinerant Indian had come together on an equal footing. The short-haired man, who turned out to be a consummate cobbler, repaired his cut-up shoes by stitching on two inches of leather to the soles and replacing most of the upper parts with the softest buckskin, which resulted in an odd sort of heeled moccasin. Finally, the children had decorated his felt hat with a colorful ribbon holding an iridescent black feather.

Moving through the throbbing desert was like sinking into the state of trance immediately preceding sleep, where consciousness summons up all its remaining strength only to register the moment of its own dissolution. All that could be heard was the thin earth—rock pulverized through the seasons, bones milled by the elements, ashes scattered like a whisper over the plains—being further ground under the hooves. Soon, this sound became part of the silence. Håkan often cleared his throat to make sure he had not gone deaf. Above the hard

shallowness of the desert, the unkind skies and the minuscule sun—a
dense, sharp dot.

And yet, despite its unbending sameness, the desert was now entirely
different in Håkan's eyes. From the compass warming in his pocket,
invisible beams radiated in every cardinal direction. The plains were no
longer blank but traversed by lines of certainty, as solid and unquestion-
able as avenues and thoroughfares. Knowing where he was going, having the assurance of finding the line of emigrants beyond the ring of
the horizon, being able to build a fire and cook proper food on it, hearing the water lap in the vats with each of the burro's steps, sensing the
weight of his full purse in his pocket, feeling the desert was not such
a foreign place anymore—all these things and impressions turned the
plains into an actual territory that could be traversed and exited instead
of a suffocating void from which everything, including space itself, had
been drained.

No change in Håkan's circumstances, however, was as meaningful as
owning a horse. On his horse, his very own horse, he had ascended to
an order high above most men—nobody in Sweden, not even the most
powerful person he had ever met, the estate manager who collected
the fee from his father, owned a horse. That Pingo—for such, according to Antim, was the horse's name—was one of the somewhat sickly
ponies the plunderers had left behind, and that he had neither saddle
nor bridle (instead, looped around his jaw, was a cord made from hide)
was of no importance to him. He had become larger and freer. He felt,
maybe for the first time in his life, proud. It was of no consequence that
out in the desert nobody could witness his ennobled condition. His satisfaction required no spectators. Still, there was one pair of eyes he did
miss. If Linus could only see him, riding through the grasslands on his
bay roan—and with a burro in tow! Within his limited means, Håkan
spoiled Pingo as much as possible. He always made sure he got enough

rest and brushed him with a piece of rough canvas several times a day. He was willing to forgo his own share of water if he sensed the horse was too thirsty. In return, Pingo seldom gave Håkan any trouble. He was a docile animal, except when his gluttony got the better of him. Whenever the thickset pony spotted a somewhat greener bush, he would head straight for it, regardless of how vigorously Håkan pulled the reins, and only when all the lower leaves—the smaller and tenderer ones— had been devoured, would Pingo notice the tug of the rope. To make sure he had caught every single scrap, he would snort on the sand, dig in, and grope for the remainders with his lips. Once Pingo was sure there was nothing else to nibble on, he would lift his head and let Håkan regain control over their course. Eventually, seeing how much pleasure Pingo got from his feasts under the thickets (and always being eager to please his horse in any way possible), Håkan ended up indulging him every time.

A few days after their departure, Pingo got diarrhea. Suspecting the leaves were the cause of the horse's illness, Håkan tried to keep him from eating them. But no matter how hard he pulled his head away from the thickets, Pingo would still suck the creeping leaves out of the sand. The pony got worse. Hoping to replicate the symptoms in himself, Håkan plucked a handful of leaves from the bottom of the brush and ate them. They were bitter and rubbery, like small dead tongues. He waited. Nothing happened. Three or four more days went by, and Pingo lost considerable weight. His hindquarters stuck out from his emaciated body. His behavior changed, too. He would stretch out, as if wanting to urinate, and remain in that position for a long time, then paw at the ground, and finally lie down and roll, with no consideration for the rider, who—after having nearly been crushed a few times—had learned to dismount with a jump at the first sign of these fits. In the end, Pingo was too sick to be mounted, and Håkan led him by the reins when he was able to move at all. He was completely puzzled by the animal's condition. He felt the horse's abdomen repeatedly without finding anything strange. And yet, it was clear that Pingo was dying. Then, one morning, overcome by despair after a fruitless examination, Håkan put his head to the horse's midline in a loving rather than a clinical way. He heard a rustling sound, the lull of waves rolling in and out of a sandy beach. He pressed his ear closer to Pingo's belly. A peaceful shore. The rushing whisper of sand in the surf. A placid seashore in his horse's entrails. He pushed hard into the animal's lower abdomen with his fist and once again put his ear to his side. The murmuring sand stream grew louder. Håkan emptied out a leather sack and, for the rest of the day, walked behind his horse. Late in the afternoon, Pingo finally evacuated his bowels, and Håkan collected a specimen with his sack. After carefully examining the manure without arriving at a conclusion, he filled the sack halfway with water, tied it shut, shook it, and let the contents settle. A few moments later, he stuck his hand in, careful not to disturb the liquid, and reached to the bottom. There was a thick layer of sand. Over the next day, Håkan repeated the test several times, always with the same result. He concluded that his horse had ingested inordinate amounts of dust while foraging for the tender leaves under the thickets. By now, Pingo was in severe pain. Håkan could see no other solution than to cut the horse's abdomen open, make an incision into the large intestine, rinse out the sand, and then stitch it all back together. Performing such an operation unassisted and with limited instruments was, Håkan knew, fraught with danger, and Pingo's chance of surviving this rudimentary procedure was slim. But he also knew that if he did nothing, the colic would kill the pony in a short time.

At dawn (he wanted to make sure he would have all the light he needed), Håkan gave Pingo several drops of Lorimer's sedative tincture with a sackful of tender leaves. Soon the horse's eyes turned narrower

and blacker. He seemed to be squinting inward. Then he started showing his teeth to the desert. Even though his hind legs became wobbly,
Pingo managed to walk away. He could not be stopped—he did not feel
the pull of the rope, and he even dragged Håkan, who was hanging off
his neck, digging his heels into the ground. Pingo cackled joylessly like
an old hen or a tired witch. Kea, kea, kea, kea. Håkan panted. The burro
looked at them, calmly surprised at their lack of decorum. Pingo sat
down, staring nearsightedly into the void. Håkan tried to get him back
on his feet with gentle words. Suddenly, as if lashed by an invisible whip,
the horse got up and resumed his erratic march. Kea, kea, kea, kea. Once
again, Håkan clung to the pony's neck. The horse's strength seemed to
increase with his disorientation. The burro had become a speck near
the horizon. Had they gone that far or was the burro walking the opposite way? Håkan managed to give Pingo a few more drops of the draft.
The gelatinous legs finally melted, and the horse collapsed on his side.
Just in case, Håkan tied up the pony's feet and then ran back toward the
burro. It had not moved.

Once back by his horse with his donkey and his equipment, Håkan
laid out a waxed canvas tarp, boiled his instruments in the murky water
(humming, like the short-haired man), washed his hands as best he
could, and took all his clothes off. After making a large cut into the
pony's abdomen, he had no trouble finding the large colon. In fact, it
was much bigger than he had ever imagined—thicker than a human
thigh. He stuck his arm shoulder-deep into the horse's belly, trying to
go around the intestine and lift it out, but it was too heavy and slippery. Additionally, it was apparent that the tissue was extremely delicate and that it would tear if handled brusquely. His body was soon
covered in sweat, blood, and viscous fluids. After gently wrestling with
that colossal snake, he managed to withdraw the most movable part of
the large colon from the horse's abdomen. The heavy bowel hung over

the animal's frame and poured over onto the tarp. He made an incision the length of his hand and flushed the contents. Pingo had swallowed an enormous amount of sand. Håkan rinsed the intestine clean, almost depleting their water reserve. Then he sutured the colon and reset it in the horse. It was remarkably lighter now that the sand had been cleaned out, and he had little trouble putting the organ back in place.

As a precaution, Håkan left the horse tied down on the ground for the first two days and kept giving him a low dose of sedative. When the time came for Pingo to get up, he proved to be stronger than expected. Still, Håkan knew it would be several weeks until the horse could walk the long distances they had previously covered every day. And they were almost out of water. According to Lorimer, they were supposed to come to a river, which—given the distance already traveled—could not be too far away. Håkan left Pingo food and water in a cask buried to the rim so it would not spill, tied him to the trunk of a sturdy bush with a long cord, and, in case this should fail, fettered his forelegs with a loose rope so as to hamper his movement. Although the animal was tethered and hobbled, Håkan was reluctant to leave his horse and kept turning around to look at his immobile silhouette until it was warped and wiped out by the distant waves of heated air.

The river, a brown line of slow, muddy waters, was a mere two days away. Although the vegetation on the riverbank showed the sternness the desert demanded of all living beings, Håkan found it refreshingly green—and the burro even discovered some bunchgrass to bring back to Pingo. Hidden in the low, entangled treetops, the only haven for miles around, several bird nests brimmed with eggs, most of them a pale orange marbled with ochre streaks. Håkan ate a few and wrapped about two dozen more of different sizes and colors in a piece of cloth. He went back to the riverbank and tried to fish with suture and a curved needle but, after a long wait, only caught a small, pungent bottom-feeder. Walking up and down the shore, he made a loud crunch with every step. He scratched the sand with the tip of his shoe and found the strand to be lined with mussels that had made their shallow homes just a few inches under the surface. He pried one open and inspected the slime within. It looked more like a single organ than a body made of many parts. He dislodged the mollusk from its shell and slid it down his throat, avoiding chewing or tasting it. With little effort, he dug out a great number of mussels and then threw them into the vats, already replenished with turbid water. The sacks were packed with grass and eggs, and soon Håkan and the burro were heading back the way they had come.

Faithful, uncomplaining Pingo stood waiting by the bush, exactly where he had been left. He was thirsty but in somewhat better shape. His stitches were healing, and although he seemed more vivacious, he found walking extremely painful.

Their bivouac gradually became a permanent camping site. Håkan cleared the center of a large thicket and spread a tarpaulin over the opening, creating a low, shady shelter where he lay most of the time, stupefied by the heat. Every three days or so, he walked back to the river with the burro and brought back water, mussels, eggs, and grass, so despite the long delay, their provisions remained, for the most part, untouched. Meanwhile, Pingo's condition seemed to be deteriorating. He got intense itching fits around his stitches. Part of his rib cage was raw after so many attempts at scratching the scar with his teeth, and he often had to be muzzled. The fits increased as he developed a swollen redness around his stitches, a hard yet somehow fragile force pushing from within. Pingo's eyes had grown larger. When he was not dressing his wound, Håkan was coaxing him to drink water or trying to shield him from the sun. He spent most of the day with his cheek to the horse's neck, feeling the flesh twitch under his coat. Eventually, Pingo's legs gave in, and he lay down. His breathing was a broken rustle, as if withered leaves were rolling inside his rusty windpipe. His eyes seemed to be about to pop out. The wound acquired a life of its own—warm and mauve, taut and throbbing.

A maggot emerged from under one of the stitches the same day Pingo started hallucinating. Håkan pulled it out and saw a confusion of worms boiling within the wound. Later that day, Pingo's ears started quivering as if they were swarming with insects. Then he began shaking his head and whipping his back with his tail, swatting invisible flies. Then he tried and failed to get up. Then he screamed. It was a sound unlike anything Håkan had ever heard. Two monstrous knife edges running against each other. Pingo sustained the scream until his lungs crumpled. Then, he screamed again. And over and over again. Håkan embraced the neck of his horse, whose delirious eyes were being sucked out of their sockets by the horizon. Pingo kept screaming, veins and tendons bulging around his throat. Håkan held him tighter and wept. The screams only stopped after a strong dose of sedative. Once Pingo was unconscious, Håkan cut through his cava and carotid, rolled up his tarp, and left.

10.

He had not seen his own face since he had left Clangston. Only splintered reflections on blades, partial glimpses on lids, quivering images on water, or curved caricatures on glass—never a complete, truthful picture of his features. And now, there it was, lying on the desert. His face.

Walking alongside the burro, he had crossed the shallow river and kept traveling north for several days without incident. Håkan was used to the illusions the desert conjured up from the dust. He had seen many pools spring up in the distance and then dispel as he advanced toward them, many hopeful or menacing shapes gather on the horizon that were nothing but the hazy ghosts of heat. But the blinding light coming from the ground was unlike anything else, and this strangeness confirmed its reality. More than a glare, it looked like a frozen blast, a detonation suspended in its flashing climax. The sharp whiteness cut through his eyes. As he approached that silent constant explosion in the sand, Håkan realized that it was somewhat elevated, although it was hard to look at it straight on. A few moments later, he reached the blaze. It was the mirror on the open door of a massive wardrobe. The large trunk was beached on its back, disemboweled, and the open door hung from its hinges at an angle. He was impressed by the dresser's craftsmanship—sensuous spirals and scrolls, lifelike paws and claws, plump cherubim and flowers. It was the softest surface he had touched during his long trip through the porous, pumice-like desert. Although there was something profoundly intimate about it—something conjugal—the dresser also called forth a crowded world and a sense of urban refinement Håkan could only vaguely imagine. In fact, the dresser was the most concrete embodiment of those civilized comforts he had ever been free to touch and inspect. While running his fingers over the turned black wood, Håkan's approach to the mirror changed. The sun was no longer on the glass, and he was finally able to look into it. It took him a moment to accept the face he saw as his own. Some of his old features were gone, new ones had set in, and he had to find himself in the image at his feet. The orange shadow of a mustache hovered over his lip, and the hesitant promise of a beard spotted his chin and hollow cheeks. At the sight of his emaciation and his protruding bones, he was reminded of his teeth. With great anxiety, he parted his chapped white lips to inspect his gums. The inside of his mouth, moist and red, was the only part of his body that remained unaffected by the arid wasteland. Relieved to find his teeth as healthy as ever, he returned to that strange face that looked up at him in bewilderment. He had withered and wrinkled—the sun had burned deep crevices into his face. His eyes were permanently screwed up, but not as the result of a deliberate frown. This was just his face now, creased by the constant squint of someone facing an overwhelming light or an unsolvable problem. And his gaze, almost invisible in the narrow trench under his knit and ribbed brow, was no longer fearful or curious, but dispassionately hungry. For what, he could not tell.

Before moving on, he was tempted to smash the mirror to take a shard with him, but the majesty of the dresser deterred him. As an afterthought, he also considered that its owners would surely come back for it at some point. He took one last look and walked away.

With every day, as he kept moving north, bunchgrass became more abundant, and eventually the land turned yellow. Water was less infrequent, but Håkan still drank it with reverence. Gadflies and mosquitoes spurred him and the burro on—the assaults when they stood still and unprotected by a smoky fire were so vicious that they once sent the burro bucking uncontrollably across the plains. Trees and thick bushes, however, grew scarce, and soon Håkan ran out of fuel. Charqui and raw wild mushrooms were his fare. Dogs, rodents, and birds became a habitual sight in that grassy extension that challenged the sky, and Håkan felt the joy of being once again a living thing among living things.

A few days later, once the desert had yielded to the prairie, Håkan stumbled upon a rocking chair swaying back and forth in the open wilderness, nudged by the breeze. For a long time, as he approached it, he could not understand the meaning of chair, as if the object itself were a word on a page made up by those signs that would forever remain a cipher for him. He kept looking at the chair. What does chair mean? He reached it and touched it. He sat on it. The vast plains receded. He felt out of place, and there was something thrilling and comical about this. But at the same time, he also felt lonelier than ever—smaller, frailer.

Although Håkan did not keep close track of time, he believed that, according to Lorimer's directions, he should meet the trail fairly soon. And sure enough, three or four days after finding the rocking chair, Håkan finally ran into a path. He was confused. If emigrant trains were like traveling cities, this track seemed nothing more than a footpath and just about one palm deep. It could never have been the result of oxen and wagons, and yet it was so regular in its construction and course, it could only be man-made. He followed the path north for a few leagues until suddenly, behind a thicket atop a small hill, he saw, for the first time, buffalo. They followed each other down their trail one by one, in single file, with a slow step and great deliberation. Beyond this stately procession, as far as the eye could see, the heath was darkened with buffalo, grazing or wallowing in muddy basins. It seemed to Håkan that these beasts were made out of two different bodies ineptly put together. Their hind legs and quarters were positively equine—slender and toned—but with the last rib began a transformation, and, as if nature had changed its mind halfway through it, the animal swelled in a stupendous, monstrous fashion, suddenly becoming thicker and taller. Its back rose steeply and abruptly, leading to a head so massive (could that dense, anvil-solid block of bone that seemed impenetrable even to sound contain a brain or any flesh at all?) that, compared to the animal's smaller back end, it seemed to have been dreamed onto the rest of the body. Below a pair of sharp horns, a pair of black eyes had been bored into either side of the skull. If any of the beasts that Håkan had seen in America had ever resembled his brother's fabulous inventions, that creature was the buffalo.

He pressed on. As the days went by, the sight of buffalo skulls, some of them bleached by the elements and scaly with lichen, became frequent. Håkan supposed that the pioneers must have hunted those beasts in great numbers, and the jettisoned goods he found over the following days—a trunk with china, bedsteads, a spinning wheel, cupboards, several cast-iron stoves, a large carpet he unrolled on the grass—seemed to confirm the proximity of the trail. Sometimes it rained, and it was always a miracle.

It was one evening, after one of those showers, that Håkan heard the church music. It came to him with the wind, in rags and tatters, like a torn flag. Although the sounds had the texture and flavor of church music, the melody was unlike anything he had ever heard—sad and incomprehensible.

Following the intermittent organ music, Håkan found three Indian lodges. He stopped a few hundred feet away and remained still, making sure he would be seen, and once he knew his approach could not be taken for an ambush, he proceeded toward the tents. Smoke puffed out of the top flaps of the lodge in the middle. They were cooking meat. As he got closer, he saw four or five men lying on the ground. Sitting next to them, a man played a harmonium. He was tall, lithe, and scrupulously

neat. His hair was coiled in a bun on the back of his head, and from
his neck descended a loose chest plate made out of coins of different
sizes. His chest was naked under this ornament, but he had a whitened buffalo robe over his shoulders. With his left hand, he pumped the
instrument while his right fingers slowly ran across the keyboard, playing an erratic melody. Now and then, he would pause to drink from a
jug, which he sometimes rolled over the keyboard, creating discordant
clusters of sound that made the air oscillate. He was drunk, and it was
clear he would soon join his unconscious companions on the dirt. He
briefly noticed and then ignored Håkan's presence. Around the tents—
tattered buffalo hides over frames of poles—meat hung to dry on hair
rope and leather cords. Going around the lodges, Håkan found a few
women on their knees, shaving the hair off newly skinned hides with
sharp flint, scrubbing out the brown flesh from the inner side, and rub-
bing the brains of the buffalo into the skins, probably to soften the
leather. When they noticed him, they were unsurprised. He was invited
into one of the tents and given roasted meat from some ribs hanging
off a rope over the fire. The women sat and watched him eat. When the
fire started to sink low, someone flung a piece of buffalo fat on the coals.
A wild blaze flashed up, revealing every last object in the tent—a stone
mallet, silverware, a portrait of a corseted lady, piles of hides and robes,
a decanter with a faceted glass stopper, arrows, a stranded chandelier,
bows, a stuffed owl in a glass dome, a mortar, a swaddled baby, a sewing machine, shields decorated with birds and buffalo, empty bottles and
jugs. The organ music stopped. Håkan finished his repast, and the women
walked him out. The drunken men were blots on the dark ground. Håkan
gave the women some flour as thanks and walked into the night.

One morning, he woke up to find that he had slept a stone's throw
away from a makeshift graveyard. The tombstones, three planks stuck
upright in the ground, bore words that had been burned into them

with a hot iron. Although unable to read them, Håkan could see the
despair in those unsteady lines. Two of the plots must have been for
very young children. The earth on all three had been torn up and
raked by hungry paws. Håkan found the contrast between the improvised, impermanent nature of the graves and the final, definite condition of those in them immensely sad. Over the next several days, shallow
graves, few of which had eluded the violation of wild beasts, and heaps
of ungainly and impractical objects strewn throughout the plain became
a frequent sight. Then the smell came. After such a long time in the
odorless desert (he had long ceased to notice the few habitual scents of
his body, his animals, and his fires), the stench of civilization hit him
like a solid mass, rather than a vapor—a smell at once slippery and
barbed, piercing and thick. And yet, despite the corruption and the
decay, the miasma brought back a sense of life. Rancid meat, feces, sour
milk, sweat, porridge, vinegar, rotten teeth, bacon, yeast, fermenting
vegetables, urine, bubbling lard, coffee, disease, wax, mold, blood, broth.
Two days Håkan traveled against the swelling reek until he saw, drawn
against the edge of the prairie, a long, low creeping line.

II.

Because the beginning and the end of the caravan curved behind the horizon, from afar the train seemed to be motionless. It was only when he got closer that Håkan made out the heavy-gaited beasts pulling ponderous wagons, and, trudging next to them, a multitude of men, women, children, and dogs. Few people rode. Nearly all saddles were empty; most seats were unoccupied. Marching alongside their teams, the drivers cracked (and sometimes applied) their long-lashed whips and encouraged or insulted the yoked animals. Everyone was young, but they all looked old. Most of the travelers were engaged in the all-consuming business of moving forward—spurring the oxen on, making adjustments to the harnesses, tightening up broken locks, replacing wheels, resetting tires, greasing axle shafts, steering their herds, marshaling their children. Some managed to share domestic moments on their moving wagons: have family meals, pray, play music, and even give school lessons. People went from one party to the next, trading and bartering. And everywhere, dogs. Some walked lazily under the wagons, hiding from the sun, but most ran in packs, prancing in between the legs of horses and cattle, snapping and yapping, pestering the oxen, sniffing the air for food, picking fights with one another, and getting kicked in the ribs by impatient boots. By the side of the rut, several emigrants had stopped by a broken wagon and were helping make a new axle out of a log. As far away from the trail as safety permitted, a group of women stood in a circle, all of them facing out and spreading their skirts to the sides, creating a round calico screen. Whenever a woman came out, arranging her dress, another one went in.

On occasion, the ignored report of a rifle came from afar. Scouts were constantly leaving and rejoining the caravan. As Håkan walked past each convoy, people quieted down and stared at him from under their hats and bonnets, their eyes invisible in the strip of shade cast by the brims. During these brief silences, all that Håkan could hear was the grinding of the iron tires, the rattle of harnesses, the dry impact of wood on wood, and the stiff flap of waterproofed canvas.

The sides of the rut were one long latrine to which men and women continually contributed bucketfuls of waste. Here and there, like irregular milestones, mounds of rotten bacon and offal emerged from the muck. Dead cows and horses—some of them skinned—shrank under the sun. Håkan kept walking against the current of wagons. It was inconceivable that the crowded procession could have an end. Lorimer had been right when he had described it as a massive city stretched out into one thin crawling line.

Some travelers nudged each other, snickering at Håkan's outfit. But for the most part, they looked at him with mute curiosity. Nobody greeted him. He spotted a young couple—not much older than he, he guessed— and, trying to overcome his shyness, changed direction and started to walk alongside them on the other side of the slimy stream. They looked at him furtively and exchanged discreet, worried whispers. Finally, Håkan found the courage to address them. He introduced himself. They politely pretended to understand his name, and he theirs. A long silence ensued. The man cheered his team on. Håkan asked if they had a horse for sale. They could not spare any of their horses, but they referred him to a man a few wagons up who had more livestock than anyone else in that company. He thanked the couple and caught up with the man in question. After a short and failed exchange, Håkan stated his request. The man quoted a massive amount that made Håkan's entire capital—which he hitherto had thought to be quite respectable—seem insignificant.

For the rest of the afternoon, Håkan kept walking up and down the train, asking if anyone had a horse for sale. The sellers always asked for prices that could never be met and bore no relation to each other—one asked almost one hundred times the already exorbitant sum demanded by another. Ever since he had landed in San Francisco, all the commercial transactions Håkan had witnessed had been conducted in the most extravagant terms, always dictated by circumstances. The pound of bacon for which prospectors in the desert paid in gold, today lay rotting by the emigrant trail. A simple piece of wood that never would have caught a trapper's attention, now, in the tree-deprived plains, was exchanged for a calf to replace a broken axle shaft. But horses were the one commodity exempted from these drastic ebbs and flows. They remained consistently unattainable. And not only that: they were, on the whole, excluded from commerce. Men were reluctant to part with their horses, regardless of the sum offered, and whenever forced to sell them, they always felt that they had been swindled, even if the amount received had been outrageously high—probably because they knew that they would be unable to replace the sold property. Realizing all this made the loss of Pingo, painful as it had already been, almost intolerable. Every day, Håkan was visited by the elation he had experienced riding his own horse, a feeling that had been intense enough (his physical frame had barely been able to contain it) to ripple through time and lap against the present.

Although far from ideal, getting to New York on foot was not such a wild notion, he thought. It rained often enough and walking against the trail solved the problem of finding supplies for the journey. He was resigning himself to this plan when an armed rider approached him. He stopped at a prudent distance.

"Evening," said the man, whose beard had not quite caught up with the mustache that must have preexisted it. In this exuberant thicket

glowed a calm yet intense smile, and below a pair of dense eyebrows—
the mustache's runaway offspring—shone a set of twinkling green-blue
eyes, which, although sharply focused on Håkan, stirred from side to
side with mousy eagerness. There was something sunny and even melo-
dious about his countenance. He looked like the happiest man Håkan
had seen since arriving in America—maybe even the happiest man he
had seen in his life. Håkan greeted him back, and the man responded
with a seemingly welcoming speech, of which Håkan understood almost
nothing. Still, he noticed that the tone, cadence, and rhythm of the
man's voice did not match his face—the natural arrangement of his features resulted in something that looked like cheerfulness but did not
reflect an inner state. After a failed exchange, the man gathered that the
newcomer's English was limited and spoke to him slowly and, as people
often do with foreigners, loudly. Håkan responded to his questions as
best he could while the man nodded along, as if with the deep dips of
his chin he could dig out from the air the words that the Swede missed.
Introductions were made (Hawk? Hawk can? Hawk can what?), and
Jarvis invited Håkan to dinner with his family.

As they moved on, it became clear that strife and resentment were
widespread among that particular convoy and that there were at least
two factions—those who warmly greeted Jarvis as he passed by, and
those who, with a hostile frown, turned their backs on him.

"I hear you're looking for a horse," the man said.

"Yes."

"Want one of mine?"

"How much?"

"You must be hungry."

Careworn and always shrouded in a mackinaw blanket, Abigail,
Jarvis's wife, was drained of all the joy and gaiety that her husband's
face, probably despite itself, so radiantly displayed. She was a rawboned

matron, slightly disfigured by exhaustion and bitterness. Her children annoyed her. The elements annoyed her. Her husband annoyed her. The animals annoyed her. Håkan annoyed her.

The sun would soon set. As if by common accord, hoots and whoops burst throughout the caravan, and the train came to a stop. With difficulty, but also with great coordination, the drivers got out of the rutted track and fanned away from the trail. The plains echoed with whistles and the few utterances the oxen seemed to understand—So, then! Yah! So, then! Wo! Gradually and (despite the arduous, plodding maneuvers) with remarkable grace, the wagons were wheeled into wide circles, the hind axletrees chained to the tongues. The oxen were unhitched and left free to roam together with most of the cattle within these large improvised corrals while the rest of the stock and horses were hobbled and left to pasture at their leisure. India rubber cloths were laid out on the ground, and cooking utensils were brought out. As the men pitched precarious tents outside the circle, the women produced hard brown discs from sacks and crates, piled them up together with some kindling, and set them alight. Håkan looked at Abigail's heap and asked what those odd cakes were. She ignored him. He picked one up from her bag and smelled it. Dung. Jarvis saw him inspecting the disc and explained that, as Håkan had surely noticed, there was no timber to be found on the plains, and that they had to rely on dried buffalo manure for fuel. The chips had a steady and smokeless burn that glowed brighter whenever the fat of the buffalo meat roasting upon tapering spits dripped down on them. That meat, together with bacon and corn flour fried in buffalo lard, was, as Håkan would learn, their daily bill of fare. Combined day after day in tinware that was never fully cleaned, these viands had solidified in a crust at the bottom of every pot, pan, and bowl, infusing whatever was put in them (including the occasional pickle and the dried apples steeped in warm brandy they had on special occasions) with the same flavor.

Over dinner, Jarvis asked Håkan everything about him and his travels. They did not understand each other easily, but Jarvis, making good use of his appearance, persevered with jovial tenacity. He was particularly curious about the Clangston lady and her gang (How many men? What kind of weapons? Where exactly was the town?). The precise destination of Lorimer's tracker and his men was another matter he came back to over and over again. In turn, his answers to Håkan's questions were vague, and he dismissed anything related to himself with a slack wave of his hand. Behind them, beyond the light cast by the fires, a child was being belted. As Håkan was trying, for the third or fourth time, to provide Clangston's location—an effort doomed by his limited vocabulary and inveterate disorientation—he was interrupted by a robust farmer who took off his hat and nervously wrung it in his hands as he approached them.

"Mr. Pickett, sir," mumbled the large man, barely overcoming his shyness.

"Jarvis," responded Håkan's host, relying once again on his cheerful face. "And drop the mistering. I told you it's just plain Jarvis," he said in a tone of friendly remonstrance.

"Mr. Jarvis, sir," the bearish man muttered, proffering a small sack. "From my wife, sir. With her compliments."

He seemed to curtsy as he bent his knees to hand the gift over to Jarvis, who, sitting on the tarpaulin, accepted it ceremoniously.

A lash and a muffled cry came from the gloom.

"Edward," said Jarvis with grave appreciation. "Thanks. Many thanks."

Edward looked at his strangled hat. Jarvis opened the sack and poured out a handful of glazed pecans. He tried one. The big blond mustache danced to each crunch. Edward kept looking at his own hands squeezing his hat. A lash and a cry.

"Gold nuggets. That's what these are. When did I have one of these last? Years?"

"From my wife, sir."

"Well, please—please—thank her." He was about to eat another nut but checked himself. "Sorry," he said, holding out the bag. "Please."

"Thank you, no, sir."

Håkan declined as well. Jarvis shrugged, ate another pecan, and put the bag by his side. Edward bid them good-night, took a few steps backwards, turned around, and left.

Similar scenes, with different visitors and different offerings, took place numerous times throughout the evening while Jarvis asked Håkan the same questions again and again ("But where are they? So rifles and pistols, eh? How many did you say they were?"). Timidly obsequious men and women approached Jarvis with their offerings—tea, molasses, a penknife, dried pumpkins, tobacco, silver. And in each case, Jarvis showed himself humbled but deserving.

"The horse, then," said Jarvis after having accepted the gift of a blanket from a girl holding a baby that could well have been either her sister or her daughter. "I've got one for you."

"How much?"

"Oh please," Jarvis said with friendly affront.

A pause ensued. Jarvis probably expected Håkan to break the silence by asking him once more to name his price.

"Do you know how to use a gun?" Jarvis asked when the lull was getting awkward.

Håkan looked confused.

"A gun," Jarvis repeated while miming a firing pistol with his thumb and forefinger.

Håkan shook his head.

"Look," Jarvis said. "Most these people are sore fond of me. You've seen it for yourself. I mean." He pointed to the gifts and shrugged his shoulders. "But there are a few who. Look. These here are hardworking

people. And this here is all they own. Some get nervous. And I fear some
may be greedy for my life."

Håkan looked down.

"You are a big fellow. You travel alone. No property. No family. I
could use your help. Just ride along with me. We'll get there in a few
weeks. And you'll have your horse. It'll be easy to make up for lost time.
What do you say?"

"I don't know."

Håkan was not sure of their location (were they closer to the Pacific
Coast or New York?) and had no way to gauge whether it would be
worth it to follow Jarvis and then make up for lost time on a horse, or
if he should set off east by foot immediately. There was, on the other
hand, the issue of the actual job he had been asked to do and the
risks it might entail. The discontent clouding the convoy was manifest,
and the animosity many felt toward Jarvis was clear. But unlike the
moody prospectors he had met along the way, or the Clangston gang,
or Lorimer's tracker and his crew, these were family men. They worked
hard, cared for their children, and read from their Bibles. However disgruntled they might have been, Håkan could not picture them shoot-
ing anyone down in cold blood. Furthermore, many liked Jarvis—the
offerings proved it. Whatever his detractors' reasons were, he could not
imagine what Jarvis might have done to justify his fears of retaliation.
Håkan thought of Linus and wondered what he, who never showed a
sign of vacillation, would do. Would his brother have accepted the elements in this dilemma—guns, horses, mutiny, the wilderness—as perfectly expectable circumstances, and therefore have an answer ready?
All Håkan knew was that this would probably be his only chance of
acquiring a horse.

"Tell you what. Just ride along for a couple of days. Think about it.
I'll throw a saddle into the bargain."

By the time the fire was dying out, a considerable pile of goods lay on Jarvis's canvas. He wrapped them all up in the blanket he had been given, wished Håkan good-night, and retired to his wagon. The belting, which had stopped for a while, resumed in the dark.

"Get up! Get up! Get up!" The screams filled the air at the first light of dawn. With these cries, the donkeys started braying, forcing even the heaviest sleepers to wake up, get out, and set to work. Tents were rolled up; flour and water fritters sputtered in lard; roped oxen were wrestled back into their yokes; teams were hitched to carts; canvas bonnets were adjusted on wagon bows. All these arrangements were made under the close supervision of the dogs roaming the quickly dissolving camp. "Get on! Get on! Get on!" was now the call echoing throughout the plains as the wagons got back on the trail and resumed their slow progress.

Later that day, Jarvis, carrying a shovel and a broken wagon wheel attached to his saddle, took Håkan for a ride. They headed south, away from the trail, and stopped when the caravan had disappeared behind their backs. After dismounting, Jarvis asked Håkan to help him bury part of the wheel and prop it up with some rocks so that it would stand on the ground. Once it was in place, they took about fifteen steps, and, from an inner chest pocket, Jarvis produced the strangest pistol Håkan had ever seen. There was nothing extraordinary about the grip or the trigger, but the rest of the gun was monstrously over-grown, as if thickened and disfigured by some morbid disease. It had six massive barrels mounted in a circle around a central axis. Seen frontally, the six muzzles resembled a gray flower. It smelled of oil and sulfur.

"That's right," Jarvis said, dreamily smiling at the gun. "Bet you never seen a pepper-box before."

He cocked the unloaded pistol and pulled the trigger repeatedly. After each click, as Jarvis squeezed the trigger, the hammer rose and the barrels turned over so that a new cylinder would get under the pin just in time for the next impact.

"See? You don't have to stop to reload. And none of that flintlock rubbish. That'll just get you killed. Twice!" He chuckled. "Twice they'll kill you while you ready one of those old things." All the while, he kept pulling the trigger, the barrels kept rolling on, and the hammer kept snapping on the empty chambers. "No, no. None of that flintlock rubbish. You just put these here like so," he explained while putting caps at the end of each barrel. "And you're good to go. Not one, not two, but six shots," he said after loading the balls. "Look."

Jarvis took aim and fired at the wheel in rapid succession. The sharpness of the shots was dulled by the curved immensity around them.

The wheel stood unscathed.

"Well, it's not an easy gun to aim, on account of the front being so heavy. You're supposed to shoot leaning it on your pommel."

He started loading the gun again.

"This takes a little bit of time. But then you have six shots." A long pause. "Six." A long pause. "Won't even feel the ball through their vitals."

Håkan sat down on the ground. The horses stared at him.

"Let's get a little closer," Jarvis said when he was done.

They took six or eight paces toward the wagon wheel. Jarvis took aim and fired. He was more deliberate this time and took a short moment before each one of the six shots. The wheel, however, remained untouched.

"Could the shots have gone between the spokes?" Jarvis wondered aloud.

He walked back to his horse, grabbed the blanket rolled up behind his saddle, went back to the half-buried wheel, spread the fabric over it, and began, once again, with the long process of reloading.

"They voted for me, you know. I was elected. Captain of the party." Jarvis never looked up from the gun. "People from other companies came to join us. I know people on the other side, you see. Important people. I can guarantee three hundred and twenty acres on arrival. At least three hundred and twenty. And I know the trail. Went out west a couple of years ago, and then back to fetch my wife and children. That totals three trips. So there it is: a man who knows the way and has something to deliver at the end of the journey. And yet. Contentions, dissent, distrust. Jealousy? I don't know."

He took a couple of steps, leaving just a yard or two between the gun and the wheel, and shot it point-blank. The blanket danced like a demented ghost on the rim. With the fifth bullet, the wheel toppled over. Jarvis walked over and finished the contraption off with his last shot.

The demanding march, the nightly procedure of driving the wagons into a circle to hold the cattle, the brief meals, the hurried morning preparations were repeated daily without change. At Jarvis's request, Håkan carried the gun at all times, always making sure it was on full display. For the most part, they stayed together, and people stayed away from them. Whenever Jarvis gave him leave, he rode up and down the train. As time went by, he noticed that on these excursions he would get the same treatment Jarvis had received when they first passed by the wagons together—some would show extreme deference (a few even uncovered their heads), but others would meet him with a scowling mien (he sometimes thought that he heard spitting behind him). While Abigail retained her shriveled bitterness, Jarvis seemed as bright as ever. Each evening he accepted, with solemn gratitude, the offerings his fellow travelers laid at his feet.

Distractions were few, and the absorbing monotony of the trip drained their days of all substance. Every step on the unchanging landscape resembled the last; every action was a thoughtless repetition; every man and woman was moved by some forgotten yet still functional mechanism. And between them and the unattainable horizon, the dust—always the dust. It burned their eyes, plugged their nostrils, and dried their mouths. Although they covered their faces with hand-kerchiefs, they felt their throats corrode and their lungs shrivel. The sun itself, red and uncertain, was suffocated behind the unmoving cloud. Several times a day, even in calm weather, the dust would make it impossible to see the oxen from the wagon. On those occasions—especially when the wind whirled around them and turned each grain of dirt into a pellet, forcing them to proceed with eyes shut—the sense of immobility and changelessness became perfect, and both space and time seemed to be abolished. Rain was a blessing, well worth the muddy trouble it sometimes caused. It settled the dust, washed away foul smells (although they returned with a vengeance when the soaked clothes, animals, and provisions started steaming under the sun), and provided them with drinking water that, for a change, was not teeming with small animals.

The last big shower on the trail lasted several days. Without inter-ruption, the horizontal rain lashed their faces and pruned their hands and feet. Their clothes got cold and heavy on their backs. Unable to light fires, they could not broil the buffalo meat that was their main sus-tenance. Deep mud; glutinous mud; slippery mud. The trail became a dense mire, and the smacking sound of hooves and boots pulling out from the clay like cupping glasses could be heard at all times under the roaring storm. Although the submissive, strong beasts—blackened and thinned by the rain—kept the train going, they moved at a snail's pace.

The trail, unable to absorb any more water, had become a shallow stream. Beasts and wagons got bogged down in the swampy rut. Some carriages sank to their axles. Every day, often more than once, men up to their knees in muck had to unpack their wagons to get them out of the mud, repack, goad their oxen, and keep going, hoping they would not get stuck a few steps down and be forced to unload everything again. On a cold morning, during which the pelting rain was briefly replaced by sleet, the wagon in front of Jarvis's got mired in a particularly deep hole. Without speaking, a group of men (Håkan and Jarvis among them) helped unburden the wagon and then lifted the wheels off the ground and pushed forward while someone laid a plank under one of the tires. Slipping hooves, screams, lashing whips. As always, there were a few children around, excited to help out, puffing, arms akimbo, with great self-importance, after each push. After a few attempts, the wagon finally was released and moved forward with a jolt. Håkan and some others fell face-first into the mud with the abrupt thrust. Everyone cheered. As he got up, he saw, through the sludge and water clouding his eyes, a small hand, and reached for it to help the boy up. The lightness of the limb was horrifying. The screams of alarm came together with the realization of what had happened. A few steps away lay the inert body of the boy whose severed arm Håkan was holding.

The unconscious child was taken into the wagon while Håkan ran to fetch his medical instruments. Only when he got to his burro did he realize that he had taken the arm with him. He rushed back and, after he returned to the father his son's limb, tried to get into the wagon.

"Go away," the man said. "We have no use for Mr. Pickett's watchdog here."

"I can help," replied Håkan.

The man drew the tarpaulin shut in Håkan's face.

"I can help," he repeated.

No response. Some onlookers had gathered around the wagon. Håkan pulled the canvas open and was met by the father's desperate and furious gaze. A woman who looked too young to be the boy's mother scrambled around the wagon with aimless frenzy.

"I can help."

Håkan opened his tin box and showed the man his instruments. In that muddy confusion, the tools gleamed with a promise of order and cleanliness. Even to Håkan they looked like talismans from the future. The man let him in.

"Fire," Håkan said as he applied a tourniquet to the remainder of the boy's arm. "Now!"

"What? The rain. How?"

"Fire now! In here. Make a fire. Boil water."

Håkan's decisiveness and precision in dressing the boy's wound must have impressed the man, because he did not question the strange request but set to it at once. He smashed a milking stool and a crate with a sledgehammer and put the splinters into a large stockpot. The wood was too damp. He frantically felt his pockets while looking around for kindling. Everything was too large or too wet. Håkan looked up from the boy with anxious eyes. Panting, the man rifled through the wagon until all of a sudden he stopped, hit by a realization. He took out a box nested within a box. The woman gasped and covered her mouth with both hands. From the inner box, the man produced a bundle, and within it, safe and dry, was the family Bible. Without hesitation, he tore out several sheets of paper so thin they crackled in his hands before being lit. Placed under the splinters in the stockpot, the paper burned with a ghostly purple glow, and the wood soon caught fire.

"Boil rainwater. Not too much," Håkan said.

The man fetched one of the buckets hanging outside, at the back of the wagon, and poured two or three fingers of water into a smaller pot, which he put on a grill he had previously rested on top of the burning stockpot. Soon, the water was boiling, and Håkan submerged his instruments into it while quietly humming to himself.

"Spirits?" asked Håkan at length, always looking into the boiling pot.

The man stared at him.

"Spirits," Håkan repeated while looking up and drinking from the imaginary glass made with his hand shaped into a semicircle.

The man got a bottle from a basket and gave it to Håkan, who rubbed his hands with the transparent liquid that smelled strongly and, except for a faint trace of beeswax and mildew, almost exclusively of alcohol. Father and daughter looked on, their faces distorted by the shock of the accident and their bafflement at Håkan's requests and actions. Håkan took the instruments out of the boiling water, let them cool down, and set to work.

He had helped Lorimer and the short-haired Indian with amputations, but he had never seen a case as bad as this. A few inches above the point where the elbow once had been, the wagon wheel had ground the flesh to a dark paste and smashed the bone to shards and splinters. With extreme care, he cleaned the wound with alcohol and clipped off the tassels of flesh and nerves at the end of the stub. He then found the main vein and artery and tied them off with suture, after which he made four vertical incisions into the healthy part of the arm, through the muscle and all the way down to the bone, and created two flaps with the skin. He pushed up the biceps and the flesh receded with it, which allowed him to saw the bone off just above the point where it had shattered. The young woman sobbed at the sound. After trimming and filing the humerus, Håkan let the flesh down, sewed the muscles over the bone and the flaps over the muscles, and daubed the stump with one of the salves the short-haired man had given him.

The rain drummed on the tarps and tinkled in the pails. Every now and then, a peal of thunder. Gently, with a fresh cloth, the girl wiped the boy's pale brow and then began cleaning the mud off his body. For a moment, Håkan lost himself looking at the scene. He had never been touched like that, cared for like that. He regained his composure and focused on cleaning and putting away his instruments. The fire in the pot had died out. With a trembling hand, the boy's father picked up the liquor bottle, took a swig, and offered it to Håkan, who declined. Then, the man stroked the girl's hair, kissed his boy on the forehead, and took Håkan by the shoulders.

"God bless you," the man said, looking into Håkan's eyes.

"I don't know," said Håkan, looking down at the boy and then away at the floor.

"I know. But maybe. Thanks to you."

They sat down.

"I shouldn't have called you a dog."

Håkan dismissed the matter with a gentle swat, surprised to realize that he had picked up that gesture from Jarvis. He felt embarrassed and looked away.

The girl was tenderly absorbed in trying to make her brother comfortable. Håkan thought that he would give his own arm to have her wipe his brow, arrange his pillow, and kiss his lips. The girl looked up, and he immediately looked down. The man kept apologizing for his rude behavior. He had lost his mind seeing his boy like that. And it was also true that the situation with Jarvis was reaching its limit. Håkan looked up, puzzled. Why else, asked the boy's father, would Jarvis need a big man with a big gun at his side? It took Håkan some time to realize that he was the man being referred to.

"First, we all fought one another. But as we saw he was up to some devilment, many of us started fighting him."

Håkan's lips quivered, trying to ask a question, but he didn't know where to start.

"So you know nothing," the man said.

Soon after they had first set out, months ago, word spread around the train that a man who had already been west had land over there and was giving it away. At first, Jarvis Pickett turned everyone down with a

chuckle, saying it was all a rumor. Then, after a few days, he admitted
to some that he did have a bit of land, but that it was mostly dust and
rocks, and that nobody could possibly want it. Then he confided to just
a few that it was a fertile valley, rivaled only by the Garden of Eden,
and that he intended to start a colony there with a select group. Then
he produced maps and deeds and started giving away plots to the most
loyal people around him. He never took money from anyone, claiming they were all partners in this venture—fellow colonists, he said.
They elected him captain. If anyone crossed or displeased him, Jarvis
would scratch his name off the deed. Each time this happened, the
rumor would spread of an opening, and the hopeful petitioners would
shower Jarvis with gifts. He pitched people against each other and had
them compete, with presents and favors, for the best plots. After a few
weeks, there were no friends in the party. But some grew suspicious of
the maps and the deeds. Jarvis's response, invariably, was that if he had
wanted to steal from them, he would have just taken their money in
exchange for the deeds—and yet, he had never accepted a penny. Still,
their convoy seemed to be moving slower than all the rest. They took
longer at rivers, made several unjustified stops, and never caught up
with the wagons that constantly overtook them. Many believed their
captain was stalling and extending the journey so that he could keep
collecting his offerings. To this, Jarvis replied that he had never asked
for anything. But by then, most people in his circle—willingly, despite
their suspicions—had given Jarvis too much. They had little or nothing left to start with on their arrival, and their only hope was the plot
of land Jarvis had promised them. His closest men, the ones who had
given him the most, were the ones who trusted him the least, precisely
because their dependence on him was absolute. Right before the big
rainstorm, the tension had become palpable, and mutiny was in the air.
Jarvis had grown distrustful. Some poor devils tried to appease him

with more gifts, hoping to displace their more disgruntled and openly hostile rivals. And that was when Håkan had arrived.

The following day, the sun resumed its place in the sky and soon baked the trail hard under their feet. Two or three mornings after the boy's accident, as their party was breaking camp and getting ready to get back on the trail, Jarvis stood on a couple of crates and asked for everyone's attention. He waited until everyone had quieted down, and then his lively mustache made a joke. Some laughed. Jarvis got serious—while retaining, somehow, his cheery countenance—and told his convoy that he had an important announcement to make.

"Friends," Jarvis said. "We all saw what happened a few days ago. Our future can't wait. Our children can't wait. Each step counts."

Murmurs.

"Our children can't wait," he repeated. "We can follow this slow trail or we can turn here. I know a cutoff."

Cheers and heckles.

"Yes, a cutoff." Jarvis was not trying to persuade anyone—just sharing the good tidings. "Follow the trail, if you wish. Or follow me."

These last statements were drowned in the rising tide of voices. For a moment, the divide between the two rival sides—hitherto only whispered about—became stark. Jarvis's supporters thanked him and congratulated each other on their good fortune, while his detractors looked sullenly at the dirt and the sky. However, most men, regardless of their faction, stayed out of the ruts and followed Jarvis's south-pointing finger. But three or four wagons decided to keep going down the trail. Everyone was surprised, except for Jarvis, who pretended not to see the defectors.

That evening, after driving the wagons into a circle for the night, in front of Jarvis's fire, there was a long line of people humbly waiting to present him their offerings. Some of them even had horses.

12.

Rather than pulling the wagons, the oxen, with drooping heads and foaming noses, seemed to be making the crust of the entire planet turn under their hooves. Journeying through the untrodden flats was like moving through a surprisingly thick substance. In addition to the boulders and holes hidden in the grass, constantly threatening (and often breaking) axles and tires, there was the resistance presented by dirt that had been packed down neither by wheel nor hoof. They were going less than half their regular speed—someone said he reckoned they were down to seven or even five miles a day. Jarvis remained as sunny as ever. He said that one mile on the cutoff was worth twenty on the trail of those stubborn tramps.

Although weakened by the loss of blood, the mutilated boy was making a good recovery. He remained sedated for a few days, running a constant low fever that Håkan took as a positive sign of his body burning away disease. Now and again, in his sleep, the boy would frantically scratch the sheets where the missing limb would have been. Håkan came by to inspect the wound more often than necessary. After he examined the stitches, the girl would often give him food or a cup of milk to make him stay a little while longer. Håkan would eat or drink in a blushing silence. When he mustered the courage to turn his eyes up, he sometimes found her looking at him with something he liked to believe was admiration.

Depending on the day, her hair could be copper or gold, and with her hair, her eyes changed from green to gray. Her freckles multiplied, vanished, reemerged, and moved around like constellations from one visit to the next. Håkan had never looked at anyone with such close attention and wondered whether all those mutations were real or just the result of his heightened awareness. He spent most of his nights awake, imagining what she would look like the following day.

Had it been left to Håkan, he never would have learned her name. She seemed to understand that he was too shy or afraid to engage in conversation and that any form of encouragement would make him withdraw further. But she managed to convey her openness through small gestures. And it was in this spirit that Helen volunteered her name, without asking for his. After a moment of apparent hesitation, he explained that his name was not Hawk but Håkan. Helen was one of the few people in America who actually tried to pronounce it. She laughed as she searched for the exact shapes of those strange vowels, but even as Håkan laughed along, he fell into a solemn trance watching her lips move around his name. That day, she also wrote his name down, unsure of the spelling, on a piece of paper that Håkan would keep for years, thinking, each time he looked at it, that he was there—in those fading lines on that yellowing scrap of wrapping through which an irretrievable past managed to persist in the present—in a more intense way than in his own body. Once, he brought dried fruits and sweetmeats. They did not dare to even touch them.

In each of his visits, Håkan tried to avoid the child's father. He believed the story about Jarvis's fraud to be true, but he still carried the big gun at his belt, and that made fraternizing with the man difficult. Håkan was eager to sever the ties to his employer, but part of his concern was that if he returned the gun, Jarvis would give it to somebody else, probably to someone more eager to pull the trigger. As Håkan saw it, as long as he had the gun, there was one weapon less to worry about. Not that he feared for himself—he had decided to leave Jarvis's party. Effective or not, the cutoff was delaying him beyond his plans. It had become clear to him that the promise of the horse was too far from being fulfilled and that he would be better off finding his way back to the trail and walking against the current all the way to New York. The situation with the gun, then, had nothing to do with his own safety. He was concerned about the wounded boy and his sister. What would become of them? Who would stand up for Helen? For the first time, Håkan was torn between loyalty to his brother and a commitment to a new person.

Although flanked by low hills, the modest basin they were traveling through barely deserved to be called a valley. It was a girl who first spotted the riders emerging behind the ridges. As in a procession, the men appeared one by one, until there were six of them on each side of the valley, about a quarter of a mile ahead. Håkan turned around and saw a similar formation emerging a few hundred paces away from the rear end of their party. He could feel their cautious, hostile gaze. If they galloped down the slope, the riders could easily cut the party off. The train was brought to a stop. A few more riders appeared from behind the hillocks.

"Circle! Circle!" cried Jarvis.

With a slowness that contradicted the urgency in the air, the wagons were brought into a circle. It was unclear who gave the order, but the men started to barricade the gaps between the wagons with crates, tables, casks, and sacks of grain and flour while the women loaded the guns—mostly single-shot pistols and muskets—and got out clubs, knives, and even swords made out of ploughshares. There was little or no talking. Slowly, the riders moved toward the barricaded pioneers along the edges of the hills. A hoot came from the group flanking the northern end. The ones in the south responded. The riders trickled down from all four sides.

"Indians!" someone cried as they got closer.

The men, wrapped in buffalo hides, had painted faces and feathered heads. They surrounded the convoy. From under their leather frocks, they produced long rifles, muskets, and blunderbusses.

"Down, everyone!" a woman screamed.

Another hoot, and all the riders opened fire at once.

As the blasts echoed away, a hoarse moan grated its way through the ensuing quiet. Håkan looked up and saw an ox kneeling down and then collapsing on its side. The dogs ran up to it to lap up the pooling blood.

"There are children here!" yelled a man.

"Fire!" Jarvis cried.

The emigrants shot back. The air became thick with powder smoke. Nobody was hit.

The riders started the long process of reloading and so did the women, ready with ramrods and pouches of shot while the men buttressed the barricade. When the guns were ready, they resumed their post.

After a moment of silence, a hoot, followed by a fusillade.

The emigrants fired back.

Nothing. Aside from a few holes in some wagon bonnets, the shots on both sides had been as good as blanks.

The besiegers broke their formation and got together to confer.

"They'll never get us," said Jarvis in a loud whisper to the whole party. "They can't get close enough. They can't."

"But for how long can we hold up?" asked a woman.

"Oh, weeks," replied Jarvis with a dismissive swat. "But they won't stay for weeks. Not worth it."

A few wagons to the right, a man began a murmured quarrel with his wife, who, from what Håkan understood, had convinced him to leave the safety of the trail.

Suddenly, and without looking back, the riders left for the hills, climbed the slope, and disappeared behind the edge. Some of the emigrants cheered. Jarvis called for silence.

"This is not how it ends," he said.

The men kept guard. The women made lunch, stirring the pots with the ramrods. Nobody spoke. There was a heightened awareness of the present. As he ate his food, Håkan felt that he was saying good-bye to something.

About half of the Indians returned. Once again, they surrounded the wheeled convoy. After a pause followed by a hoot, they opened fire. The emigrants responded. No one was hit. Everyone reloaded, and there was another volley of guns. Bullets whistled and whined by, missing their targets by a long way. There were three or four of these loud and harmless exchanges.

All of a sudden, a group of white men came galloping down the slope, screaming, roaring, and brandishing their rifles. Confusion and dread rippled through the Indian circle. Caught between the fire pouring from the wagons and the wider ring the newly arrived rescuers were forming around them, the Indians started hooting and shrieking and galloped south down the valley. A few of the newcomers chased after them but desisted as soon as the Indians turned right and disappeared over the brow of the western hills.

Inside the barricade, there was a profusion of embraces, tears, and invocations. Some congratulated Jarvis. Håkan went to see Helen and the boy. Undisturbed by the commotion, the child slept in his astoundingly clean bed. Håkan put his hand on the boy's forehead. Still a low fever. Helen put her hand on Håkan's. The softness, the wonder, the desire displaced everything—the world, his own self. She rested her head on his shoulder. He caressed her hand with his thumb, hoping it would not offend her. She came closer. Their thighs touched. They sat looking at the boy, ignoring the sound of moving wagons.

"Hawk!"

Jarvis wanted him. Håkan summoned all his courage to look at Helen. Her eyes were still on the boy, but the smile on her face was for Håkan.

He got out of the wagon. Jarvis was waving at him from the opening they had made in the circle to let their rescuers through.

"They're coming. I want you here."

Clustered by family, the emigrants stood in one expectant line. The sun stung like an open wound. Two mating dogs looked up with dejected piousness. A little boy fired his carbine-shaped stick at the hills. A few birds circled over the dead ox.

"Thank you, friends! Welcome! Thank you!" cried Jarvis on behalf of the whole party as the men rode into the open circle.

Some women flattened their aprons. Some men rearranged their hats. The riders were quiet.

"Thank you," Jarvis repeated, sunnier than ever. "Please. What can we do for you?"

"Bread. Haven't had bread for ages," replied the leader, a man in a hat with the crown belled out, while discreetly gesturing his companions to specific positions.

"Somebody! Bread!" shouted Jarvis.

There was a moment of hesitation. Finally, two of the women headed toward their wagons, running with short steps and gathered skirts. One of the riders took his post by the opening, next to Håkan. Nobody said a word. There was an anthill by Håkan's foot. He looked at the insects, then up at the sky, and then at the man next to him. The rider's face was dotted with those yellow, red, and blue spots that dance in front of eyes that have just gazed into the glaring sky. Håkan blinked. The dancing spots faded. He blinked again. The dancing spots were gone. Still, on the rider's face, there were yellow, red, and blue stains. Paint stains. Håkan felt weightless. His knees trembled. He stumbled and stepped on the anthill. The little boy fired his stick carbine. The women returned with their short steps and gathered skirts, carrying round loaves of bread. Helen looked out of her wagon and smiled at Håkan. The rider followed her gaze, looked down at Håkan, and understood that he had seen his yellow, red, and blue paint stains. Both men were paralyzed during this moment of mutual recognition. The rider smeared the paint off his face and then looked at his fingers. Across the circle, the leader, in the process of breaking a loaf in half, saw the last part of this scene. His eyes shrank to slits. He dropped the bread and leveled his rifle at the line of emigrants.

"Charge, by Jehu!" he cried.

They shot at anyone in their line of fire—armed or unarmed, man or woman, adult or child. The rider next to Håkan was transfixed. Håkan's skin tingled with terror as he drew his pistol and shot him in the heart. Winded and horror-stricken, Håkan found cover behind some sacks of grain. Smoke. Ringing ears. Crawling silhouettes. Whinnying. Frightened dogs and greedy dogs. Cries. His own blood throbbing. That sense of weightlessness.

From behind the hills right next to them, the fake Indians reemerged and streamed into the circle, joining the riders and opening fire on the emigrants. Those who were able to fired back. One of the Indian imposters, shot in the chest, fell next to Håkan. He was alive but would soon drown in his own blood. Håkan crawled up to him. He could hear the sound of the sagging lung flopping around in his rib cage. Håkan stared into the man's blue eyes as he gave his last shallow breath.

The gunshots grew sporadic. There was no time to reload. Guns were replaced by blades, clubs, and fists. The mutilated boy's father lay dead a few steps away from his team of oxen. Håkan saw three men climbing into the wagon where Helen and her brother were. He got up and grabbed a loose kingbolt from a wagon. One of the Indian impersonators intercepted him. He had a knife. For the first time in his life, Håkan felt, in his flesh, in his bones, in every limb, the full extent of his own size and the power that came with it. He raised his arm, swung the kingbolt, and knocked the man's brains out. After picking up the knife, he reached the wagon and looked in. The boy's throat had been slit. Two men, naked from the waist down, were hunched over Helen. A third man held a blade to her neck. No one noticed Håkan. He stabbed the one who was moving back and forth on top of Helen. Surprised, the one with the knife slashed her throat. Håkan drew his gun and shot them both.

Håkan was pulled out of the wagon by the vortex of violence that still spun around the wheeled camp. He screamed and sobbed like a child as he fought the pillagers. He was only aware of each one of the bodies in front of him that needed to be destroyed. He had no clear rec-ollection of his deeds, but his impressions endured. He remembered thinking of his own face, disfigured and reddened by his screams as he made each one of the three shots left in his pistol count. He recalled a new part of his conscience coming into existence and perishing as he brained a man with the butt end of his gun. He had a keen memory of his departure from himself as he stabbed someone in the liver. He knew he had killed and maimed several men, but what remained most vividly in his mind was the feeling of sorrow and senselessness that came with each act: those worth defending were already dead, and each of his kill-ings made his own struggle for self-preservation less justifiable.

They were drunk. One song kept coming back, interrupting their bois-terous ramblings. Håkan could not make out the words, but for some reason, it made him think of a wedding. They had put a garland on his head and called it a crown. "To the Hawk," they cried before each drink. Jarvis insisted that he celebrate with them, and Håkan could only make him stop by putting the vile bottle to his lips and pretending to take a gulp. "To the Hawk!" Håkan stared at the fire as if the flames were fueled solely by his gaze.

The land was hard and rocky, and they had buried their dead in shallow graves. Parents and widowed spouses stared at their mounds of dirt. Håkan placed Helen with her family in a site far away from the rest. He was about to put his lips to her forehead but was sickened to discover that he found it easier to kiss her now that she was dead.

Their enemies were left to rot. The majority had died by Håkan's hand. Jarvis said the plunderers had retreated once they saw that they stood no chance in hand-to-hand encounters. And that had been thanks to Håkan. He made it too costly for them. Or something like that. Håkan was not sure. "To the Hawk!"

They interrogated the only survivor who had been left behind. Håkan understood most of what the dying man said—he spoke slowly, making long pauses to catch his breath.

"Soldiers of Jehu. The Wrathful Angels. There are more of us," he said defiantly.

"Where?" asked Jarvis.

"The prophet's militia. We'll take you over the rim of the basin yet. You. All the other cursed gentiles. Even your president. Over the rim. The brethren."

"Where? Where are the other brethren?" insisted Jarvis.

The man smiled.

"Why attack us? We got nothing. We're poor," said one of the emigrants.

"Like the prophet said, there are three kinds of poor." Although exhausted by pain, the man clearly relished in the words he could not yet utter. He coughed and wheezed. "Prophet said: There are three kinds of poor. The Lord's poor, the Devil's poor, and the poor devils." He laughed and coughed.

"This man here can cure you," Jarvis said, pointing at Håkan. "Speak."

"Over the rim."

The man gave a series of muffled coughs, looked at the night sky, sputtered out a blotch of thick black blood, and died.

A beamless glow floated in the east. There was something sinister about the bodies of the emigrants strewn around camp, sleeping off their drunkenness by the paling embers. A few women were already at their chores. The horses of the fallen attackers had been hobbled and grouped together. Håkan found the bay that had belonged to the first man he had killed. He adjusted the stirrups and led the horse over to his packed burro. Jarvis lay nearby. Håkan left the gun next to him. The women stopped working and looked at Håkan from the black holes of their bonnets. He mounted and slowly rode away.

13.

Would he ever confess to Linus what he had done? Håkan remembered his brother's boastful stories, full of heroic deeds and displays of courage, and the mere thought that Linus might be impressed by his killings saddened him. Having experienced violence firsthand, Håkan realized now that all those childhood tales had to have been made up. Nobody could commit or witness those barbaric acts with such giddiness. And he preferred to think the stories were false rather than to even consider that his brother had felt such frivolous delight at bloodshed. In either case, his lies or his enjoyment darkened, for the first time, Linus's image. But so much time had gone by, and so many things must have happened to him. Surely, he was a different person by now. What would this new man make of his younger brother and his sins? For Håkan did believe that he had sinned. Not against god, whose fading presence he barely considered anymore, but against the sanctity of the human body into which he had so recently been initiated and then, just months later, utterly violated. There were no exceptions, no excuses, no attenuations for this violation—not even Helen, whom he had been unable to save. What would these killings turn him into? What would he become?

Because he did not wish to see other people, he decided to travel east along a parallel line a few days south of the trail and ride up only when his supplies ran out. But he did not stay this course for long. His mind would drift off, and it was his horse who for the most part set their erratic course. Often, the three of them—burro, horse, rider—would simply stand in the middle of the plains. Aside from the occasional sigh or the halfhearted attempt at swatting away an insect, they all stood still, staring into the void. Brown flats, blue wall. From his animals, with their serenely sad, bulge-eyed gaze, Håkan seemed to have learned to gape into space. To this absent expression, he added a drooping jaw. They merely stood, completely absorbed by nothing. Time dissolved into the sky. There was little difference between landscape and spectators. Insensible things that existed in one another. Suddenly, Håkan would come out of his long stupor, consult his compass, and set out again, only to lapse into empty thoughts a moment later and once again relinquish his command to the bay. He barely ate—charqui, a biscuit. His fires at night were small. Sleep seldom came to him. He lost all count of time and had no clear idea of where he was. Still, he believed that, with luck and an extra effort, he could reach New York in a matter of weeks. And yet, he felt no desire to rush on. His thoughts weakened until they were just lethargic spasms in the thick fog that clouded his consciousness. Gradually, his reason quieted down, became a murmur, and finally ceased.

He was overwhelmed by an active, all-consuming hollowness—a corrosive shadow wiping out the world in its progress, a stillness that had nothing to do with peace, a voracious silence craving total desolation, an infectious nothingness colonizing everything. All that remained in its soundless, barren wake was an almost undetectable vibration. But in the absence of everything else, this faint drone was unbearable. Håkan had neither the will to make it stop (a simple task carried out with some sense of purpose, like keeping his course or cooking a meal, would probably have been enough) nor the strength to endure it. With the last dregs of consciousness he was able to scrape up, he managed to find a more or less hospitable spot with some water in it, surrounded by decent pasture fields. He tied the horse and the burro with long ropes, unpacked his tin box, and, from one of the vials kept there, took a few drops of Lorimer's sedative tincture.

For a few moments—it was so fleeting—he did not matter, and that did not matter. There was a sky. There was a body. And a planet underneath it. And it was all lovely. And it did not matter. He had never been happy before.

And it did not matter.

Like a sphinx, the burro was stretched out next to him. He thought it was a dream, since he had never seen the burro lying down. They looked at each other. Dawn hummed on the horizon, but how many nights had preceded this daybreak, he could not tell. His piercing sunburn reached his bones. The lines defining the things around him— the bush, the beasts, his feet—were brittle. His body felt tingly and hollow. He walked to the pond and drank the cloudy, creamy water. After making sure his animals had all they needed, he ate some charqui and a lump of sugar. With a blanket, the saddle, and a few bags, he built a simple shelter to block out the sun. He crawled under it and took another dose of the tincture.

This time, he did not experience the bliss of irrelevance. He was merely snuffed out. His eyes rolled back, but he was surprised to discover they were still able to see in the dark. They looked back into his cranium, at his own brain. With the part of his perception that was not involved in the process of seeing, he understood that his brain was receiving the images of itself from the eyes attached to it. It took his brain a moment to understand how extraordinary the situation was.

"What brain has ever seen itself?" it thought.

It also thought that its crevices, color, and texture were unique and entirely different from other human brains it had studied in the past. For a moment, the brain found the vertigo of having its own image of itself within itself dizzying and even amusing. Then it thought that it should pay attention and learn. And with that, the brain's surface turned from gray to brown. While retaining their shape, the pearly waves became bristly knolls, and the gelatinous surface was harshened by dust and sagebrush. A gang of buffalo came out from behind the eyes and ambled through the hills.

Now Håkan knew he was dreaming and lost interest. He sank into annihilation.

The unstable shelter had collapsed, and the blanket had wrapped itself around his upper body. Slithering sweat stung his chest and neck. It was the afternoon. An afternoon. The pond had shrunk to a puddle of brackish water. For no particular reason, that well-known patch of land where he had been for days now sickened him. He did not want to stay but lacked the will to move on. The only way out of his apathy, he thought, was to make it deeper by extinguishing himself again with a few more drops of the tincture. The lack of water for his animals, however, made another prolonged absence impossible. With weak, unsteady hands, he packed the burro and saddled the horse and set out, itchy from the sun, his sweat, and insect bites. Scratching his face, he realized that his beard was now thick and full.

The next morning, the earth was hard with frost. The sky was lower, and the sun indecisive. Håkan knew that the emigrants chose the warm seasons for their journey and that the trail would soon be deserted. It was time to head up north and get provisions for the remainder of his trip before winter set in. He rode leisurely, hoping to regain strength and clarity of mind along the way. The cold air cut through his head. Every evening, he had a proper dinner and made sure to stay warm and get a good night's sleep. He would set out at sunup, always at an unhurried pace to spare his animals. When he least expected them,

like noiseless detonations, images of the killings struck him with overwhelming vividness, obliterating the physical reality around him—he
often found himself reenacting some of the events of that day (he would
be on his horse and suddenly brandish an invisible knife, or cover his
eyes with the back of his hand, or scream out, or duck). Although the
hum, the constant vibration he had felt since leaving the caravan, was
still there, now he was able to think and hear himself over it.

There was no way to tell how long he had been on his own—his long
vacant spells, the days spent under the influence of the potion, and his
general numbness rendered all calculations vain. But since the air had
cooled and the days shortened, he assumed that he had been drifting for
several weeks. He picked up his pace to make sure he did not miss the
last stragglers on the trail before the cold finally set in, and a few days
later, he made out the broken line of a meager caravan. He approached
it slowly and rode along the wagons for a while, keeping a few hundred
paces from them. The train was much less populated, and unlike a few
months ago, there was ample space between convoys. After some time,
enough for the emigrants to see that he was alone and harmless, he
turned toward the trail. By now, he was used to the impression a stranger
in the plains caused. He was also accustomed to the reaction his attire
and, above all, his height brought about. This time, however, something
was different. Through the usual bewilderment ran a streak of recognition. They looked at him with that particular squint that tries to penetrate the past, as if they found him vaguely familiar while impossible to
place. Meanwhile, some men grouped together, holding shovels and axes.
A few fetched their rifles. The women gathered their children. A group
of armed emigrants got on their horses and rode out to meet Håkan. As
they approached, he held his hands up and rode in a circle to show them
he was unarmed. They stopped at a prudent distance from each other.

"Are you the Hawk?" one man asked.

With these few words, reality was overturned. How could this be? How could these men out in the wilderness know his name? A current of astonishment tickled his skin from within and then dissipated, yielding to a terrible realization. Perhaps the story of his deeds had traveled from Jarvis's party back to the trail and then passed down from wagon to wagon. The truth was awful enough, but who knew how the narrative had been distorted along the way? He did not know how to respond. Lying was hopeless—his appearance was far too conspicuous.

"Håkan," he responded. "I am Håkan."

"Right, the Hawk," someone responded. "You killed all those people."

Håkan looked down. For the first time since the killings, he felt something other than pain and guilt. He felt ashamed. It would almost have been a relief to trade his torment for shame, had the humiliation not burned so much. Ashamed, embarrassed, dirty. Soiled in front of everybody.

"We don't want any trouble," said one of them with a trembling voice.

"What are you saying? The man's a hero!" responded someone with more assurance. "Those could have been our daughters there!"

A heated but hushed debate ensued. Håkan could not look up. Naked and soiled. Always staring down, he turned around, touched up his horse, and, with the burro in tow, left at a canter. A few moments later, he was overtaken by a small group of riders. They all stopped. Håkan's burning face never looked up. They left a few sacks with supplies by his horse, thanked him for ridding them of those bad men, wished him good luck, and turned back to their families.

14.

He learned to wrestle the horse and the burro down. It started like an embrace, with his cheek to the animal's neck. He would then force it to bend one of its fore knees with his own leg while pushing down and to the side with the full weight of his body. At first, it was a contest, but in time the beasts understood that, with an embrace and the slightest push, they had to lie down on their sides and stay until Håkan got up. He did this each time he thought he spied someone on the circular horizon. Had Håkan and his animals ever been spotted, the distant travelers would have taken the vanishing silhouettes for a mirage. But there were no such travelers—the moving shadows he saw almost every day in the distance were illusions. With the double intention of getting away from the trail and the cold, he had traveled south for days. He passed no settlements or paths, and there were no signs of trappers, prospectors, or Indians. For weeks, the only human forms in sight had been his own extremities and his own shadow. The flats around him allowed for no ambushes or surprises. Sounds seemed to travel faster in the freezing air, and if anything happened to escape his eyes, it quickly reached his ears. His solitude was total in the shoreless plains. And yet, he felt cornered. The slightest stir in the skyline, the feeblest rustle in the scrubs sent him down with his animals. They stayed quiet with their ears to the ground and the dirt in their nostrils. Håkan measured time with the artery throbbing underneath the living leather of his horse's neck. After at least one hundred beats (double if he thought the threat was grave), he would look up, and the three of them would get back on their feet and resume their march.

So great was his fear of running into anyone who might know about him and his deeds that, in addition to the illusory shadows that sent him diving with his animals, he started to detect signs of human presence at every turn. A few broken twigs (and there were many broken twigs throughout the sagebrush steppe) signaled, to him, the passage of a rider; a few stones in a somewhat regular pattern (and he saw patterns everywhere) represented the remnants of a campfire whose ashes had been scattered by the wind; a pale weedless streak on the ground (and streaks striated the plains in every direction) was taken to be a trail; a well-traced circle in the bunchgrass (and whim had drawn countless circles all over the flats) meant that cattle had been left to graze within rounded-up wagons. Several times a day, he dismounted and picked up some dry dung to make sure it was not horse manure—and if it happened to come from a horse, to establish how old it was. He inspected carrion and blanched bones, looking for evidence of human method in the way the bodies had been butchered. The air, which he had always found odorless, now seemed to carry all kinds of human smells, from cornbread to gunpowder. Multitudes had just left the circle of his reality or were just about to invade it. With the advancing cold, the ground got harder, and instead of the mossy, muffled thud Håkan was used to, the hoofbeats acquired a wooden resonance. He made eight pouches out of tarpaulin, filled them with dry grass and old rags, put the horse's and burro's feet inside, and tied them to their ankles. The boots rendered the hoof-falls inaudible, which gave the journey the lightness of an unfulfilled idea. For the most part, Håkan rode almost sideways, with one ear forward, listening for other travelers in the soundless expanse. The plains that first had seemed to him impenetrable in their barren sameness, and then a source of knowledge, now became a ciphered surface, saturated with coded messages that pointed to one single meaning: the presence of others—men who would see him in his rotten,

infected condition. They were always just behind the horizon. And so
was winter.

Seeking to avoid further encounters with the last stragglers on the
trail and looking for milder weather, Håkan headed south, always with a
slight slant east. Winter was a giant wave gathering in the distance, surg-
ing over the plains, ready to break and wash away the minute rider in
a whirlwind of darkness and ice. Already, the shadow cast by this massive wave had caught up with him. The days had grown shorter. The sun
had lost its authority. The brown grass was crisp with frost. Firewood
became immune to tinder. Water lapped under glass cobwebs. Game
grew scarce. Provisions had to be rationed. He ate different plants that
got him sick, until he finally found a succulent stalk that he would grind
with the butt of his knife into a bittersweet, slightly salty pulp that
reminded him of the licorice candy his mother had given him with great
ceremony three times in his life, and that he had pretended to like. For
some time, he ate crickets, but soon the supply grew scant until they all
vanished completely as the cold set in.

Since he had only a few blankets to wrap over the hodgepodge of an
outfit the Indians had made him, peltries quickly became as valuable
as meat. Most animals had migrated south or holed up for the winter,
but some dogs, rodents, and cats still rambled around, their eyes convex with hunger and despair. He caught his first badgers and rats with
a deadfall trap. Smashed to a mass of hair and flesh under the heavy
rock, the smaller creatures—most of his catch—were hard to skin and
impossible to eat. One afternoon, as he was discarding a particularly
damaged rabbit, he remembered his father's glue. A few times a year,
his father would gather the skins and carcasses of dead animals (mostly
mice and hares snared around the house, although he had once used
parts of an elk he had found rotting in the forest), scrape the hides, and
boil the shavings together with bones, tails, and tendons for a couple

of days, adding as little water as possible, until it was all reduced to a viscous syrup, not unlike resin. He would then remove the bones and use the paste for minor repairs. Once, particularly satisfied with the results, he challenged Linus to split up two planks he had bonded together with his concoction. Linus—proud of being treated like an adult and, moreover, eager to perform a feat of strength—grabbed the planks and, without any visible effort, snapped them asunder. It was so quick, he was unable to even blow out the big breath he had taken in preparing for the effort. After the initial surprise, Linus smiled proudly, until he looked up and saw their father's face. He told the boys to clean up the mess, then turned around and left. Even if the glue was not strong enough for wood, Håkan thought that it might be used to hunt small game. The main obstacle for making the paste was to keep a fire going for all that time—not only because of the scarce firewood and the intense wind, but mainly because it increased his chances of being seen. Having spent the next few days stocking up on fuel, he devised a screen out of blankets and tarpaulins that had the double virtue of shielding the fire from the wind and concealing its glow through the night. After boiling down the shavings and scraps of his pulped prey for almost two days, he poured the glue on a piece of oilcloth and baited it with biscuits. The first victim, a gopher, managed to escape. A second gopher also broke free from the sticky trap but was slowed down enough for Håkan to be able to deal a clean blow to its head. Most animals, although confused by the sudden thickness under their feet, succeeded in fleeing with their biscuit. Even if he was disappointed, Håkan felt closer to his father with every defeat. In time, however, between the deadfall and the glue (which, once cool, became an amber block that could be melted and reused over and over again), Håkan managed to catch a decent number of prairie dogs, ferrets, weasels, badgers, rats, hares, and even small dogs.

He started making a coat out of the pelts. All the dissections Håkan had performed under Lorimer's supervision had turned him into a consummate skinner. With no more than a few incisions, the furs almost slid off the frame, as if they had been lined with silk and the flesh they covered had been made of wax. In some cases, he was able to leave the empty skin almost intact, which gave the impression that the body within had simply melted and evaporated. After skinning his prey, he scraped off the flesh and fat from the hides and strapped them up to dry across his horse's saddlebags and the burro's croup. Remembering those Indian women he had seen tanning buffalo hides while their husbands lay unconscious from drink, Håkan rubbed the brains of the freshly caught animals into the stiff furs to soften them. Since most of the brains were so small, he mashed and mixed them with water. During a drought, he discovered that his urine produced better results.

After some pounding, the dry sinews from the larger animals split into fibers that Håkan separated and used as thread to stitch together the disparate patches of cured leather with his surgical needles. It was a slow process (hunting, curing, threading, sewing), and the first snow had already fallen. Without a gun, there was no hope of getting one of the last few bears or larger cats he sometimes saw in the distance eating the carrion he had left behind. He once smeared himself with gore and lay down, pretending to be wounded, hoping to knife a bobcat that was on his trail. The bobcat never came. Not too many days later, however, something better made up for this failure.

Through the light snowflakes that melted before touching the ground came the cry of a baby. As always, Håkan's first reaction was to wrestle his horse and burro down. In the mist, the weeping continued. The small, airy drops felt like a cold halo hovering over his face, contrasting with the warm glow coming from the horse's muscles twitching under his cheek. No voices of men or women. No jingling of harnesses or creaking of springs. No rumbling of wagons or tramping of beasts. Just the lonely wail. Håkan's horse got restless, but he pressed on his neck and made him stay down. A long time went by. The weeping never stopped, always issuing from the same spot in the white mist. Other than the cries, complete silence. It stopped snowing. The fog thickened. Cramped and soaked, Håkan got up, mounted his horse, and rode into the crawling clouds. With each step, the wails grew louder. The plains barely insisted against the fog. Håkan got out his knife. As he moved along, the ground ahead of him faded into reality from the whiteness ahead. Then, in a slight depression by some shrubs, a lion took shape. It was lying in a pool of its own blood, lightened by the snowfall. Next to it, a wailing blind cub. It was getting hoarse. Håkan dismounted and immediately saw that the cougar had died trying to give birth to its second, breech offspring, still stuck halfway out. Håkan rolled the mother over and put the crying kitten to one of her teats. From its out-stretched hind legs to its head, the lion was taller than Håkan. The cub nursed greedily. After a few moments, realizing that nothing came out, it started crying again. Håkan tried to milk the lion. Then, he went through his provisions and offered the kitten everything he had—charqui, sugar water, dried meat from different animals, oats, bacon, and moistened biscuits. Håkan now heard rage in the cub's desperate cries. He made a cut into his own forearm and put the kitten's snout to the blood, but it would not taste it. Håkan looked into the crying mouth and saw the ribbed vault of the palate, the sharp little teeth, and the white scales on the pink tongue. He smelled the clean breath coming from the empty stomach. Then he looked into the creature's watery eyes and wrung its neck. Mother and cub were skinned.

His animals were exhausted and ill fed, but Håkan knew their only hope was to outrun the northern cold. He gave up all aspirations, how-ever small, of heading east. The constant gales made him feel as if he

were falling rather than walking. His face was windburned; his hands
scabbed; his feet frostbitten. The horse proceeded with his head tucked
low, almost bent into his chest. Every so often, Håkan had to stop and
turn around to rest from the relentless, deafening, insane howl that left
no room for a single thought in his head. There was no way to light a
fire, and he slept wrapped in his lion skin. When this was insufficient,
he wrestled his horse down and huddled up next to him. One night,
when the horse refused to stay down, Håkan learned that the burro was
happy to have him sleep against his rib cage, and in this way they shared
each other's warmth through several storms. During those days, his only
relief came from thinking how unlikely it would be to meet someone
else in that obliterating scream. His loneliness was perfect, and for the
first time in months, despite all the roaring and lashing, he found calm.

A modest mountain range emerged on the horizon. After months
and leagues of desert and leveled grass, the rugged undulations rolled
up into the sky like an otherworldly phenomenon. Some of the sum-
mits were even lost in the low clouds. The sides, unbelievably, were
green. Perhaps he could find shelter there, and maybe the winds would
be milder on the other side. Two days later, he was halfway up the
most accessible of the sierras. Relieved by the change from the invari-
able flatness of the steppe, Håkan rode on up with joy. And the trees.
The evergreen trees. The vertical trees. In the canopy, friendly birds
(not the desperate, demented scavengers that sometimes overflew the
plains) chirped and labored on their nests. Sliced and opened up by
branches and needles, the ashen sunlight recovered some of its glow as
it landed in thin, discrete rays on lichen-lined stones. Life bustled in the
underbrush—chipmunks, earthworms, foxes, insects. By a fir, Håkan
found some buttery mushrooms that reminded him of the chanterelles
he used to pick with Linus. In Sweden, these were not winter mushrooms, but Håkan plucked one and, recognizing the fresh yet overripe

smell, took a cautious bite. He teared up and suppressed a sob. Toward sundown, he found a narrow cave where he cooked the mushrooms in lard and ate them with his eyes closed. The following day, he rested. When he woke up from his long, mossy sleep, he set a few traps and got to work on his coat.

Inevitably, the garment came together around the skin of the lion. Håkan had taken good care to strip it off making as few incisions as possible to preserve the integrity of its shape. With a few leather patches sewn or glued to some essential spots hidden on the reverse of the fur (ears, forehead, snout, jaws), the cougar's head, which had been reduced to a rag, regained some of its majesty. It hung behind the wearer's neck but could also be fitted as an ominous cowl. The forelegs, thrown around the neck, were meant to be worn as a scarf, which the weight of the paws, stuffed with dust and pebbles, kept in place. The lion's back draped down on Håkan's, so that the cat's tail looked like the continuation of the man's spine. From this so-far sleeveless robe, Håkan hoped to make a proper coat, for which he was sewing together all the smaller pelts he had tanned along the way. During his stay at the cave, he caught a fox that made up, almost on its own, a full sleeve. Because the cougar's skin covered nearly his entire body and the game in the little mountain forest had been abundant, he now had spare leather, with which he devised a small foldable shelter.

Had the pasture not been so scarce, he would have spent the entire winter there, peacefully sewing, trapping, and eating mushroom stew in the den that was quickly becoming the most homelike place he had known in his travels.

Once he went over the cusp and climbed down the southern face, he was glad to have moved forward. On the other side of the mountain, the winds were gentler, the grass more tender, and the sun less remote. It still snowed every now and then, and the nights were long and bitter, but according to his calculations, winter should have been half over, and if this was the worst, he was sure to survive. Although he was still heading south, he gave his course a modest pitch toward the east. The sierras were far from insurmountable, but somehow Håkan was more at ease knowing that they stood between him and the trail. He still scanned the plains for signs of men, but there was not a single trace left by fire, tools, or cattle.

Although he had ridden through unmarked plains in the past, this time something was out of place. He. He did not belong in that landscape. He wondered when those fields had last been in someone's consciousness. He felt them staring back at him, aware of this encounter, trying to remember what it was like to be looked at in this way.

"Gräs," Håkan said out loud, sensing the wonder and the injustice of making all those individual blades of grass that swayed into the edge of the earth come together for the first time under the domain of that single word.

He feared sunset and often spent the entire day worrying about night. The lack of firewood and the violence of some of the gusts sometimes made it impossible to build a fire. Anticipating this, back at his cave in the mountain, he had taken the precaution of building his little tent. Made of flexible sticks, leather, and quilts, it was an elongated, curved triangle with two convex sides, like the inverted bow of a small rowboat (or like the head of certain fish or the beak of certain birds), and an opening. He would pitch it windward and crawl in, lying on the base to keep the structure in place. The tent covered only his upper body, but the streamlined prow cut through the gales, always about to crush the little hull of the upturned craft that seemed to move at a dizzying speed despite being completely motionless. Whatever sleep he got during these wild, fireless nights was thanks to his small refuge.

From daybreak to sundown, he marched on, never dismounting to eat and pausing only when he came to a stream or some standing water to refresh the horse and the burro. On these occasions, he would lay a few traps. As he drifted south through that unknown land, a growing discomfort rose in his body. It had an abstract origin, like a mysterious humor rising from his innards that became denser as it ascended through his esophagus, until it coagulated into a lump at the end of his sternum, right between his clavicles. The semisolid ball made him want to vomit. Even though he had ingested plenty of rotten meat and too many noxious plants, he somehow knew that his sickness had not been caused by something he had eaten. The source of his malady was outside him. It was the plains. It was his constant motion through the void. Perhaps the lack of proper food and rest exacerbated it, but the undulated expanse itself had become sickening. Just looking at the plains made the lump denser, and it got harder and more asphyxiating as soon as he started to move across the steppe. The brown, the knolls, the murmur, the glare, the dust, the hooves, the horizon, the grass, the hands, the sky, the wind, the thoughts, the glare, the hooves, the dust, the knolls, the hands, the horizon, the brown, the murmur, the sky, the wind, the grass made him queasy. Sometimes he tried to make himself throw up but only felt the veins in his head bulge and threaten to burst as he retched. Minor events interrupted the nauseous monotony—buffalo, a rainbow—but after their dispersion, the illness only returned with renewed force.

Håkan kept traveling south for a few weeks. Life got easier as the air warmed up. Still, he was surprised to see that despite the milder weather, the vegetation became sparser. Hard, razor-sharp grass grew only in patches. The bushes turned bristly and hostile. Scaled animals soon outnumbered furred ones. A red desert was overtaking the brown desert. As he moved forward, the terrain acquired familiar features—the crimson dust fading into purple as it reached the jagged skyline, the heat coming out of that white hole in the firmament, the general indifference toward life. Had he been here before? It reminded him of part of his journey with the Brennans. Or was it the wasteland where Lorimer and his party had found the plundered Indians? Håkan was stunned by the realization that he could not tell these two places apart, and his confusion frightened him. Had he, somehow, despite the fact that he checked his compass regularly, managed to get lost? Had he returned to one of those places he had already been to? How many deserts could a country have? Lorimer had taught him that, against everything his senses told him, the earth was a globe. Had he already made his way around it? Had his journey south (and slightly east) taken him all the way back northwest, from where he had come? Comparing the length of his ride with the time he had spent sailing north from Cape Horn on the ship that had brought him to America, it did make sense. He wept. Had he traveled around the world for nothing? An even more terrifying thought sank in. Was reason abandoning him? Was his brain sick?

There were no plants, no fuel, no water. He did not know where he was. He did not know if he was sane. The only choice was to turn around, go back into the grassland, and then, no matter what, head straight east.

15.

A bee. It circled the horse's ears, buzzed behind Håkan's neck, and then escorted them for a while, cautiously inspecting the saddlebags and the burro's load. Håkan's first thought was that, at last, spring had arrived. Then, immediately after, he realized that he had not seen a bee in years. In fact, this was the first one to cross his path since he had left Sweden. So far, the American wilderness, with its lavish range of species thriving in extremely divergent conditions, had been unable to produce a bee. He had experienced every season in different climates. And these prairies were the same prairies he had been riding through for ages—at the very least, since first meeting the emigrants on the trail. Why, then, now, suddenly, a bee? Farms. That was the only explanation he could come up with. In all this time, since landing in San Francisco, he had never seen anyone working the land. No plowing, sowing, or reaping; no fences, haystacks, or mills. No beehives. So there had to be farms close by. Since everything else, beginning with the terrain and the elements, had remained constant, this had to be the explanation for the unexpected appearance of the honeybee.

He was still concerned about other people, but he hoped that after all the time that had passed since the killings, he would have been forgotten. Sometimes, when his spirits were at their highest, he even trusted that he was far enough from the scene for anyone to even know about what had happened. The news could never have reached these parts, so removed from the trail. And even if reports of this unlikely possibility proved to be the case—even if reports of his shameful deeds had traveled through the seasons and through the plains—he believed that he had become stronger and that he was ready to face anyone with the truth. Whenever these arguments failed, he told himself that he was either mad or lost, trapped in the great grasslands between the trail and the desert, and that if he ever wanted to see Linus again, sooner or later he would have to turn east, and should he not meet other men along the way, he would surely have to confront a multitude in the great city of New York.

For the moment, however, even if the bee—and the many others that followed it—was a herald of civilization, there were neither farms nor villages in sight, and Håkan traveled forth undisturbed. Moreover, despite their threatening implications, the bees gave him great joy. A few days after spotting his first specimen, he saw the air thickened by a swarm overflying a fallen log. The bees thronged over a hollow in the trunk, which turned out to hold a honeycomb. With great care, but unable to avoid a few stings, Håkan reached for the wild honey. His forearms burned with domed yellow blisters as he took a flake to his mouth. He barely recognized the flavor as honey. It had less to do with taste than with touch, smell, and sight. The waxy, silken paste went straight to his nose, where he saw a thousand flowers.

When he shed his fur coat, Håkan also took off the horse's and the burro's tarpaulin boots. The hardships of last winter had become a memory—a series of vivid and yet partial recollections. He knew that he had been cold but could not invoke the cold in his bones; he knew that it had been windy but could not relive the wind slicing through his flesh. Likewise, he knew that he had lived in constant fear of running into other people and remembered how exhausted he was from his never-ending precautions but found it impossible to summon the fear itself. These things—the numbing cold, the gritty gales grounding into the skin, the relentless and inarticulate dread—could be brought back as words or pictures, but not as experiences. And it was this impossibility that made him believe that now, when spring had set in, he was prepared to meet his fellow creatures.

Having traveled north until the last red vestiges of desert had vanished from the greening plains, Håkan made an abrupt turn east. Each time he consulted the silver compass, he caught a partial glimpse of his face reflected on the clouded lid, which his fingertips had darkened over time. He always looked at his teeth first. With their untainted whiteness, they were the only part of his body that reminded him of who he used to be. As soon as he shut his mouth, those relics vanished under the yellow and orange disorder of his beard. He was always stunned to find that brutal thing on his face. His eyes had shrunk from so much squinting and were barely visible at the bottom of the depressions between his protruding cheekbones and his prematurely wrinkled forehead. His features were only revealed to him one at a time as he scanned his face with the dim compass lid. If he pulled it back to see the whole, it all vanished. He wondered what people would make of that face. What had the wilderness done to it? Were his murders drawn on its surface? Although there was still no sign of settlers or travelers, Håkan foresaw that he would learn the answer to these questions soon enough.

The sun had just risen above its own red glow when Håkan spotted four orderly plumes of smoke separated from each other by the same distance. He would have been unable to say why, but there was something in the density, texture, and color of the smoke that spoke to him of hearths and hobs. Those were comfortable fires, not urgent ones. He paused, indecisive, and then resumed his march. As he rode toward the narrow, upright clouds, an orchard came into view. Beyond the trees, a church steeple took shape. The beat of a hammer, the first man-made sound he had heard in ages, echoed above him, as if a remote hand were nailing something into the sky. He was unsure whether the smell of

bread, apple blossoms, dogs, and jam was in the air or in his mind. Did
he hear a woman laughing? Feeling he would look less threatening on
foot, he dismounted and walked his horse toward the village. The treetops swayed yes and no. He could make out some of the houses. They
were painted Swedish red.

Håkan stopped, sensing he had reached an edge beyond which he
would be seen. White linen waved on a clothesline. One of his scabbed,
scarred hands scratched the other. Behind the red walls, there were
beds—beds that would be made with the sheets drying out on the
clothesline. He had not been in a room in a long time. Maybe some of
the sheets were tablecloths. Behind the red walls, there were also tables.
There were also chairs. There could be a sofa. There was milk in jugs,
and there was crockery. There could be someone sweeping the floor.
There could be children in bed. How would he speak? What would his
story be? A wretched man out on the plains by himself. How would he
account for his condition? Could he lie? He looked at his bandaged moccasins. The thought of conversation—and knowing he would be unable
to carry any form of deception through—made his heart drum in his
ears and the blood crawl around his face.

Something moved in the orchard. A second hammer joined in. The
sun had whitened and soured. Håkan got on his horse, turned around,
and, for the very first time, set out at a gallop.

His eyes got watery from the fast, dry wind. He discovered that he
was not a good rider, but the fear of falling off the horse was nothing compared to the terrors he was fleeing. The horse seemed to have
remembered something about himself and was happy about it.

The plains took them back in.

When the horse decided to stop, it was Håkan who was out of breath.
Having always been told that horses ought to be spared, he had never
indulged in anything beyond a canter. The feeling of speed, which he had

never experienced in his life, had not stopped with the gallop. Panting, he still sensed the horizontal plunge. He may have laughed. Little by little, as his breath evened out, he understood that the world had come to a still, and finally his woes caught up with him. He would never be able to face other people. This was clear to him now that he stood, once again, by himself, in the void. But then how would he pass through all the towns that surely lay between him and New York? And how would he ever make his way through the throngs of people that crowded that gigantic city to find Linus? And even if he did—even if he somehow managed to handle every one of these hundreds or thousands or millions of encounters—he would still have to face his brother.

Suddenly, he realized that he had left the burro behind. Going back was unthinkable. He waited, ready to give up the burro and its load rather than return to the edge of the village. Moments later, the burro came into sight, walking, resigned and dignified, toward his companions.

West again. The grass, the horizon. The tyranny of the elements. Undefined visions wafting through his brain, seldom amounting to thoughts. Relinquishing command to his horse. Barely eating. Clearing his throat to remind himself of himself. Sunburned. Smelling, occasionally, his own body. A vague and vacant interest in flowers and insects. Enough rain. No tracks, no threats. Sometimes, a fire leaping under his fingers. The burro and the horse in their perpetual present. His hands doing things. Riding on. Breathing, somehow. Benumbed, yet never finding rest from a thickening sense of desolation. Sponged up by the starry sky each night.

Summer came. Without a clear destination or purpose, there was no reason to keep trudging in the stupefying heat. When his horse led him to a pool, Håkan pitched camp—tarps, oilcloths, and hides stretched out over a cluster of low bushes, under which he would crawl and lie, unable to sit up, for most of the day. Now that Linus was beyond his reach, he saw no reason why he would not end his days there, languishing in the scrubs. The years would go by. His animals would die. Then, no creature (except, perhaps, a clubbed fowl or an ensnared rodent) would look into his eyes ever again. Old age would overtake him. Sickness would shrivel his innards. Once beasts and maggots were done with his flesh, some of his bones would remain scattered on the plains for longer than he had lived. Then, he would be erased.

He was sick of the sun and would often lie on his stomach, drowsy and almost feverish from the stale air under the low-hanging skins and canvases, to avoid its sight. Still, it would pierce through his refuge and bore into his skull, igniting all the past suns that had hunted down and degraded him and everyone else he had met throughout his journey— the sun, deceitful in Portsmouth, implacable over Brennan's mine, cold-hearted against his Clangston window, shrieking across the salt lake, complicit through a wagon's bonnet, excessive when unwanted, and far from its creatures when most needed. To distract himself, he looked into the crisscrossed disorder of the brambles. Many insects had dug their homes in the duskier recesses of those mazes. Barely realizing it at first, Håkan started to study the insects' daily habits, distractedly mapping their itineraries. Slowly, as the days went by, his interest grew, and suddenly he found himself collecting beetles. He caught them under the dome of his hand, held them up for inspection. They remained uniformly frenzied, regardless of what was done to them, until he pierced them through with a suture needle. Håkan believed that the white paste that oozed out of the hole had to be some sort of liquid organ. But this was a fleeting thought. It was not moved by the naturalist's curiosity that he gathered all those inflexible bodies; he did it because he found them pleasing to the eye. Arranging the iridescent shields in different patterns, but always by color and size, Håkan experienced a sort of pleasure that was entirely new to him. He had never experienced delight in color. The way each shade vibrated with a resonance of its own; how certain sheens seemed to emit light and others to absorb it; what neighboring hues would bring out in one another—these were all novel wonders to him. And he was surprised by the joy he got from organizing the beetles. He was consumed by the work on his designs, an effort with no end other than to stimulate his sense of sight. Sometimes he woke up to discover that a gust of wind had scattered his collection or upset his arrangements, but he was almost grateful to have to start from the beginning. In time, he was walking around camp, looking for new specimens. Unaware of it, he often spent the entire day wandering about, going farther each time. He regained some of his former vitality. He resumed some of his trapping and ate better. New pelts were tanned, and once again he took up work on his coat.

Still, he had no desire to travel on. He had not decided to stay there, in the bushes. But he had not decided to move forward, either. The mere thought of other people made his heart pound in his throat. And he still had no idea where he was. Was the desert he had last seen going south the same he had walked through in the north? If so, it would be senseless to move through the plains in either direction—he would just go around the world, from grassland to wasteland and back (and meet the emigrant trail in the middle). Proceeding farther west, he would run into prospectors and homesteaders, and he might even stumble upon San Francisco.

During one of his beetle-hunting expeditions, Håkan was bitten by a snake. Although he was stung on his right heel, he first felt it in his upper left gum. The sting made him jump, and he was lucky enough to land on the snake with the other foot, which allowed him to pin it down and stab it. He had heard that one should cut an X over the bite and rinse the venom out of the wound, and so he did. Back at the camp, he skinned the snake, thinking it would greatly embellish his coat. He made a stew with the flesh. After dinner, when he tried to get up, he noticed that his foot had purpled and swollen. He got colder. Dragging his numbed foot, he replenished the fire and lay down next to it. The snake meat did not seem to agree with him. His stomach felt like the center of a spiral, and his whole body was starting to spin around it. He made himself vomit and after a few attempts got it all out. It did not help, and now, while being colder than ever, he was soaked in sweat from the effort. His mind was shaking, but in the brief segment of quiet in between shivers, he could see that his condition had nothing to do with the food. It was too late for a tourniquet. All he could do was wait and hope that the poison would not be lethal. Keep his eyes on the fire. Try to find friendly faces in the flames. With a jolt, he realized that he had forgotten to breathe. He gasped for air, curled up, and tried to concentrate on the fire. But his body would not breathe. It was only through a colossal exercise of will that he could inhale. His lungs were inert, alien things—completely external devices, bellows he had to pump by hand. He feared he would die if he failed to actively produce the next inhalation. The fire became two fires, beyond which two burros and two horses grazed with indifference. His tongue, putrid and desiccated, tried in vain to push saliva down his crumbling throat. Shivering, he started crawling toward the pond. Although the edge was just a few paces away, the trip felt longer than his entire journey across America. He thought (although those dark ripples in his mind were barely thoughts) that the poison would soon bite into his heart and kill him or that he would die of cold or that wild animals would devour him or that he would faint and drown in the shallows of the pond. The blackness above would take him. Fear had always been loud for him—as soon as the feeling took over, he was deafened by the blood and air rushing through his body. But now, for the first time, terror was suspended in a silent void. Between each distant, laborious breath, Håkan barely felt his heart beat. Every now and then, he heard his animals cropping grass, their molars making the sound of pebbles in the water. There was something almost peaceful about this quiet horror. Then, a sudden gulp of air, and he would clutch a tuft of grass, crawl forward, and lie there, breathless. Whatever little remained of his consciousness was entirely devoted to taking in air and feeling panic; still, he managed to discover one thing—he feared death.

The sun, burning deep into his neck, woke him up from a nightmare in which he was being beheaded. It was noon. He had never made it to the pond. His foot looked better, and he was breathing normally. He drank some water and looked around his camp. For months, he had led a crawling existence in those bushes, hoping that by staying there, without actually deciding anything, he would return, through a motionless path, to the peace of an inanimate state. Yet, when the gift of death had been presented to him, he had used every single one of his poisoned muscles to push it away. Remaining in his degraded condition after this realization was impossible.

He struck eastward as summer came to an end.

16.

Fall hardened into winter. Håkan had marched on slowly, taking advantage of the last temperate days to compose himself before the inevitable encounter with travelers and settlers. He was glad that by the time he saw the first sign of civilization, it was cold enough for him to wear his coat. It made him feel safe. With each turn of his body, the lion merged, like a fabulous creature, with a fox, a hare, or a gopher. Around the neck and down the chest, the snake's silver streak.

Some cows surfaced and sank on the horizon.

It was the first time he saw cattle out on the plains, away from the trail. After a while, however, the herd turned in Håkan's direction. He stopped. Moos and bells. As he was wondering what to do, the drove changed course again, slouching along the skyline. Some time later, a group of riders, shimmering in the distant gleam, came into view—the first human forms Håkan had seen in many seasons. He knew that the wranglers had spotted him, too. They may have hesitated for a moment, but never halted, and soon they were out of sight.

A few days later, Håkan saw a city.

He was unable to tell at what point the road had appeared under him. By splitting them in half, the dusty stripe abolished the sense that the plains were infinite. There was now this side of the road and that side of the road. And at the end of it lay the city.

Several riders, wagons, and even carriages passed him in both directions. He kept his head low and never greeted anyone back. Even if he fixed his eyes on the dirt, he could feel the turning heads and the staring eyes. Like a froth corroding his organs, terror rose within his body. Each time he was about to turn around and gallop away in fright, he forced himself to think of his squalid shelter in the bushes and the bestial life he had led there. If he did not press on, that would be his only other option.

Chin on chest, Håkan made it into town and proceeded down its main street. He could see the small city dissolve back into the plains a few blocks down. The furtive glances from under his brow revealed buildings not too different from the ones in Clangston—simple wooden boxes of up to three stories high, most of them white or unpainted— except for the fact that here, most houses were older than the people walking around them. A few grander buildings were made out of brick. Håkan realized that those were the first brick constructions he had seen in all his years in America. Another source of surprise was the unreasonable profusion of flags, banners, pennants, and banderoles of all kinds and sizes. Later, he would learn that the white stars on a blue field with the red and white alternating stripes was the ensign of the United States of America.

A block or two down the avenue, something changed. The people who until then had stopped to gawk at him now scurried away at his sight, seeking refuge in shops and taverns. Still, Håkan felt everyone staring from behind the dark windows. Was it that he was filthy and wild? Was it his lion coat? Was it that they saw a murderer? To his surprise, his fear momentarily gave way to indifference. He did not mean to stay there. The town, a mere obstacle on his journey east, was just an opportunity to try himself in society, and it would fall behind him forever in a matter of instants.

A saddlery caught his eye. After so much tanning and stitching, he had developed an interest in leather and was curious to see what could be achieved with better materials and tools. There was a pair of boots in the window. Håkan was practically barefoot—his outgrown moccasins, already unable to prevent numbness and chilblains during the previous winter, had been replaced by precarious canvas and leather wraps. Also, New York could be closer than he thought, and he did not mean to go through that big city and meet his brother shoeless. Although these arguments barely convinced him, he tethered his animals and walked into the store, hoping that the money Lorimer had given him would be enough. The delicate bell on the door startled him. As soon as he walked through the threshold and smelled the perfumed wax, he knew he would not be able to stay. The neatly displayed goods, the polished curves of the counter, the lustrous leather, the general sense of order overwhelmed him. He had never bought anything at a shop in his life. What had made him think that going into a store and conducting a transaction in a currency he was unfamiliar with (and was unable to read) was the best idea for his first exchange after such a long period of solitude? As he was getting ready to leave, a door in the back opened, and through it came the shopkeeper, who stopped at the sight of the stupendously tall man. The smile he had brought from the back room did not match the awe that now widened his eyes. Håkan was about to turn around when he saw his own picture on the wall. Could it really be his face? It seemed to be his portrait, under some bold letters and numbers. The drawing was rudimentary, and he had not seen his own face in a long time, but his main traits were there. Surely, it was a coincidence—it had to be someone else. Still stunned by the resemblance, Håkan turned around and walked out.

The street was now deserted, except for three men with their rifles pointed at him.

"Your gun."

The man who had spoken held out his hand. His hollow cheeks were pitted with smallpox, and his head seemed to simply rest between his shoulders like a ball on a shelf. No neck. A silver star shone on his narrow chest. His voice reminded Håkan of the squeaky tones Linus sometimes used for imaginary forest people, witches, and twig dolls.

"No gun," Håkan said, surprised to find that language worked.

"Right. And how did you get that lion?"

"I got it."

"You got it?"

"Yes."

"Without a gun?"

"Yes."

"With your bare hands?"

"Yes."

The man sighed, annoyed, and with a nod asked one of his assistants to search Håkan. One of them made the gesture of walking over, but stopped, visibly afraid, before even setting out. The man, now more irritated, patted Håkan down himself.

"What's your name?"

"Hawk."

"That's him all right," the man told his companions.

At first the men had been intimidated by Håkan's height, and now that they knew his name, they seemed even more unwilling to approach him. The man with the star stepped back and all of a sudden hit Håkan in the stomach with the butt of his rifle. He fell in the dirt and was kicked until he no longer moved.

He woke up clutching a fistful of dirt, which made him think that he was still on the street, but he lay on a wooden floor, and gradually, the narrow space resolved itself into a prison cell. Over the scent of lamp oil, it smelled of tobacco, onions, and dogs. His hands were fettered to a metal rod, which, in turn, was chained to the wall. His feet were cuffed. Boots walked about beyond the bars. When he tried to look up, pain brought his head back to the ground. He feared things had been broken, torn, and punctured inside him. Quite some time must have elapsed since the beating, because the blood on his skin and clothes had coagulated into small desertscapes. Slowly, one by one, he tested his limbs. They hurt but did not seem to be fractured.

"He's moving, Sheriff," someone said.

More boots came into the room, and they all lined up in front of Håkan's cell. A jingle of keys, the turning of a lock, someone standing right by his face. Håkan knew it was the neckless man. Someone poked Håkan in the shoulder with the muzzle of a rifle.

"The Hawk," said the squeaky voice. "The terrible, the famous Hawk."

After a pause, he added something that Håkan did not understand. Someone laughed.

"So it's true," the sheriff resumed. "Your English is bad. Or is your brain soft? Hello? Hello? Hello? Hello?"

Chuckles.

"Tell me. Why did you kill them all?"

Håkan was sucked into an airless abyss. They knew. Everyone knew. Maybe even Linus knew by then.

"No. Wait," the sheriff burst out, interrupting himself. "Why is not the question. How. How did you kill them all? The brethren, those emigrants, those women, those boys, those girls?"

Håkan heard this from some distant place within himself. He never knew it was so vast and desolate in there.

"You even enjoyed some of them. And still managed to slaughter everyone and flee unharmed. I suppose only a giant, right?"

Snort.

"Another thing I don't get. Why did you ever leave the territory? No one could get you there. The brethren tried, of course. But where to start? And there's no law. No law, no crime. Now here. Here we have laws. The laws of the United States. They're in the Constitution. And

you've broken most of them. Not to mention the divine laws. You'll be
destroyed and cursed. To come into the States. Ha! It must be your soft
brain. You're going to hang. Upon my soul, I would put you to death
myself and burn your beastly bones. But the brethren want you. More
money alive. That's the only reason I haven't spoiled your features. So
they can see it's you. I even have this tin box here to prove you're the
doctor they say you're meant to be. The doctor! The giant killer doctor!
By Cain's curse."

Sniggers.

"Slaughtering good men of God," the suddenly somber sheriff said.
"I can abide an honest murderer. But this? Brethren spreading the good
word." He paused, considering the immensity of the crime. "They sure
want you in Illinois. Good men of God."

Håkan finally managed to turn around and look at the head deposited on the shoulders. It looked down at him with disdain.

"Hello? Hello? Hello? Hello?" the sheriff suddenly croaked in rapid
succession.

Laughs.

Space kept swelling within Håkan. He was now an unlit universe.
How could he ever have thought the world an enormous place? It was
nothing compared to his expanding emptiness. Details that once would
have concerned him disappeared into the void. Did the sheriff say he
was in a new country? Then where had he been before? Who had fab-
ricated that story about those evil deeds he had not committed? Who
were those brethren? All these questions faded behind Helen's image.
She had once touched his hand. Linus looked at him from afar. But
these last pictures were shredded into hazy tatters and vanished in the
blackness.

"So, the tin box. What do we have here? Little pliers, little knives,
little bottles. Funny needles. Thread. You've healed so many people.

Maybe I can heal you now. Because you're sick, you know. You have a bad heart. You have a bad heart, and I will fix it."

Håkan was turned on his back. He realized that he could see only out of one eye. Through a watery veil, he made out the sheriff threading one of his needles with suture.

"I'm no doctor, but I'll cure your sick heart," the sheriff resumed after getting the thread through. "Jesus is gone from your heart. That's why you're sick. But I'll stitch him right back there. Grab him, boys."

The sheriff kneeled over him and stuck the needle into Håkan's chest, right above his heart. For a moment, the pain obliterated his consciousness, his shame, and his sorrow. But they all came back with his howl. The needle surfaced on the other side, and he could feel the thread burning as it ran through his flesh.

"I know, I know," the squeaky voice said. "But you'll feel better."

Another stitch; another scream.

"You'll be healed. Purified from the dross of depravity. Cured."

Another stitch; another scream.

"Dang! That was a rib, right? Say, Doc, should I sew over or under it? Let's see. Darn it! No. I'll just have to go over. Hope that'll do. Just one." Stitch. "Two." Stitch. "And." Stitch. "There. Now we just need to go across."

Gasping, Håkan stared at a stain on the ceiling that looked like a cloud that looked like a troll. The astonishing pain. The sheriff was the one holding the needle, but the pain was his own. How could his body be doing this to itself?

"Josiah, pour some water here. I can't see what I'm doing under the slime. All right. We'll stitch him right back on there."

This was eternity—this pain, this now with nothing behind and nothing ahead.

"There. Anyone can be saved. You just need to let Jesus back into your heart."

Before fainting, Håkan managed to lift up his head and see a coarse, irregular cross stitched onto his chest, right over his heart.

A cold, soothing cloth on his forehead woke him up in the middle of the night. One of his captors was gently wiping his brow. He put his fingertips to Håkan's lips and shushed. They looked into each other's eyes. There was something imploring and at the same time giving in the man's gaze. He wiped Håkan's face and then his chest. Although shorter than Håkan, he was still tall and, judging from the firm hand with which he propped him up, strong. His clearly traced features inspired confidence, as if that orderly and proportional face had been carefully designed by the mind behind it according to its own image.

"I brought your box," he whispered. "Can you cure yourself?"

Håkan pointed to a salve and with gestures instructed the man to daub it on the stitches. Then he asked him to take the tincture.

"Two drops," Håkan murmured, opening his mouth.

The bitterness was already a relief.

"I killed those men," Håkan managed to say under his breath.

"Quiet," the man said softly.

"But not the girl. Not the friends. Just those men. Nobody else."

"I know."

"But I did kill those men."

He fell asleep in the man's arms.

The clanging and the pain in his chest woke him at the same time. The sheriff was hitting the bars with a cudgel. Everything was tingly from the drug, as if reality were a limb that had fallen asleep.

"Up! Up! Up! Up! The circus is in town! Up! Up! Up! Up!"

One of his captors, Josiah, giggled. The other one, his benefactor, looked on from a dark corner. The sheriff walked into the cell and unchained Håkan while the giggling man pointed a gun at his head.

"You'll need your costume," the sheriff said, tossing Håkan his coat, which landed on his face. "Good Lord, this reeks," he added as he wiped his hands on the back of Josiah's shirt.

They dragged Håkan up.

"Asa!" yelled the sheriff. "What the blazes are you doing there? Come over here! The half-wit is a giant, in case you forgot."

Asa came out of his shadowy corner and helped get Håkan on his feet. They tied his hands with rope, led him, stumbling, down a staircase, and pushed him into the deafening morning light.

The rotten vegetables and eggs hit him before the screams did. Through his single eye, he saw a vociferous mob standing at a prudent distance but close enough to reach him with the garbage they had brought, seemingly for the sole purpose of hurling it at him.

"That's right!" proclaimed the sheriff, standing on a crate. "That's him! The giant sinner! Like I said, caught him myself! The giant murderer!"

Insults, hisses, boos. Someone threw a rock. Covering his head with his arms, the sheriff leaped off his crate and got between Håkan and the crowd.

"His face, boys! Don't let them get his face!" he said to his deputies, who made Håkan duck. "No stones, ladies and gentlemen. Trash only. Remember, we are all with sin. So no stones."

With a gentle and firm hand, Asa kept Håkan down as long as possible.

"That's right," the sheriff went on, dragging Håkan back up by his hair. "The brethren slaughterer! The beast! And just look! Isn't he truly a beast?"

The sheriff pulled up the lion's head from Håkan's back and fitted it on his head, like a hood. His face vanished in the dark.

Gasps and a sudden silence.

"That's right. Step right up, ladies and gentlemen! Take a look! The very beast that roamed our fields and killed our brethren." A pause. "All partakers of glory at the time." He looked at the sky, mournfully, and then, with renewed energy, pointed at Håkan. "But this beast from the underworld! Behold the predacious lion that butchered our flock! He's not a criminal. He's an animal! The unhung brute can barely talk. Look at him!"

The crowd stood in silent awe.

"It was I who conquered this Amorite, whose height, as you can see, is like the height of the cedars, and whose strength, you can believe me, is like the strength of the oaks. Now, I, after hunting this malefactor down, will take him to the brethren in Illinois, where he will face the awful majesty of the law."

Isolated mumbles of approval.

"There, this son of Belial will be tried in a court of law and hanged to death. Now, this bucket here is for donations for the brethren's gallows. Who'd like to give? Contributions? Here is the hawk that preyed upon our doves. Let us wring its neck. Donations for the brethren's scaffold? Help cast this unrighteous freak out into the outer darkness, where there's only wailing and gnashing of teeth. Don't be shy now!"

One by one, farmhands, homemakers, shopkeepers, schoolchildren, and other townspeople approached the bucket and deposited the money inside—never tossing it in, but always placing it carefully at the bottom, as if it could break. Some, mostly women, paused and gave Håkan a furtive glance, but most quickened their step after making their donation without daring to look up at the prisoner.

"Thank you. Thank you all," the sheriff said as the crowd started to disperse. "Thank you in the name of the brethren."

He got the money out of the pail, counted it, and secured it in his pocket.

Håkan had not seen his burro since his capture, but they put him on the same horse. It turned out that the stallion that Håkan had taken was dear to one of the victims' relatives, and there was an additional reward for bringing the fugitive with it—dead, alive, with horse, in increasing amounts.

"You boys can split the horse in half," the sheriff had said to convince his two assistants to escort him across the state border to deliver the prisoner.

Because Håkan had his hands tied to the pommel and was barely conscious, he was loosely guarded. In the endless expanse, there was nowhere to run, so for the most part, Håkan, too weak and wretched to attempt anything anyway, was left alone. Sometimes, seldom, something like a thought pulsated in the blackness within him. Mostly, he hoped—if those muted throbs in the dark ever amounted to something like hope—that Linus would think that he, Håkan, had returned to Sweden after they had been separated. Or that he thought him dead. These vague illusions aside, Håkan had only a dim awareness of the pain in his chest and of being, again, in the convex plains. But the plunge into senselessness was not solely the result of his maimed mind and his battered body. Every night, at great risk for both, Asa gave him a couple drops of the tincture. It was the greatest kindness anyone had ever done him.

Time had frozen within him, but somehow external reality seemed to move, shred, and disintegrate into nothing at great speed, like fast-sailing clouds. There was only a tenuous connection between his inner vacuum and the rags of reality flapping intermittently around him—flickers of understanding (this was his body, that was not his body, this hand could touch that hand, this hand could not touch the sun).

Most of what happened during those days was told to him later.

They reached a town. Håkan was paraded down its main street.

"Come and see!" the sheriff announced. "The brethren killer! Come and see the beast! Caught it myself! Like the valiant Benaiah, who struck down both a giant and a lion. Step right up, ladies and gentlemen! Just look! He must be five cubits tall, just like the Egyptian giant. And he is fierce, just like the lion in the snowy pit."

They stopped in front of a tavern. The sheriff put up the same placard Håkan had seen at the saddler's.

"That's right! Spotted him over Winthrop's Creek. Snuck up on him. Shots were fired. We emptied our guns. He had a knife, but I threw some dirt in his eyes and disarmed him. Then I overmanned him in single combat. Look at him! A beast, verily! I almost got myself killed, but if he's big, I'm cunning. Like the king of Israel against the giant Philistine! But unlike David, I couldn't take this Goliath's head because the brethren want it. Yes, we're taking him to Illinois, where he'll get a fair trial and hang. Now, this bucket here is for donations for the brethren's gallows. Who'd like to give? Help send this sinner down into the lake that burns with quenchless fire and brimstone. Contributions? Let's feed him to the undying worm. Let's make sure this monster does no more violence to the earth we tread upon, to the air we breathe, and to the heavens that shelter us. For the brethren's scaffold? Come on, don't be shy!"

He pocketed the money, rolled up the placard, and led his men and the prisoner out of town.

Back in the wilderness, there was little talk. When Håkan refused to eat, the sheriff said that he would be blasted if their food went to waste on an animal that surely preferred scraps and trash anyway. Håkan simply sat there, abstracted and slightly wide-eyed, as the garbage after every meal was dumped upon his lap, to Josiah's always fresh amusement.

After a few days' travel, as another small town started piling up on the horizon, the sheriff had his party dismount and asked his assistants to hold Håkan tight—an unnecessary precaution, given his soft inertness. He weighed a few pebbles in his hand and finally found one around which he could wrap his fist firmly. Then he spat, looked up at Håkan, and swung with all his might. Håkan's cheekbone burst open like a plum. The blood hesitated briefly in the gash before pouring out.

"But what? Hey!" was all that Asa could utter as he recoiled with surprise and disgust.

"What?" the sheriff asked icily.

They mounted, rode on, and got to the town, where the sheriff, once again, displayed Håkan and told everyone how he, single-handedly, had captured that most wicked of Nephilim, even though the demon had charged at him like a ravening and roaring lion. This time, Håkan had a fresh scar to show for his captor's valor and strength. The sheriff made sure to point at it as he asked for donations.

As they were leaving, on the last block of the short road, a small shop arrested the sheriff's attention. The window glistened with gems of every color and pearls of all sizes set in gold and silver necklaces, watches, rings, brooches, lockets, pocket guns, tie pins, wristbands, and cigarette cases. Because it was so small, the store looked like a jewel box—a dazzling little world that could only be looked at but never entered. Nonetheless, the sheriff ordered everyone to stop, dismounted, straightened his clothes while discreetly looking around for bystanders, and walked into the jewelry shop.

His men waited under the sun for a good while.

Finally, he emerged from the shop wearing a smug smile and a gold watch chain that dangled from one of the buttonholes in his waistcoat before diving into the fob pocket.

Back out in the plains, the sheriff took some of the money from a pouch hidden deep under his clothes and called his men.

"Here, boys. A little taste before the reward."

Josiah took the money with meek greediness, giving profuse thanks. Asa rejected it with a polite but almost invisible gesture and turned around before the sheriff had time to release the wrath gathering in his face. After this incident, Asa and the sheriff barely exchanged a word for days. Meanwhile, Josiah and his boss grew closer, the former showing the most abject and sycophantic submission to the latter.

They continued their journey over the plains. Håkan still refused to eat and, despite Asa's gentle entreaties, consented only to having some water. After a few days, they arrived at another town, where the sheriff, once again, put Håkan on display next to the placard and gave a detailed account of the capture. This time, the sheriff, through his tremendous heroism, had managed to defeat not only the Behemoth but also several laws of nature in the process. People gave generously.

Håkan, now too weak to stay in his saddle, had to be tied to the horse. He would not take any food. They had even given up teasing him with the scraps and the garbage. Had the sheriff not made those detours to stop at the last two towns, they would already have reached the brethren in Illinois. When the sheriff announced that they were headed for a city that took them in the opposite direction, Asa finally spoke up.

"It would be a sin to have this thing executed without making an example out of it," the sheriff explained. "Before we take him in, I intend to edify everyone in every town between us and the brethren."

"And make good coin while at it."

"Watch that tongue of yours, you rascal."

"He'll die."

"Of course."

"Before we get there."

"I'll guard him."

"No. Of hunger."

"Bah!"

"He'll never make it. Look at him."

The sheriff was not a man to take orders from anyone, so it was despite himself that he turned to the heap collapsed on the ground.

And it was also probably against his will that Asa's words sank in. He grabbed Håkan, propped him up, and then shoved a spoonful of left-over grits into his face.

"Get up, you stinking sack of sins! Eat!" he squealed, prying Håkan's mouth open and stuffing in the food, which just lay there, unswallowed. "Eat, you reeky, hell-hated reprobate!"

Håkan, covered in food, did not seem to feel the hand that slapped him back and forth across the face.

"Stop," Asa commanded.

The sheriff did not deign to respond. Instead, he pointed at Asa's chest with a firm finger and glared at him sternly. Josiah, dumbfounded, took a few steps back and looked on. Muttering to himself, the sheriff walked over to his horse, rummaged through one of his saddlebags, and returned with Håkan's tin box, from which he produced a scalpel. He leaned over Håkan with the spoon in one hand and the scalpel in the other.

"A notch in your flesh for each uneaten spoonful."

Again they tried to feed him; again the food dribbled down his chin and onto his chest. The sheriff pushed up Håkan's sleeve and carved a deep line into his forearm.

"One."

The pale white of fat and bone was visible for a moment, but soon the gash filled and overflowed with blood.

"Here comes two," the sheriff squeaked, sticking the spoon into Håkan's mouth.

"Sheriff!" Josiah cried.

The sheriff turned around to find Asa pointing a gun to his head, which, twisted back, looked more than ever like a shapeless ball on a trunk. They stared at each other in silence.

"Asa, Asa, you'll hang."

"Stand back, Sheriff."

"Oh, Asa, Asa," he said with ostentatious calm, but his wrath was as solid as a body.

"I'm taking him away."

"Oh, Asa. When the brethren hear about this."

"Yes, when the brethren hear about this. And they'll hear it from me. I'll take this man to them directly and tell them how you've profited in their name. I'll tell my uncle. The elders will listen to me."

"Here's my money. All of it. Please take it," Josiah said. Stunned with fear, he threw the money on the ground, as if it had suddenly turned into a snake or a spider.

"You must be moon-hit," the sheriff hissed, eyeing Asa narrowly.

"Lord knows plenty of people saw you take that money," Asa continued, ignoring the sheriff's interruption. "They gave it to you in the first place. You will claim you took it in good faith, on behalf of the elders. I will send them to that watchmaker of yours."

"You mean to keep the whole reward to yourself, don't you? You covetous misbegotten hound."

"Plattsville's the closest town. Five days on foot? By the time you get there, I'll have told the elders everything."

"I will dismember you, feed your limbs to the pigs, and piss on their excrement."

"No, you won't. You'll run. They'll come after you. You'll hide."

For a moment, the sheriff's features, contracted and twisted by anger, revealed that he knew Asa was right.

Asa covered the sheriff's and the assistant's heads with sacks and then helped Håkan mount. Dulled by the burlap, Josiah's incoherent implorations were a soft, wet mumble. The sheriff, his sharp voice cutting through the sack, told him to shut his mouth. Once ready, Asa rode off with Håkan by his side and the two other horses in tow. The sheriff took his hood off and hurled insults at the riders, but they were already so far away that his shrill imprecations seemed to be addressed only to the plains. Josiah still had the sack on his head when they vanished from sight.

17.

Blue and cold were one. Håkan felt the crisp blue sky on his skin and eyes. And with this consonance of sight and touch, he realized that his consciousness had returned. His cramped limbs were an indication that he had been gone for a good while. He tested his other senses (the swish and swoosh of grass, the smell of old coals and manure, the sourness of sleep in his mouth); he confirmed the hardness of the soil under him (so unlike the viscous pit down which he had been slowly sliding for days); he conjured up a few memories (friendly pictures he could summon and dismiss at will, not like the ghosts that haunted him in his dreams); he tried language in his head (jag är här därför att jag kan tänka att jag är här). Dots of bright but undefined colors popped in and out of the sky as he tried to look deeper into it. He was still in the plains.

"Are you in pain?"

Asa came over from behind him and sat by his side. Håkan had not been in pain until asked. Now, the fire in his chest started burning, and the cut in his forearm throbbed with a life of its own.

"Yes."

"If you can bear it, we should stop those drops. I thought I was losing you."

"Yes."

"Let me know."

"Yes."

Håkan looked at his forearm, not knowing how he had hurt himself but noticing that the wound had been rudimentarily, yet efficiently, cleaned and bandaged. Asa put a soaked cracker to his lips. Håkan ate it with relish. He was spoon-fed some stew. Someone had made it for him, he thought before nodding off.

The last phosphorescence on the horizon was dying away as he woke up. There was a fire going, and Asa slept next to it. A pot simmered at the edge of the embers. Having eaten those morsels after his long fast had revived Håkan's appetite. He coughed and thought his chest would split open. Asa woke up.

"You look better. Hungry?"

"Yes."

Asa propped him up against a saddle on the ground and gave him a cupful of stew. They ate in silence. Håkan had only a blurred recollection of what had happened after being stitched up in the prison cell, but he did remember that he was being taken to Illinois so that the brethren could hang him. Where was the sheriff? Had he dreamed up that squeaky head pelted with smallpox? Why were his hands no longer tied? Would he dare to ask?

"Where are we?" he finally asked. It sounded like an apology.

"Back in the territory."

Håkan was confused.

"West. We've left the States," Asa explained.

"Illinois?"

"Not Illinois."

"The sheriff?"

"No sheriff."

Asa told him what had happened.

"I believe you," he concluded, filling Håkan's cup. "Many of us guessed what had happened to those emigrants on the trail. The Wrathful Angels. They've been roaming the country for years, at war with all gentiles. The brethren's militia. By now, they're just a band

of outlaws. Some of the elders support them, but most want nothing to do with them. My uncle is an elder. He wants nothing to do
with the Soldiers of Jehu. There were all these stories about you and
what you'd done. But then I met you and saw it just couldn't be true.
They'll still want you for the dead brethren, though. But they'll never
find us."

There was a confusion of anguish and relief in Håkan's throat. He
could barely breathe. Redemption was impossible, but at least someone
knew he had not killed Helen and all those innocent people. His eyes
blurred, and he tried to swallow to let air in.

"I was quitting west anyhow," Asa said after a pause.

Evening had deepened into night, and Asa's face was barely visible in
the glow of the sinking embers. He stirred the fire, sending blue flames
leaping into the sky in the midst of an effervescence of sparks.

"Will you tell me your story?" Asa asked shyly, as if the answer to
this question would reveal something about himself rather than Håkan.

Håkan finally managed to swallow and wiped his eyes.

"I come from Sweden. I lost my brother. I'm going to New York to
find him. The people on the trail. I met them. They. After."

The lump in his throat thickened. He coughed and felt that his lungs
would burst out through his wound. The pain released the tears.

"Let me get you up here," Asa said, putting his arm around Håkan's
back and folding a blanket behind him.

"I'm tired," Håkan said in a soft moan, his face disfigured behind
the tears.

Asa held him tighter.

"I'm tired."

Håkan rested his head on Asa's shoulder, sobbing.

"So tired."

Asa wrapped his other arm over Håkan's chest.

"So tired."

It was Håkan's first embrace.

They traveled on westward, mostly in silence. Now and then, however, they would look at each other from their horses and smile fleetingly. No one had ever smiled at Håkan like that, for no reason. It felt good. After a while, he learned to smile back. Every evening, when they bivouacked, as they built a fire and made dinner, he found it almost miraculous to be seen by someone, to be in someone's brain, to reside in someone's consciousness. And Asa's presence also affected the plains, which no longer were the oppressive immensity whose existence, for such a long time, had somehow been entrusted to Håkan's lonely gaze.

Even though Håkan was still rather weak, he insisted on removing the stitches from his chest as soon as possible—the recollection of Pingo's maggot-infested sutures haunted him. Asa offered to do it, but Håkan wanted to perform the procedure himself, even if this meant he would not be able to take the tincture. As Håkan plucked one stitch after the other with a pair of tweezers and cut the sutures with a scalpel, Asa stared on, uttering disjointed words of encouragement, which only made Håkan tense. But once he was done and the pain had receded, he realized how much Asa's presence had helped him.

Asa loved food. Håkan found this pleasure utterly baffling. Of course, he preferred some foods to others (strawberries with milk to charred prairie dog) and ate with delight whenever a meal to his liking came his way. But he had never pursued this enjoyment or even felt particular cravings. Eating was something one had to do to stay alive. So he was surprised by the care with which Asa prepared every one of his meals. He selected the ingredients throughout the day, constantly stopping to pick up herbs, flowers, mushrooms, and eggs. Only the finest of Håkan's game ever made it to the pot, and Asa was always experimenting with different cooking methods—roasting, smoking, burying, curing. Asa made him look at food in a way similar to that in which Lorimer had made him see bodies—revealing depth and meaning where there had been none (even though when it came to food, Håkan knew that he lacked the inclination and the aptitude he showed for anatomy). And as with Lorimer, Asa's passion made Håkan discover wonders in what had hitherto been a monotonous wasteland. In this apparent empti-ness, Asa managed to obtain a wide variety of ingredients. Given the shortage of herbs and condiments, he had learned to season his food with flowers. Not only could he distinguish every nuance between spe-cies and families, but he also knew exactly how to use each part of each flower—he seldom put the entire blossom into a dish, preferring to use the petals from this flower and the stamens of that, while sprinkling only the pollen from another. If spices were scarce, sweets were almost impossible to find once they had left the last bees behind. Throughout their entire journey, Asa was on the lookout for a dwarf tree of sorts, which he tapped by screwing a gimlet into the knotty limbs. It was hard to conceive that such a rugged, thick-branched bush could yield such sweet sap. Asa used it in cakes and confections and boiled the rest down to sugar. There was something extraordinary about eating candy in the plains—something that, for a moment, annulled their immen-sity. But the ingredient for which Asa, who otherwise was a very dis-ciplined traveler, would go far out of his way was a certain quail-like bird. Unlike most of the other fowl, these birds were almost impossible to catch. They even made a habit of taunting their pursuers, waiting until the very last instant to take off in a strangely vertical flight, as if some-one had pulled them up with a string. Whenever he spotted one of these birds, Asa would dismount and run around like a madman, trying to throw a blanket over it, and cursing under his breath each time it got away. Consistent with its mocking nature, the quail would fly away and land just close enough to keep Asa's hopes up. But it was well worth the humiliation. Those tender birds tasted like chestnuts, whipped cream, and, Asa would say, the very skies that surrounded them. Asa's favorite recipe was a quail and mushroom stew. Håkan admired his precision as a cook and, above all, the confidence with which he used the ingredients that had cost him so much time and effort to obtain.

When he cooked, Asa was too absorbed in his work to talk, but during the meal they had brief conversations, usually about their itinerary and immediate plans. After cleaning up, they fell back into their friendly silence. One night, long after the fire had gone out, Asa came over to Håkan and lay next to him. At first, the proximity of Asa's body frightened him. Not daring to move, he looked up at the stars, wondering if Asa, who held him from behind, perfectly still, was also awake. Not knowing why, Håkan matched his breathing with Asa's. They breathed together. Slowly, he fell asleep, safe, warm, and happy. From that night on, always around the darkest hour and after the embers had paled under the ashes, Asa would come over to Håkan and lie by his side.

They always got up before sunrise, erased every trace of their camp, and set out at a brisk pace. By that time, the brethren surely would have heard the rumors and pieced together the story of the Hawk's capture, the sheriff's fraudulent scheme, and Asa and Håkan's escape. They were probably looking for them already. Asa's plan was to head out far west and hide for a while. Then, after a year or two, they could travel on and try their luck in California. He knew people there who could help them start up—get a job, save up, and then go and make their fortune. How he would get Håkan there unnoticed, Asa did not know. But he did know that, somehow, they would get there together.

Traveling with someone who knew the land and had the eye of a tracker transformed Håkan's perception of the plains. Where Håkan had once spotted threats and proliferating signs of foes, Asa saw nothing—

except, perhaps, some sort of aromatic wood ideal for smoking meat, a prized root vegetable, or one of the soapstone-like rocks he was always picking up for his makeshift pit ovens. Conversely, Håkan would often be surprised when Asa stopped in the middle of what seemed a void—identical, in its nothingness, to every patch of land in any direction—dismounted, looked around, pointed in a new direction, and had them trot away from a faint but, to him, eloquent sign of riders. Even if these sudden stops and turns forced them into intricate snaking patterns, Asa, who did not own a compass, unfailingly kept piloting them west. But more impressive than his ability to decipher the plains and his perfect sense of direction was the fact that Asa's knowledge of the terrain, acquired through numerous trips, allowed him to anticipate every stage of their journey. Hitherto, Håkan had been traveling away from the past but not into the future. He had remained in a constant present, leaving landscapes and people behind but never heading toward a more or less certain destination that he could foresee. New York, his only true goal, was as abstract and fantastic as a city on some distant moon, never a clear destination in his mind's eye that he could look forward to. So far, he had journeyed only from one now to another. James Brennan had roved about the country following whatever traces of gold he found in the dirt; John Lorimer had been as new to those tracts as Håkan was; and Jarvis Pickett's directions had not proven trustworthy. It was only Asa who, over and over again, had been able to predict the world to come. Tomorrow, we'll get to a river. In about three days, we'll find good firewood. Should we ride that way, we'd hit a town before sundown. When Håkan learned that the earth was round like a ball, his idea of the world and how to move around it had changed in ways he never imagined possible—in fact, each time he considered this, he felt his mind curving to somehow accommodate this new idea. Asa's ability to predict the future had a similar effect. Reality no longer ended at the horizon.

Before being captured by the sheriff, Håkan had feared that he might have circled the globe, missing New York, and remained eternally trapped between the plains and the desert. Since he had followed his compass, the other possibility he had considered was that he was going insane. It took him several days to form the question in his head and muster the courage to ask it.

"The world is round," he said. Håkan's tone was both that of a statement and a question.

Asa looked down. He had either nodded or was waiting for Håkan to continue.

"After the ship, we walked. Then I was in the desert. For a long time. First it was red. Then it was white. Then it was red again. For a long time I was in the desert. Alone. Then I was in the plains, also for a very long time. Then I saw the desert again." He felt he should explain himself. "Before the sheriff and you, I saw the desert again but turned around."

He thought that what he had said made little sense and wished he had never started. A long silence.

"Did I go around the world?"

Asa looked up, as if someone had pulled his head back by the hair, and stared at Håkan for a moment. Håkan flushed, overwhelmed by embarrassment. He was not crazy; he was just a fool. Asa smiled.

"No. You did not go around the world. It's just a big country."

The shadows of winter were gathering, and soon they would be immersed in one long, cutting night. Because the sheriff had paraded him in it, Håkan still had his coat, but Asa, who initially had set out on a brief trip, shivered under a couple of threadbare blankets that kept sliding off his shoulders. Håkan convinced him that trapping was their priority—he had started a coat for Asa, but being constantly on the move had made work difficult. They made a sharp turn south, toward warmer lands where game would be more abundant. The detour would set them back, but it would also baffle their pursuers.

Once they reached a brown, hard forest, they camped and trapped for a week or so. Asa was an excellent hunter, and they made good progress, which Håkan was almost sorry about—he was happy to rest and feel, in a manner, at home. During those days, Håkan derived great joy from seeing how impressed Asa was with his skills—skinning, dissecting, tanning, threading, sewing. Not since Linus had Håkan cared about dazzling anyone in this way. Not even Helen. Now, to his amazement, he realized that he wanted to impress Asa. And he did. Most times, he would pretend not to know that he was being watched while making his delicate incisions and pulling the skin with such ease that the dead animal seemed to be grateful to have been rid of the fur, but now and again, after indulging in some flourish with the scalpel, he could not help looking up to confirm that his movements had been followed with awe, and then, after meeting Asa's wide eyes, he would smile, blush, and look back down. Whenever he was able to overcome his shyness, Håkan pointed out the different organs and their anatomical functions. He knew that something had affected Asa deeply whenever he stepped back and shook his head in disbelief. There was no greater validation for Håkan than that head shaking no.

One night, encouraged by the respect Asa showed for his knowledge, Håkan decided to share Lorimer's ideas with him. He had been rehearsing his speech in his head for days. The best occasion would be toward the end of dinner, when Asa was no longer fully engaged with cooking or tasting, but merely enjoying the last bites, which always put him in a particularly placid mood. With the help of bones and organs he had saved for this purpose, Håkan outlined the main aspects of the naturalist's theory. Asa listened carefully, but it was unclear whether he was focused on the words or on the food. It was not easy to explain the

nature of that vesicle of sentient substance and how it evolved and created a protective crust and then a body and limbs around itself to further
its own life. Håkan arrived at the hardest part of his exposition—the
one that required doubting that god had created man. He paused. They
could hear the resin hissing as the cinders fell between the logs. Håkan
resumed his account. He stuttered and faltered at times but was quite
sure that he had been clear and faithful to Lorimer's system. When it was
apparent that he had concluded, Asa put down his plate, cleaned his
teeth with his tongue, and, slowly, started to laugh. There was no malice
in his chuckles, no mockery, no disdain. He simply laughed, innocently
and wholeheartedly, in good faith, as if Håkan had shared a joke with
him. Håkan's tongue dried up and his hands tingled. A new feeling—
sharp quills coming out of his pores—traversed his body. He had never
been indignant before. Staring into the coals, he was shocked at how far
Asa suddenly felt from him. Håkan was also disappointed in himself for
having been unable to convey the importance of Lorimer's discovery. An
open confrontation or even derision would have been better than Asa's
frank laughter. The one thing that made him happy was that not even
Asa's laughter could shake his belief in Lorimer's truth.

They had all the pelts they needed. Some would have to dry out for a
few more days, which meant that Håkan would finish the coat along
the way. In preparation for the winter gales, he also brought additional
furs and flexible branches to make another portable shelter, big enough
for two. Throughout their stay, Asa had smoked many of the skinned
animals and made abundant charqui. He also had gathered and dried
mushrooms, along with a large sack of bitter, oily nuts he had found in
the forest.

The grass got drier and sharper as they moved west. They changed
horses more often and had to make frequent detours to water and feed

them. Asa was now wearing a fur vest. Håkan was working on the sleeves and on their tent, which was finished only a few days before the first blizzard. They spent their first night in the storm-pelted shelter, huddling together for warmth. The wind screamed and shook the leather frame. Håkan thought that it was their first time sleeping together under the same roof. He knew that Asa, behind him, awake, calm, was thinking something similar.

"Why did you do this?" Håkan asked.

"What?"

He felt Asa's soft breath, first on his neck and then in his nose. It smelled like warm, wet soil.

"This."

"What?" Asa laughed under his breath.

"This. Help me. From the sheriff. And then run with me. Leave everything. And now you're here. Why?"

"Because of you."

"But why?"

"Because I saw you and I knew."

18

It took them the entire winter to travel north along a mighty mountain range, searching for a pass, and then back south, all the way down to their initial position, but on the opposite side of the sierras. They had intended to head straight west after the crossing, but the pass was quite busy, and some people recognized Håkan. Soon trappers, prospectors, and homesteaders were abuzz with stories. The giant who had strangled seven priests. The lion killer. The monster who had slain all those defenseless women and children. There was talk of a colossal reward. Håkan and Asa left immediately and kept riding through the night, hoping that farther down south, away from trails and travelers, they would be able to resume their westward course in solitude. Despite all the bluster and the threatening looks, nobody followed them.

With the arrival of spring, Asa thought they should make their final push west and devise a plan to get Håkan safely into California. There were, however, a few obstacles. Although he trusted his own instincts, Asa did not know his way on the other side of the mountains. To make matters worse, their encounter with the travelers at the pass had shown that Håkan's notoriety had grown into a myth. Even if he was no longer wearing his lion coat, with his prodigious size, he hardly went unnoticed. It was only a matter of time before word of their whereabouts reached the brethren—and bounty hunters serious enough to take the risk. While they were considering solutions to these problems, yet another difficulty arose.

Asa had climbed up a crag to get a better view of their surroundings and find a shortcut through the particularly rough stretch they were traversing. As he descended, he slid and rolled down the cliff. He looked like a thing as he tumbled and bounced against the rocks. Håkan saw it from afar, and as it happened, he felt the weight of reality draining out of the world. Later, he was embarrassed to recall that his first thought had been that now he would be completely alone again. The initial shock overcome, he ran to the base of the crag where Asa lay, badly bruised and bleeding but conscious. His left tibia was disfigured in a zigzagging fracture.

"I can help," Håkan panted, holding Asa's head in his hands.

Asa did not respond. The pain had canceled out whatever it is that makes eyes human. They moved around frantically, looking at nothing. His chest heaved. He gasped like a fish.

Håkan ripped Asa's trousers. The bone had almost broken through the skin. He thought that he might be able to set it but was concerned about the fever and the rot that often followed wounds of this kind. Asa started shivering. His teeth chattered. The horses could not get up there. Håkan would have to move him down. Make a stretcher. But first, the bone. He needed the sedative. He held Asa's head tightly to his chest and then, very gently, put it down. Asa's eyes still stirred, staring beyond the sky. Håkan took a step back. He could not leave him there, alone. Not even for an instant. He wished he could ask Asa what to do.

"I will come back," he said and, before becoming paralyzed by doubt again, turned around and dashed downhill toward their horses.

He got his tin box, blankets, and rope, and ran back.

Asa's jaws were now clenched in a sinister smile, as if offering his teeth up for inspection to a remotely distant being. He looked lost. Asa had never looked lost before. His frame shook. Håkan managed to pour a few drops of the tincture down the corner of his mouth. The shaking subsided. Håkan touched the skin over the fracture. It was tight, like a full bladder. For the first time, he was scared of a body—of hurting it, of the power its frailty had over him. Gently, he got Asa on a blanket, dragged him over to a tree, sat him up with his back against the trunk, and, after padding his armpits and chest with another blanket, tied him to it. He studied the fracture, then looked at the mountains, then at the sky, then down. He closed his eyes and covered his face with his hands. A hawk called; another responded. He removed his hands from his face. As if waking up, he opened his eyes and kneeled at Asa's feet. He grabbed his ankle, delicately moved it up and down and side to side, and suddenly, with abrupt violence, pulled. The bones shifting through the flesh sounded like horses chewing corn. He kept pulling and twisting the ankle, holding his breath, blinded by his sweat. With a deep moan, he let go. The bone seemed to be in place, but blood kept pooling under the skin. He could only hope no major vessel had been torn. With some branches, blankets, and rope, he improvised a stretcher on which he pulled Asa down to their camp. The slope was littered with sharp stones. They slowly clambered their way down. The sun had long set when they got back to their horses. Håkan pitched camp.

The following morning, Asa had a fever. He raved and constantly tried to get up to repair a ladder. It was an important ladder. It had to be fixed. What would they do without the ladder? With a lancet, Håkan drained the slow blue blood from his leg, always fearing to find pus. Most of the day was spent going back and forth to a nearby creek to cool the compresses he applied to Asa's forehead, lips, and wrists.

After coexisting for a while, the moon prevailed over the sun. Håkan built a fire but cooked no food. Asa wrestled with himself for most of the night, but when he finally calmed down and fell asleep, his face acquired a calm and stern expression, showing a serene strength that made Håkan think of a king. Up to that moment, this word, king, like so many others, had had a pictureless meaning for him—he had never seen a king, not even in a portrait; but now, as he watched Asa sleep, those sounds merged, forever, with his face. He put some salve on Asa's rope burns and then lay next to him, resting his head on his chest. Asa's heart beat slowly. Even unconscious, he managed to comfort Håkan. Out of the night and in between heartbeats, Linus's face came forth in his mind. The picture of his brother, who had protected him from hunger, cold, and pain, had always come to him as the very image of safety. Until now. This time, as Linus's features became clearer, he saw something different—a child. The Linus he had loved and lost was a child. It was true that Linus had protected and cared for him, but Håkan had never before understood how young and innocent his brother had been at the time. His stories, his bravados, his knowledge, his boundless confidence—vain constructions of a little boy. The realization made him cry. He had outgrown his older brother. Never again would he find that comfort and safety in Linus's image. He listened to Asa's calm heartbeat and felt its throb against his temple. Asa was not a child. Fleetingly, Håkan wondered what Linus would make of him. What would he make of them? Although he still loved his brother dearly, Håkan discovered that he did not care.

The next morning, Asa woke up hungry and without a fever. Håkan's knees almost faltered with relief.

"You will live," he said, turning away from Asa when he felt his eyes well up.

After breakfast, Asa asked him to get ready to leave. Håkan refused. They could not risk aggravating the wounds and having the fever return. Asa did not listen. The brethren, the Wrathful Angels, the bounty hunters, the law would all close in on them soon. Their only hope, he believed, was to get to the cañons. If they did not get lost there themselves, they would surely manage to lose their pursuers. The discussion ended when Asa tried to ride his horse. With great difficulty, Håkan managed to get him on. The pain distorted Asa's features as he sat on the saddle, and his face turned white when his injured leg started bouncing against the moving horse. Håkan helped him dismount before he fainted. They tried different kinds of splints and straps, but once he got on the saddle, the pain was always too intense. Defeated, Asa picked a more secluded recess where they would settle down for a few weeks.

Time went by slowly. At first, Håkan thought that they would enjoy their rest in that benign spot—close to fresh water, surrounded by plentiful trees and bushes, in the path of easy game—but the first few days, Asa was so vexed by his condition that he barely uttered a word. Håkan went on short expeditions in search of some of the ingredients he knew that Asa liked. For the most part, they would rot by the fire pit. Gradually, Asa's irritation turned into anxiety. He would not allow Håkan beyond a narrow area around their crag. They were coming, he said. No doubt. Someone was coming. It was a matter of time. Håkan believed him—as he always did. After all, he owed Asa not only his life but also the world, which he had lost after the killings. Still haunted by the lives he had taken, Håkan felt sullied and fallen. The shame of being, for almost everyone, a murderer, a murderer of women—Helen's murderer—was enough to make him want to shun the society of men forever. But the world had returned. Asa had brought it back to him, brimming with meaning and purpose.

Despite his constant uneasiness and his somber mood, Asa never failed to express his admiration and gratitude for Håkan's healing abilities. He had seen too many people perish in similar circumstances—a fall, a fracture, bleeding, gangrene, amputation, delirium, death—to take Håkan's talents lightly. The story of how he set his leg fascinated him, and no matter how many times he heard it ("Tell me about the leg, and what you did," he would ask Håkan over and over again, like a child), Asa always listened with gaping reverence. Each compress and salve that Håkan applied, each bleeding, each suture was received with solemn devotion.

When he was not looking for food or tending to Asa's wounds, Håkan worked on new crutches and different kinds of splints, whittling, stitching, and patching together all sorts of materials. Eventually, Asa started cooking again. They had to stock up on cured meats and preserves for their trip to the barren cañons.

"The cañons are our only hope," Asa repeated every evening. "Too many days lost here. We can't outrun anybody. But maybe we can lose them."

One night, after much hesitation, feeling foolish for having waited for so long, Håkan asked, "What is the cañon?"

"I've never been myself," Asa responded. "They say it's a land like no other. Like a bad dream. Red tunnels carved by long-gone rivers. Like old scars in the ground. Very deep. For leagues and leagues. Few go in. Fewer get out."

Later that night, long after they had gone to bed, Håkan woke up. He could feel Asa thinking behind him—his thoughts had woken him up. He could also sense that Asa knew that he was awake.

"We can't go to California now," Asa said at last. Then, after a long pause, "They'll be looking for you. You'd never make it. We'll go to the cañons. Wait there." He was quiet for a while, as if his silence were a small sample of that wait. "Then, to San Francisco. I don't know how, but we'll make it." Another pause. "There, I'll find my friends. They can get us on a boat." Another silence. "We'll sail to New York. Nobody will be looking there. You'll be safe there. We'll be fine." Pause. "And we will find your brother."

Something within Håkan melted. Only now, as it softened and evaporated, did he realize that for years he had lived with a frozen lump in his chest. Only now that he knew he would see Linus again—for there was no doubt that, with Asa's help, he would see him again—did he feel how much pain this cold shrapnel had caused him. And he understood that up to that moment he had never had a chance of finding his brother. Getting to New York? Finding him in that endless city? How would that ever have happened? Love and longing had kept him going, but now, with Asa by his side, he saw how hopeless his search had hitherto been, and how doomed it would have been without Asa's aid.

How could he respond to Asa's words? Like a magic spell, they had changed reality just by being uttered.

19.

The day to leave came at last. Asa's leg had improved enough for him to move around with a pair of crutches Håkan had made him. Out of bones, wood, leather, and tarpaulin, he had also devised an articulated brace that allowed Asa to mount with greater ease and dulled the impact of his leg against the horse's side while helping the bone stay in place. Their two spare horses were loaded with the water and provisions they had gathered during the past few weeks.

It got warmer, redder, and drier. The mountain chain was reduced to a few crooked pillars. The forests died out, and only some prickly gray things sprouted every now and then. Birds no longer flew in flocks—only a bird here and then, later, maybe, a bird there. The air felt tense, as if the entire sky had inhaled and pulled back while holding its breath. And the sun, always the sun. Small in the sky, immense on the ground.

Asa reckoned they would travel about one hundred leagues through the cañons, making a stop halfway, before reaching the forests. The horses were his main concern. The country had few watering places and was almost barren of feed. Luckily, the animals were quick to spot edible desert scrubs and a fleshy, almost harmless variety of prickly pear. They also fed on forbs and shrubs and learned to nibble on malformed piñon pines and stunted tree yuccas. When everything else failed, they licked salty rocks and ate dirt. Their ribs started to show, and there was something increasingly deranged in their bulging eyes, but they kept going. One of them, the one that had belonged to the sheriff, had a great talent for detecting water underground. He would stop, snort, and dig with his forelegs. Håkan helped. The horse was never wrong.

It was sudden. Somehow, without ever having climbed up, they were looking down. It took their eyes a few moments to adjust to the darkness below. Cool air came wafting from the depths. The feeling was so pleasant, Håkan had to take a step back when he pictured himself plunging into the shady chasm. The deep gorge, branching out in angular streams, looked like a black horizontal flash of lightning.

They walked along the edge, looking for a way down at each angular fork, but the incline was always too steep for the horses. Never had Håkan witnessed desolation at such a scale. The deserts he had crossed so far had felt alive compared to this landscape. They were wastelands, yes, but they had been created that way, and perhaps their emptiness was only the first stage of a long process toward a lush future. They were perfect blanks. They were full of promise. But the cañon was done. Some great force had tried; it had broken the ground up like a loaf; it had, at some point, poured water into those ravines; it had even arranged the gulches and streams in pleasing patterns. And then, for some reason, it had desisted and withdrawn. The rivers dried up. The dirt hardened, yellowed, and crimsoned. All that was left was a majestic hopelessness.

The sun was setting, and they still had failed to find a path down into the cañon.

More angered than weakened by their thirst, the horses refused to go on. They bivouacked by the edge of the precipice, ate some charqui, and went to bed. The following morning, however, their luck turned. Before noon, they found a more or less gentle scree slope, and as soon as they scrabbled down to the bottom of the bluff, the sheriff's horse darted around a bend, where there was a small stream. Asa laughed. He confessed that the night before, as he lay down, he thought that they would die in a few days. While the horses drank and Håkan washed, Asa walked up the gulch. A moment later, he returned, excited beyond measure. There were some bushes and small trees upstream on which the horses could feed. All they needed was a hideout close enough to the springs and the shrubs. Toward nightfall, they found a curved passageway leading up to a hall of sorts, part of which was covered by a smooth orange dome. Too magnificent to be human, too intimate to be natural, it was an eerie yet inviting place. It was neither a fully enclosed nor an entirely open space. The vault, covering about three-quarters of the chamber, was big enough to shelter and hide them and their horses, but the far end of the refuge was open and looked down onto the ravine, offering a view of the entrance to the passageway from above, so no one could approach them unseen. They concealed the access to the cave with some rocks, which could easily be removed as needed. Asa said they could not have wished for a safer hideout.

Days and weeks went by. Asa believed that if they waited long enough, their pursuers, seeing how hostile the conditions were, would abandon that course and head west ahead of them—and there was nothing better, he said, than being behind one's chasers.

Håkan found bliss in their austere life in the dome. They lived frugally on the victuals gathered in the mountains and spent their days in almost complete silence. Asa told him they should make as little noise as possible, since sound traveled fast, loud, and far through the cañons. Håkan did not mind. The orange vault, marbled with pink and purple, kept the air cool during the day and warm at night. He liked to spend entire mornings lying down with Asa, staring at the dome, and, in whispers, pointing out faces, animals, and all sorts of fantastic scenes that popped in and out of the intricate swirls on the cupola. Examining the colored layers on the wall, Håkan found some remarkable fossils (legged shields, spiral shells, thorny fish) but never showed them to Asa.

Once a day, in the afternoon, when the bottom of the ravine was shady (and therefore less visible from above), they took the horses to their feeding place and fetched water from the spring. Since the boulders that blocked and concealed the entrance could only be removed and replaced from the inside, they had to take turns. At first, Asa refused to let Håkan go at all. It was, Asa said, the only moment they could be found and killed. But Håkan insisted: they should share the risk. In the end, and not without reluctance, Asa agreed. Although he missed Asa when they were apart, Håkan also enjoyed that daily hour of solitude, either walking down the gorge with the horses, looking at the earth from below, or staying in the dome, pacing around, humming ever so softly— fearing Asa would hear him from the brook—and listening to his own voice bounce back from the most unexpected corners.

It was one of these afternoons, when Asa had left with the animals, that Håkan, who was humming to himself, heard a big commotion. Galloping. Many horses. Asa whooping. A gunshot. Another. Asa hooting. Galloping. Håkan crawled to the open end of the refuge from which he could see the entrance while remaining invisible in the shadows. The hoofbeats, the screams, and the shots grew louder, and one echo resounded over the other so that it became impossible to tell where the sounds came from and in what order they had been produced—cause and consequence, past and future were overturned and scrambled in the reverberations. For a moment, in the swirl of sounds, Håkan thought that Asa might have been shot already, even if his screams were still in the air. But as the wave of echoes surged, Asa emerged from behind the bend, galloping at full speed. Raising himself on the stirrups, his body leaned forward, touching the horse's neck. When he was not whipping the animal with a piece of rope, he brandished it in front of its eyes, so that the horse became as frantic as the rider. He sped by the hidden entrance and turned up his head to the dark balcony from where Håkan was looking down. Asa could not have seen him, but his upturned gaze and his furtive smile, warm and serene for a moment (a moment during which the chase, the noise, and the world came to a halt), told Håkan that he knew he was being watched. An instant later, Asa was out of sight. Immediately after, three riders galloped by. They, too, vanished. The screaming and the gunshots continued. Then they stopped.

Håkan was pulverized and scattered by the ensuing silence. There was no room for him—or anything—in it.

Someone laughed. It was not Asa.

There was too much air, too much light.

Hooves echoing in the distance. At a walk. Getting closer. Then, the three riders leisurely making their way down the gorge. Chatting. Laughing. Asa's horse in tow. Asa's body strapped to it. Right under Håkan. Asa's head shining with blood.

Håkan remained there as the sun set, the stars came out, and morning dawned. Thrice.

20.

How many years had passed since he had left the cañons, he did not know. A few winters back, he had found the first gray strands in his hair. Some of the logs and boulders he used to lift effortlessly now made him grunt. At some point, his voice, which he heard only when he coughed (or on the rare occasions when he hummed or said a few words to himself), had started to sound to him like that of an old man. Maybe older than his father.

He seldom left his dwelling. A long time before, when first settling in those parts, he had decided to dig and build down. He thought it would make his refuge less visible. It took him a few months to dig the main trench that dead-ended at a roughly square cell. Even so, he moved into the hole as soon as it was large enough to fit him and had lived there ever since, while expanding and improving on his shelter. As the trench got longer, so did the pitched roof that covered it. Although it barely stuck out from the ground, in the early days, it made him uneasy to have that protruding structure, but those four feet or so, he soon discovered, were necessary for proper drainage away from the tunnel. During the first rainy season, he was forced to pave the floors and tile the walls with stones and logs to keep them from swamping and crumbling down. He proved to be particularly skilled at tiling and even found some pleasure in coming up with different designs—and perhaps this was one of the reasons why he kept enlarging his refuge throughout the years. Regardless of the season, he had several fires burning at the same time, at least for a while, to keep the walls and the floor dry. This took up a considerable portion of every day, but he did not mind. It gave him something to do. The inlays, together with the daily fires, made the tunnels and the chamber habitable and the air in them less foul. He even devised a leather funnel connected to a flue, and several of these chimneys were installed throughout the burrow.

For as long as he lived there, he kept digging. Even though he knew that a larger dwelling would be more noticeable, the inexplicable sense of safety he derived from multiplying its forking trenches outdid common sense. After the main passageway and the square cell were finished and furnished (flooring, walls, smokestacks, a rustic bed, some stumps and boulders as tables and chairs), he started on a new channel that would connect with another of the chamber's sides. He worked piecemeal, beginning at the farthest part of the new trench, and, in the end, connecting it with the finished structure, so that his living quarters remained clean during construction.

He had chosen that spot after discovering that underneath a tough superficial crust, the ground was made of malleable clay. To break through the top layer, he had made a battering ram of sorts with a long branch and a heavy pointed rock. With a few blows, he broke down the clusters of pebbles, roots, and dry dirt, and then used different kinds of hollowed-out tree trunks to shovel the soil out. Once he got through to the muddy layer, he was often able to use a big, flat triangular stone to slice through the clay and remove massive slabs at once, instead of having to scoop the mud out. He would shove the sharpest tip of the triangle—a large, smooth arrowhead—in at a slight angle, and then, with the help of two staffs, stand on top of it and jump on the edge until it was completely buried, at which point a big block of mud would come off. He toiled ceaselessly, losing his sense of time and of himself as he dug and logged. Night would come, unnoticed, while he kept excavating in the dark. Once in bed, he often discovered wounds he had failed to notice during the day.

His compulsion had him start on different passageways at the same time, and in a few months, he had a complex network of tunnels. Certain trenches were interconnected; others were completely isolated; a few were linked to the square cell. Many tunnels were narrow gutters, mere sketches of more ambitious undertakings. However, there was no way to keep such a vast maze from collapsing. There were not enough boulders and beams to prevent avalanches, and it was impossible to keep all the fires needed to dry out the mud. The elements prevailed. Remoter tunnels fell into disrepair and caved in after floods and slides, a fate that many of the outer sections of the burrow shared in time. In the end, he retreated to the original square and kept only a few subsidiary tunnels. He spent months filling up the abandoned trenches.

After Asa's death, Håkan had remained in the dome until winter. He barely ate and left the chamber only a handful of times to fetch water. The world was reduced to the orange figures in the vault. Each instant was a prison, barred away from both past and future. Now-here, now-here, his heart pounded in his ears. His indifference toward himself and his fate was complete. His pain, intense and deafening as it was, came to him as a remote echo of someone else's scream.

Later, looking back at those months, he pictured himself as one of the fossils encrusted in the rock face.

One night, he almost died of cold. The orange dome had long been overtaken by blackness. Instead of the whimsical images swimming in and out of the swirls in the stone, he saw people he knew. His parents, the estate manager, neighboring farmers. He also saw animals. The colt his father had sold to the miller. A motionless buzzard staining the desert sky. The lady who had held him captive, her guards, the fat man. Jarvis Pickett and the short-haired Indian. A white pig. The woman churning butter next to the schoolchildren. The schoolchildren. The horse he had taken from the brethren. Lorimer, Antim, the sailor who had told him that the brown city on the coast was not New York, the tracker, the Brennan family, the sheriff, Linus, the Chinese seamen having lunch in Portsmouth. At that exact moment, as Håkan was staring into the dark, most of them were probably alive. At that exact moment, most of them were doing something—the schoolchildren, now young men, plowing and milking; the sailors securing mooring lines; the horses staring into space; Linus walking down a busy street; women and men sleeping; some aching; all of them with some picture in their brains; a few talking; someone having a draft of cold water. But Asa was dead. Håkan's stiff and shivering frame suddenly relaxed, and he felt his consciousness sink, like a dull red ember disappearing into the ashes. Why he fought this pleasant release, he did not know. But the next morning, he was on his way.

Asa's killers had taken the horses, so Håkan had to travel light. With a series of leather straps and canvas, he managed to load blankets, provisions, guns, and tools on his back, over his fur coat. He walked out of the cañon and headed northwest, where, according to Asa, there were trees and rivers. Like before, he stayed clear of trails and every sign of human presence, but this time it was exhaustion, rather than fear, that moved him. Questions, accusations, threats, verdicts. Talk. He wanted no talk. Without a clear destination and having no purpose other than solitude, it was easier to elude everyone. Being on foot allowed him to travel through wild, otherwise inaccessible tracts.

He crossed deserts and forded rivers, climbed mountains and traversed plains. He ate fish and prairie dogs, slept on moss and sand, skinned caribou and iguanas. His face became wrinkled by many summers and furrowed by many winters. His hands, burned and frostbitten year after year, were crossed and recrossed with lines and creases. Once, he saw the ocean but turned around immediately, thinking there would be settlements along the coastline. Whenever he stopped, it was at an inhospitable location—never in a meadow, by a water source, or in a plentiful spot—barely pitching camp and seldom making fires. It was dead quiet in his mind. He rarely thought of anything that was not at hand. Years vanished under a weightless present.

Through countless frosts and thaws, he walked in circles wider than nations.

And then he stopped.

Years of marching almost barefoot had turned his feet into dark knotty things. Blisters, splinters, and wounds had affected his gait, and now he walked by resting mostly on the outer edges of his soles. This bowlegged stance had damaged his knees, as a result of which, his legs were not as agile as they used to be. Even if, in time, he had learned to get by with almost nothing, he had always packed a few essentials on his back, and now he suffered from permanent discomfort in his spine and neck. Still, battered and exhausted as he was, these were not the reasons why he stopped. He stopped because it was time to stop. He had not arrived anywhere. There simply were no more steps to take. So he put his things down and started digging.

Aside from the malleable properties of the soil, there was nothing remarkable about the spot—and that was why he chose it. A few knolls assured him that travelers would not pick that particular course when the surrounding grounds were flat. There was a water source nearby but not close enough for him to run into thirsty wanderers. Game, berries, nuts, and mushrooms were not hard to come by, although they were not so abundant as to make anyone go out of his way. Without being hostile, the weather was not attractive. Springs fleeted by, yielding to sweltering summers that burned the green out of every plant in a matter of days. During the cold season, the hills, weeds, and few surrounding trees turned into rust-stained steel. For a few weeks a year, the soil became one big unbreakable rock.

Silence and solitude had clouded his perception of time. A year and an instant are equivalent in a monotonous life. Seasons went by and returned, and Håkan's occupations never changed. An abandoned ditch had to be filled. More glue had to be boiled down. A trench had fallen into disrepair. An extension to an old passageway was necessary. Traps had to be set. A gutter overflowed. Tiles had slid out of place. Drinking water was needed. The coat had to be mended. A roof could leak less. Some meat had to be jerked before it spoiled. A leather flue was too decayed. Firewood had to be gathered. A new tool had to be made. Cobblestones had come loose. Before one of these tasks had been completed, the next one demanded his attention, so that at all times he was engaged in one of these chores, which, together, over time, formed a circle or, rather, some sort of pattern that, though invisible to him, repeated itself, he was sure, at regular intervals. These recurrent duties made every day resemble the last, and within each day, from sunup to sundown, there were few markers to divide time. He did not even eat at regular hours. In fact, his diet had been reduced to the absolute, life-sustaining minimum. Since Asa's death, he had become averse to food. He had his quick, small repasts—charqui, whatever the soil yielded, some bird or rodent barely roasted on a spit—only when he got light-headed and inexplicably angry. Asa's quail abounded around the burrow, which confirmed their penchant for mockery. At first, the birds, their mere presence, infuriated him. In time, he came to ignore them. Not once did he try to catch them. He did, however, trap other creatures. Fearing a shortage of game that would take him far from the burrow, he was always smoking meat and drying it in the sun. Here and there, by the edges of some tunnels and next to a few distant fires, strips of browning flesh and entire carcasses hung on crosses and racks. The dried meats were stored carefully. But he never felt hungry—only that dizziness and irritation that signaled his body's imminent collapse. Sometimes he was surprised that his health was so robust. He had not lost a single tooth—and he had never met an adult with a full set of teeth. This could only be explained by another fact that he found equally puzzling: even though he did not know how old he was, it was clear to him that he had reached the age at which the human body has matured and starts its decline. Still, he had never stopped growing. Tight shoes were the first sign of a new spurt. They were hard to make, and he constantly had to cobble them or put together a new pair from scratch. Since he had started to spend most of his time in the burrow, he could manage by wrapping his feet up in leather, canvas, and furs. But when-ever he went on one of his rare excursions beyond the creek, he needed more protection, and the shoes he wore on those occasions fit him only a few times before they had to be enlarged or replaced. His clothes, a confusion of rags and pelts, were too loose to be outgrown, but he had lengthened his fur coat's sleeves several times. The burrow itself, however, provided the best standard to measure his growth. It was not that he became too large to fit any of the chambers or trenches, but rather that, at some point, certain spaces that used to be comfortable started to become oppressive and eventually felt so tight that he was compelled to dig down for more headroom or sideways to widen a given cell or tunnel. Some of the additional passageways he had excavated had been born out of this feeling of confinement. Something similar happened with his few pieces of furniture. One evening, a stone stool would make him bend his knees too high. One morning, he would find that his heels touched the end of the bed. Since he had not seen another human being in years, he had no sense of how tall he would feel next to someone else, but he did know he would be conspicuous—an added reason for staying out of sight. But these were only fleeting thoughts. He seldom considered his body or his circumstances—or anything else, for that matter. The business of being took up all of his time.

Every thought of ever finding Linus, of traveling to New York, had long abandoned him. Practical impediments—he was a wanted man who would never fail to be noticed; he had no money or means to obtain it; he did not have a horse—had nothing to do with it. There were simply no goals or destinations anymore. Not even the desire to die that he had experienced after the most crushing tragedies in his life. He was just something that kept going. Not because it wanted to, but because that was the way it had been built. To keep going with the bare minimum was the line of least resistance. It was natural and therefore involuntary. Anything else would have required a decision. And the last decision he had ever made had been to dig his burrow. If he kept going at it endlessly, it was simply because he could not muster up the strength to decide to stop.

During the long years spent there, not a soul passed by. At first, he was on the lookout for riders and even built a small platform to make his stays on top of a tree that commanded a view of the surrounding area more comfortable. He barely lit fires and spent the larger part of the day listening against the wind for hooves and wagons and scanning the horizon for smoke and cattle. As the seasons went by, it became apparent that his plot was far removed from every route and trail and that nobody would ever expressly come to that rather sterile gray land with the intention of claiming it.

Little by little, his fears dissipated, and he withdrew into the maze, which he seldom left. When he did, his world did not reach far beyond the creek. He always took a different route there to avoid creating a trail. Aside from fetching water, he roamed about, setting traps and exploring the surroundings to erase any trace he might have left. But for the most part, he avoided leaving the burrow. After having spent most of his life outdoors, walking, he liked being inside. It was not that he feared vast expanses. Rather, he felt about open space the way he did about rain—something he would prefer to get out of. Staying in the dugout, however, did not mean a motionless life. All day long, Håkan walked up and down the covered trenches, repairing tiles, digging, and fueling fires, always smelling the resinous scent coming from the pine-tree ceilings. Perhaps, without knowing it at the time, he later thought, he had opted for that particular kind of dwelling so that he could keep walking without leaving his home. Night used to catch him working, and although his body throbbed with exhaustion, sleep came only after going into long trances, staring at the neglected flames, which sank to embers, which sank under the ashes, which sank into darkness. His mind was empty, but somehow that void demanded all his attention. Emptiness, he discovered, wants everything for itself—it takes the fraction of an atom (or the flicker of a thought) to put an end to a universal void. Exhausted by the vacuum, he would often get up, build a new fire somewhere in the burrow, and work on the tiling, adding pebbles around the boulders and slabs on the walls. This was of modest help in keeping the clay in place, but it gave him some pleasure. There were no predetermined designs. He just liked to insert the small stones as close to each other as possible and then step back to see what patterns chance had created. Finding, sorting, and inserting the stones was a slow process, and because there usually were more urgent chores to tend to, only a few segments in some tunnels and parts of the main cell had been completed.

A year and an instant are equivalent in a monotonous life. Seasons went by and returned, and Håkan's occupations never changed. A gutter overflowed. Tiles had slid out of place. Some meat had to be jerked before it spoiled. An abandoned ditch had to be filled. Drinking water was needed. A trench had fallen into disrepair. Cobblestones had come loose. An extension to an old passageway was necessary. More glue had to be boiled down. A roof could leak less. Traps had to be set. A new tool had to be made. The coat had to be mended. A leather flue was too decayed. Firewood had to be gathered. Before one of these tasks had been completed, the next one demanded his attention, so that at all times he was engaged in one of these chores, which, together, over time, formed a circle or, rather, some sort of pattern that, though invisible to him, repeated itself, he was sure, at regular intervals. These recurrent duties made every day resemble the last, and within each day, from sunup to sundown, there were few markers to divide time. He did not even eat at regular hours. In fact, his diet had been reduced to the absolute, life-sustaining minimum. Since Asa's death, he had become averse to food. At first, when he was still traveling, he used to look at Asa's spoon, and the almost acoustic intensity of its presence would make him weep. The scrap of paper on which Helen had written his name was still in his tin box of medical supplies. It was appropriate that he could not read those signs, he thought, since neither the person who had traced them nor the one they referred to existed anymore. In time, he stopped conjuring up Helen's and Asa's faces, and they withdrew further into the blackness that had claimed them, although now and then they returned in flashes that Håkan always welcomed. These visits were brief but so vivid that they challenged the surrounding reality. Other figures occasionally haunted him. The men he had killed stared at him in his dreams. Sometimes, Lorimer's features took shape around his spectacles—the spectacles came first, then the beard around his smile, followed by the rest of his gentle, savage figure—but this apparition was not like the echoes that the dead leave behind, which resonate with a lifelike ring when the surrounding space and things vibrate in conjunction with them. The naturalist returned, rather, as a question. Håkan was certain Lorimer was alive—he just wondered where he was. As time went by, these visits became more sporadic, and now, for the most part, his memories seemed to have dissolved in his mind. The past seldom came back to him. Gradually, the present took over, and each moment became absolute and indivisible.

Since the cobblestones set into the dirt evened and dried out the more they were trodden on, the original part of the burrow was also the most comfortable one. The clay on those walls had been baked hard by countless fires and acquired the texture of earthenware. Sounds down there felt like solid little objects. Nothing echoed. Life existed only as a murmur. Loud noises were muted, yielding to the whooshing of canvas and the creaking of leather. Sometimes, the hairs on his forearms rose with pleasure at the clack of wood on wood and the clink of stone on stone. Every aspect of fire was audible—crunching kindling, rustling leaves, snapping sparks, hissing sap, popping pinecones, crumbling logs, exhaling coals. Whenever Håkan coughed or said a word out loud, his own voice sounded monstrous, like that of an ungainly giant, an invader

in his own home. It was a relief that the clay walls sucked in these awkward growls immediately, without leaving a trace. In this subterranean
quiet, his movements became more deliberate and softer. Everything
took more time, and there was a full awareness of each action as it was
being performed—as if to expand the present to which he was confined.
The tin cup was not merely put on the table, but placed there with the
utmost care, so that when the tin and the wood touched, the moment
was prolonged enough to give a slightly miraculous feel and create the
impression of a gentle yet momentous meeting of alien worlds. He was
reluctant to split firewood indoors, feeling there was something irrever-
ent and even tasteless in the loud snaps. When he made a stew or glue,
he was careful to stir the liquid without clanging against the pot's walls.
Without being fully aware of it at first, he often found himself scratching his beard just because he enjoyed the sound.

If the clay walls, threatening to slide, crumble, or even collapse in
extended avalanches, demanded constant attention (tiling, retiling, but-
tressing, propping), the pitched roofs required, perhaps, even more work.
They were mostly made out of pine branches that he had learned to
entwine while they were green and supple, interlacing them with leather
where needed. The result was a tight enough thatch to keep the floors
in the passageways more or less dry—but seldom sufficiently water-
proof. In whichever trench or cell Håkan took residence, he reinforced
the roof with some waxed tarpaulins and oilcloths. He also made rect-
angular frames out of sticks tied together with tripe, which he then
fitted with skins, creating movable panels, some of which could be
opened and shut with leather hinges. In varying combinations, branches,
cloth, and leather panels were mounted on beams buried obliquely on
either side of the trench and joined, at the cusp, to a ridgepole with rope
made of braided leather straps. His glue, perfected over the years, sealed
the cracks between the disparate parts. These were rather precarious

structures, and some of the rare events that interrupted the sameness of his existence over the years resulted from problems with the roofing. Sometimes, under the weight of rain or snow, or merely because the wood had decayed, a section of the roof came crashing down. Once, the whole construction, beams, joists, and all, collapsed on him while he was sleeping. A big bough stabbed him in the leg. Through the yellow fat, he could see his femur. At first, it did not heal properly. He feared for his leg and considered different devices to amputate it himself. Then, he feared for his life. Despite the fever and the stupefying pain, he managed to drain the wound, keep it clean, suture it, bind it, and, eventually, cure himself. Since then, all his beds were covered by a sturdy canopy.

A few years later, however, there was another incident, from which no canopy could have saved him. The roof of one of the lateral passageways was hit by lightning. To prevent the fire from spreading, he tore down all connecting sections. Isolated, the straight line of fire kept burning after the short storm had blown over, and, for a moment, as dusk set in and the flames died down, it looked as if there were two horizons, each glowing with its own twilight.

Less grand but more profound was another phenomenon, involving a different part of the ceiling, that lasted for some time. He was working on a distant tunnel, making a deep cellar for his tanned skins, which demanded watertight roofing. After securing a few pieces of leather and tarpaulin to the protruding structure, he climbed down into the hole to inspect the results. To his complete bewilderment, on one of the walls he saw an image of the sun setting among the treetops—upside down. A perfect picture of the world outside of the hole. In lifelike colors. And it moved. The trees swayed; birds flew by; the sun continued its descending course. Upward. It felt like someone else's hallucination; as if someone, far away, were dreaming up that place (wrong side up), and Håkan, for some reason, were able to look into that dream. Overcoming his bewilderment, he dislodged one of the leather panels to see if there was something abnormal outside. As light streamed in, the image on the wall vanished. He looked out of the hole. The same ashen landscape as always. Nothing out of the ordinary. He ducked back in and fitted the panel back into place. The hole darkened, and the image reappeared. As he leaned across it, his own shadow revealed that there was a hole in the tarp through which a beam of light came filtering in and, it seemed, became that inverted moving picture as it hit the wall. There was no room in his mind for superstition or magic. Astounding as this image was, he knew it must be a natural occurrence. But he failed to understand what was behind this prodigy. For a few days, the picture appeared on the wall as the sun started to set and vanished before it had fully sunken. Even if he knew every last detail of that patch of land, Håkan never tired of looking at its slightly watery inversion on the wall. Then, one evening, it was gone. He tried everything, but never managed to bring the picture back.

These events provided him with a vague calendar—before and after the accident or the lightning or the moving picture. And there were a few more incidents that loosely divided his monotonous life into different eras. The bear that kept him distant company for one fall. A shower of stars. The fox that gave birth in one of his tunnels. Those times the moon turned red. The birds whose feet froze into the ground. Some bad storms. In time, however, the order of these events got confused in his head. Looking back, his life in the maze seemed a completely uniform period. The few extraordinary moments were lumped together in a cluster of their own, unrelated to the sameness that ruled those years. Seasons went by and returned, and Håkan's occupations never changed. A roof could leak less. Traps had to be set. A gutter overflowed. Tiles had slid out of place. An abandoned ditch had to be filled. The coat had to be mended. A trench had fallen into disrepair. Firewood had to be gathered. An extension to an old passageway was necessary. Drinking water was needed. A new tool had to be made. Some meat had to be jerked before it spoiled. Cobblestones had come loose. A leather flue was too decayed. More glue had to be boiled down. Before one of these tasks had been completed, the next one demanded his attention, so that at all times he was engaged in one of these chores, which, together, over time, formed a circle or, rather, some sort of pattern that, though invisible to him, repeated itself, he was sure, at regular intervals. These recurrent duties made every day resemble the last, and within each day, from sunup to sundown, there were few markers to divide time. He did not even eat at regular hours. In fact, his diet had been reduced to the absolute, life-sustaining minimum. Sometimes he was surprised that his health was so robust. He had not lost a single tooth—and he had never met an adult with a full set of teeth. This could only be explained by another fact that he found equally puzzling: even though he did not know how old he was, it was clear to him that he had reached the age at which the human body has matured and starts its decline. Still, he had never stopped growing. Since he had not seen another human being in years, he had no sense of how tall he would feel next to someone else, but he did know he would be conspicuous—an added reason for staying out of sight. But these were only fleeting thoughts. He seldom considered his body or his circumstances—or anything else, for that matter. The business of being took up all of his time.

21.

Those flailing arms sticking out of the upright trunk. Those legs, like ridiculous scissors. Those forward-facing eyes on that flat face with that beakless, snoutless hole for a mouth. And the gestures. Hands, brow, nose, lips. So many gestures. Those misshapen and misplaced features and their wasteful, obscene movements. He thought nothing could be more grotesque than those forms. His next thought was that he looked just like them. Then, he ran for his gun.

Because he had lost the ability to think about the future, he had stopped considering what to do if someone ever came to the burrow. And now that five men were approaching, it seemed the most obvious thing in the world. Of course someone would come at some point. With the oncoming men, a forgotten dimension of reality suddenly reappeared, defying his senses. The world was new, complex, and frightening. His hands shook as he readied the gun.

He reached toward the ceiling, slid a leather panel to the side, and peered out. The men rode about leisurely, inspecting the burrow and pointing out this and that detail. They were alert and, at the same time, relaxed, as if they knew that he lived there, but also that he was outnumbered. Had they been spying on him? Where from? How could he have failed to notice? Everything in their approach—their loud voices, their occasional laughs, their slow pace and the sagging reins, the casual way in which they held their rifles—indicated that they were certain he was alone. They had the arrogance of the conqueror who knows that merely showing up will be enough.

Three of them were soldiers, but they seemed to belong to two different armies. Two were in loose-fitting gray uniforms and matching forage caps, while the other soldier wore blue and a slouch hat with some sort of adornment pinning the brim up. His left sleeve was empty, folded up, and attached to the elbow. On his right arm were three yellow stripes. Regardless of color and rank, the uniforms were torn and tattered. The remaining two men looked like so many others Håkan had seen on his journeys—deerskin leggings, flannel shirts, wide-brimmed hats. The civilians were on regular bays, but the soldiers rode thick, tall draft horses—stout, muscular, almost neckless, their fetlocks and hooves covered by thick tufts of hair full of burrs and thistles. Håkan knew nothing about breeds, but it was clear that those beasts were meant for the harness and not the saddle.

"Friend!" the blue soldier cried. "Hey, friend! We're friends!"

Håkan realized that he was panting. Out of nowhere, a colony of little incandescent dots started bubbling, popping, vanishing, and reemerging before his eyes. His body felt less dense. Even if he had wanted to respond, his tongue, glued to his palate, was too dry and heavy to allow him to speak a single word.

One of the soldiers in gray muttered something, and the others laughed. They rode by some meat that was being jerked on frames. The other gray soldier took a piece, tasted it, and spat it out. He rubbed his tongue with his sleeve while cursing and making grotesque noises. More chuckles.

Håkan thought that he could smell them. Human stench. To what savagery would he be subjected? Because these were wild and unkind men. He could tell from their scars, their snickers, and, above all, their calmness—the calmness of people who know they can always rely on absolute violence. He looked at the gun in his hand as if someone had planted it there while he was distracted. Taking another life.

They stopped about fifteen paces away from him. Had he been seen? After conferring—in signs more than in words—one of the civilians put his rifle into his saddle holster, dismounted, and took a few steps toward Håkan.

"We mean no harm, mister. No harm at all. Just a few words."

Showing himself unarmed was the only option. Perhaps his size would intimidate them. Perhaps his size would make them want to shoot him on the spot. He was reconciled with the idea of dying, but he did not want to share that singular, final experience with these brutes. Before putting the pistol down and proceeding to one of the exits, he realized, fleetingly, that it was the first time in his life that he was scared of men younger than himself.

The lion coat hung on one of the posts at the foot of the bed. It was not cold, but he put it on. After removing a section of the roof, he stepped on a table and climbed out.

Because he was crouching when he emerged from the trench, his height was not revealed at once, but as he uncoiled and came to an upright position, he looked ahead and saw amazement gradually overtaking everyone's expression. Håkan himself was surprised. It had been years since he last stood next to another person or something of a more or less constant size—something that was not in nature or that he had not made with his hands. The men were like children. The horses looked wrong. Håkan and the men stared at each other; he, remembering what a man was; they, discovering what a man could be.

One of the civilians cocked his gun. The soldier in blue raised his single hand without looking away from Håkan.

"It's you," he said.

Håkan stared at his own bare feet. After so many years looking down at them, they had become objects removed from his own self. Even more, callous and insensible to touch, they had ceased to mediate between the world and his consciousness. They were one more everyday article.

"It is you," the one-armed man in blue repeated. "See?" he cried, turning around to his comrades. "It's him!" And then, facing Håkan once again, "The Hawk."

The disgrace, the guilt, the fear came rushing back, wiping out all the years spent in solitude. He was back where he had left off.

Perhaps as a reaction to his shame, for a moment he forgot how recognizable he was and thought that if the blue soldier knew who he was, they must have met at some point. In the fraction of an instant, all the faces he could remember flashed through his mind. None of them matched the blue soldier. Perhaps the soldier had been one of the children on the emigrant trail. Maybe he had been one of the boys who had flung rotten vegetables at him when the sheriff had him on display. But there was an expression on the soldier's face that Håkan knew well. It was the stare of people who had heard about him but never actually seen him. Briefly, he wondered if those uniforms meant that the newcomers were lawmen.

"The brethren killer, lion skin and all."

The blue soldier's explanation was unnecessary. The awestruck, frozen expression of the four remaining men showed that they had realized on their own who Håkan was.

"He's alive?" asked one of the civilians to no one in particular.

"Abundantly," said the blue soldier, gesturing to Håkan from head to toe.

Håkan looked around, pausing on the different sections of the burrow. Knowing that he would soon leave it forever, he understood its magnitude for the first time.

The blue soldier had rejoined the others, and they were having a muted discussion. Every now and again, they turned around and, still mesmerized, stared at Håkan.

"Do you have a gun?" someone asked.

"Inside."

"Quite a place you got here," a gray soldier said. "Quite a place."

"How did you do it?" the blue soldier asked, ignoring his friend's remark.

"I dig," Håkan responded.

"No, no. How did you do it? All those things. You know, the brethren, escape from the law. Stay away for so long."

"I walked," he said, addressing only the last part of the question.

The men laughed.

"He walked," someone said and giggled like an idiot.

"How long have you been here?"

"I don't know."

"You're a legend, you know."

Again, his feet.

One of the civilians took a swig from a flask and offered it to Håkan, who shook his head.

"Quite a place," the gray soldier said again.

They dismounted, escorted Håkan to his cell, and, after taking the guns they found there, walked around, inspecting the burrow and claiming different sections for themselves.

Night came. After the men had had a long conversation by a fire removed from Håkan's quarters, they asked him to join them. The one-handed soldier in blue spoke for all of them.

"We have some business to discuss with you. An offer." He paused, peering into Håkan's eyes. "We all admire what you've done. Like I said, you're a legend. Getting those settlers. And then those heathens—those brethren. And then." He laughed in advance. "And then getting away on the sheriff's horse! I mean. Hell!"

Talk. This was what Håkan had been running away from. That he was being complimented did not make it better. He wanted no more talk.

"We have our own stories to tell, all of us, from the war. But nothing like you. Anyhow. Ever since peace reigns again," he said, looking at the gray soldiers with a smirk, "we've been riding about, trying to survive. You know. Plenty of opportunities out there."

Someone kept spitting into the fire. The embers hissed each time.

"So we were thinking. Thought we could use you. You wouldn't have to do anything. Unless you wanted to, of course. All you do is show up. You just show up in your big lion skin. We walk into the place. Store, tavern, bank, whatever. Then you walk into the place. People see you. They freeze. We take it from there. It would even be your gang. The Hawk Gang or The Hawks or something. Take all the credit. But with your name, reputation, and. And. Well." Failing to find the right word, he just pointed at Håkan. "With you. With you, no one would stop us."

Håkan looked straight into his eyes.

"No."

During the silence that followed his response, Håkan could feel some inner mechanism cock in the men—they did not load their guns, but themselves.

"Right, sure," the blue soldier said without losing his composure. "I'm not done. Like I said, you could come with us as our. What's the word here? Leader. You could come with us as our leader, or we could take you back. There's still a price on your head, you know. A power of money. Not as much as we would make if you came with us but still a handsome amount. Like I said, you're a legend."

Although he kept staring into the fire, Håkan knew that the men were ready to spring and strike at the shortest notice.

"Now look here," the blue soldier said at last. "We like your place. We're tired. We'll stay for a few days. You let us know in what direction we all set off when we leave."

The following day, the men rested, watered their horses, and drank spirits, but always had someone watching Håkan. He walked about the surrounding fields and woods, making sure his guards could see him at all times to dissipate any suspicion. First, he gathered mushrooms, nuts, a few herbs, and some flowers. Then, he started chasing the quail around, hunched over with a blanket. The birds always took off at the last second, only to land a few steps away and stare at him with their heads insolently tilted. The men looked on and laughed, slapping their thighs and holding their bellies. They pretended to sympathize, offering long cries each time he missed and then made fun of him with condescending words of encouragement, most of which referred to the disparity in size between hunter and prey.

The sun was setting when he had finished gathering all the ingredients. He built a fire over the ashes from the night before. While he plucked the quail, he went through the order in which things had to be prepared and cooked. With a stew, order is everything, Asa used to say. It surprised Håkan how well he remembered each detail and how vivid Asa's image was, guiding him through every step. Once the birds were cleaned, the flowers sorted, the nuts peeled, the lard in place, and the mushrooms chopped, he headed back to his cell, always making sure he was seen. He even caught the eye of one of the civilians and pointed down to the trench to let him know what his intention was. The man, busy with his flask, ignored him.

Once in the square chamber, he took the tin box out of a hole concealed under a pile of firewood. Next to it lay Asa's spoon. Håkan paused. Then, he opened the box. There, among his medical instruments, was the little bottle with the tincture. After so many years, whatever was left of it had evaporated. All that remained was a caramel cloud darkening the inner walls of the bottle and some crystallized dregs stuck to the bottom. He took Asa's spoon and hid the bottle in his sleeve. With a loud grunt, to make sure someone would turn toward him, he climbed out of the trench, waved at the guard with the spoon, put the pot on the fire, and started to cook.

It was the first proper meal he had made since Asa's death. Mushrooms cooking in lard. The scent of herbs and blossoms. The browning quail. Some of the men approached the pot and stuck their noses in it. The civilians were already drunk. Finally, he added some water. All surrounding heads turned to the fragrant steam. As the liquid boiled down and became more viscous, Håkan got the little bottle out of his sleeve and put it into the pot, making sure it sank to the bottom.

The civilians walked over with their tinware. Håkan served them. They sat down by the fire, heavy and stupid with drink. Their initial merriment had turned into a focused form of confusion—knit brows, determined eyes, carefully calculated yet extremely ineffectual movements. They ate with relish and kept drinking between bites.

"Dudley! Fellows! The giant can cook!"

Håkan forever remembered that name, although he never learned whose it was.

"Ah. This feels real good," the man said and lost consciousness, followed shortly after by the other civilian, who quietly closed his eyes.

The three soldiers approached the fire and laughed at the civilians. The man in blue made the sign of the cross over them.

"In the hope of a glorious resurrection," he said with mocking solemnity.

"In two days, maybe," added one of the gray soldiers.

More laughs.

"That does smell good. Let's have some," the blue soldier ordered Håkan.

"Not for me," said the other gray soldier. "I had his dried beef. And that was enough."

Chuckles.

"But this is good stuff, this is. Like home or something," his gray companion said.

Håkan proffered a spoonful.

"Didn't you hear? None of that for me."

"Well," the blue soldier muttered between bites, "more for us."

The man who refused to eat spat over his shoulder. The other two kept devouring the quail.

"Let's get some of that," the blue soldier said and got up to fetch the flask by the civilians.

He stumbled, and his single hand was not enough to catch his fall. The gray soldier sitting next to him tried to get up but failed. All at once, the remaining man understood everything and reached for his gun. Before he could draw, Håkan hit him in the head with the pot. He never checked whether he was unconscious or dead, preferring to live with the uncertainty rather than with the knowledge of having killed another man.

22.

After years of restless rambles followed by years in a stagnant haze, having a purpose felt like being possessed by a spirit. If in the burrow he had lived in an inescapable present, now he existed only for the future. He was at war with each instant. Each day, once finished, was one more obstacle overcome. He barely rested. He had a plan.

He intended to go back west and find James Brennan's hidden gold. To do so, first he must locate Clangston, from where he could easily reach the mine and then Brennan's secret hole. An eternity had gone by since the Clangston lady and her men had taken over the mine, and Håkan was hoping that by now it would be exhausted and forgotten. And even if the place were bustling with activity, his former captors would be too old or dead. Either way, Brennan's hideout was sufficiently removed from the quarry and had probably been left untouched for all those years. With gold, he would find a way into San Francisco—his first thought was to get a covered wagon with a hired driver. He would then get on a boat, buying the captain's silence, and sail away.

To outdistance his pursuers, he had taken all five horses. A few days after leaving the burrow, when he felt safe enough, he let four of them loose, keeping only the biggest of the draft horses. He was yellow and orange, and massive enough to belong in one of those dreams where familiar things are unsurprisingly alien. His flesh seemed to be made of some material that was beyond the distinction between living and inert. Each muscle, clearly defined under his coat as if he had been skinned, felt like a bag tightly packed with sand, barely yielding to the touch.

There was a certain resignation in his demeanor and in his gait that contradicted his immense strength and size. Together, Håkan and the horse made an impressive but, in a way, reasonable figure. They canceled each other out. Mounted on him, Håkan was almost unremarkable.

Knowing that his skins and rags would draw too much attention along the way, he took most of the civilians' clothes. Each night, he worked on a pair of trousers and a shirt, enlarging them by sewing in patches here and there. One of the wide-brimmed hats, which he also had to make bigger, eclipsed his features. The lion coat was rolled up and tied to the saddle.

The only certain thing was that Clangston lay east of San Francisco. He regretted that he had paid so little attention during his trip with the Brennans. But after all those years drifting around the country, he could guess that while going east they also could have steered a bit north—they never went too deep into the desert. Therefore, since he knew he was south of San Francisco, he intended to find the sea and then head northeast in a snaking diagonal line that must, at some point, put him near Clangston.

The journey was like so many of his other journeys. He had grown too accustomed to privations to feel them. The few wonders he encountered seemed old and tired. Nature was no longer trying to kill or to amaze him. But although he had spent the greatest part of his life in those prairies, deserts, and mountains, he still was unable to feel that they were his own. After thousands of nights under those same stars, he woke up as many thousands of mornings under that same sun and trudged for as many thousands of days under the same sky, always feeling out of place. That land—its beasts and plants—had fed him for such a long time that it had become, in a strict sense, part of his body. If Lorimer was right, the vastness around him was now his flesh. And yet, nothing—not the countless footsteps taken or knowledge acquired, not the adversaries bested or the friends made, not the love felt or the blood shed—had made it his. Except for his brother, there was little he missed

about his Swedish childhood, but sometimes he thought that that brief
period (which, compared to the long and eventful years that had followed it, was so short that he had yielded to the illusion of believing that
he could remember every single day spent at the farm since he was old
enough to be aware of his surroundings) was like a pinhole in the unend-
ing expanse, and everything—the plains, the mountains, the cañons, the
salt flats, the forests—had drained down through it. Immense as they
were, those territories had never held him or embraced him—not even
when he dug into the ground and found shelter in the earth's bosom.
Anyone he met, including children, had, in his eyes, more right to be in
that land than he did. Nothing was his; nothing claimed him. He had gone
into the wilderness with the intention of coming out on the other end.
That he had stopped trying did not mean that this was now his place.

For the first few weeks, he kept up his habit of avoiding people. It
was easy to stay clear from the few houses and hamlets he spotted in
the distance, and in those tracts, where robbers and vandals presumably abounded, he, a shy stranger minding his own business, was invariably left alone. Still, there were strange indications of human presence
in those regions. One morning, he found himself facing a line of tall
poles. They were about twenty paces from one another, strung together
with a cable tied at the very top. Some birds perched on the black rope.
The line was long enough to bend with the surface of the earth in both
directions, shrink, and vanish. He felt an unaccountable kind of apprehension riding under the cable, as if he had crossed the border into an
unimaginable territory.

Once close to the sea, he turned north. The scattered hamlets became
neighboring villages and even towns. Riding around them undisturbed was
not too hard, but it became difficult to evade wranglers with their cattle,
farmers with their produce, and merchants with their goods. Normally
a tip of the hat was sufficient. But traveling on, a new obstacle put him

face-to-face with strangers—fences. He had barely seen them in America before, and only around houses. Now they sliced through the plains in every direction. Some railings were long enough to divide the horizon in two. A few times, it took him a couple of days to find his way around them. Long or short, these detours inevitably led to a brief exchange with some laborer leaning on a wooden post. During his first conversation, he could barely utter a word. He could not hear anything over the inner rumble of fear, and his face refused to do what it should. But that day, Håkan made a great discovery: it did not matter. Most men were as laconic as himself, and the rest were too eager to tell their own stories to listen to anybody else. Whether Håkan spoke or not—whether he even seemed engaged at all or not—had almost no effect on others. Still, he never dismounted during these conversations, convinced that once on his feet, his height would become apparent. That aside, there was not much else to do. When greeted, greet back; when spoken to, look down; for most questions, a vague grunt. Throughout the following days, he asked a few of these cattlemen about Clangston. The first ones he spoke to had never heard of the place, but farther up north, most people knew about it. The mining town, they called it. He was headed the right way, they said.

Ever since those five men had come to the burrow, Håkan had been surprised to discover that almost everybody out west was young. Perhaps this had always been the case, and he had failed to notice it when he was young himself. But now he seldom saw anyone his age. The vigorous men he encountered seemed to acknowledge his years with a respectful bow of the head. Taking advantage of this, Håkan made himself look older, weaker, and smaller by slouching and shrugging on the saddle. His bepatched attire added to the character. Sometimes, when spoken to, he pretended not to hear. With each new performance, he perfected his role. He started to droop his head and squint from underneath his calculatedly furrowed brow, barely visible behind the long strands of hair that, with great deliberation, concealed his face. His voice became a trembling, creaky mumble. He knew it was his imagination, but it seemed to him that his yellow draft horse was playing along with his character, looking down and sighing despondently each time they stopped. The orange mane even poured over his forehead—like Håkan's hair over his—when, with dejected apathy, he reached for a blade of grass. The more Håkan played the role of the infirm, the more he enjoyed it. Not only because he felt safe in the disguise of his shriveled and shrunken body, but also because he found an immense and unexpected pleasure in deception. Falsehood was a new experience for him. During those days, he realized that, except for the incident with the tincture and the quail stew, he had never lied or betrayed anyone's confidence. He did not think this was because he had been an exceptionally virtuous man. It was just the way things had turned out.

Farther up north, the black soil turned into pale dust, the fences vanished, and the country went back to its own kind of order—an organization that Håkan never understood but always revered. He slept in one of his portable leather shelters and ate only a few pieces of charqui a day. The impulse to trap, skin, and tan was almost impossible to repress. Those tasks had defined his life for so many years, and he barely knew what to do without the daily contact with those small bodies and the surprise of their anatomies freed from fur. But he abstained. He wanted to keep his clothes clean and would rather not look and smell like a trapper with his musky spoils hanging off his saddle. Just a poor old homesteader on his workhorse.

One afternoon, as he reached the top of a hill, he saw a road penciled in the distance. Horsemen and wagons in puffs of dust. Even coaches. According to the last man he had spoken to, the road had to lead to Clangston. Håkan turned around and looked at the desert. He would never see it again.

23.

He rode into Clangston at dusk, making himself more decrepit and smaller than ever. Gothenburg, Portsmouth, San Francisco, and the sheriff's town were the only cities he had ever set foot in. Having spent only a few moments in each of them, he had no accurate notion of their size, but Clangston was infinitely busier than all of them. For a while, he sat on his horse amid the tumult and the din, stunned. Then, at a foot pace, he rode into town. Wagons and carts overloaded with clanging wares rushed by, their drivers jerking the reins, vociferating, and insulting their own horses and distracted passersby alike. They hurled imprecations at him for riding so slowly and erratically, and someone even lashed him on the shoulder. People of all sorts walked briskly up and down the streets. Workers with shovels and pickaxes, ladies in the finest dresses imaginable, boys on errands, youths on arrogant horses, crews of Chinese miners, gentlemen in coats shinier than any of the ladies' dresses, men with hungry eyes and slipshod shoes, waiters with trays full of food and drink, tight packs of sternly dressed and heavily armed couriers carrying boxes and briefcases. And every foot—covered in patent leather or rugged buckskin, resting on the thinnest soles or the highest heels, wrapped with rags and twine or laces and buckles—had to tread on the black, brown, and red slime that covered the street from threshold to threshold like a stagnant river of mud, excrement, and rotting food. But the sludge did not slow anyone down. Even the numerous drunkards and beggars seemed to be in a hurry, stumbling from one side of the street to the other with pointless resolution or, with businesslike expeditiousness, soliciting money and food from strangers. In dusky public houses, drinking was not a matter of leisure but either an excuse to conduct various transactions or an activity undertaken with the utmost rigor and dedication. Around green tables, cards were dealt, received, and played with brisk earnestness. Wild melodies coming from unseen instruments whose sounds Håkan did not recognize clashed against each other like simultaneous arguments in different languages. Behind a window, pink faces were being shaved. Grown men with boyishly naked cheeks. Mustaches, whiskers, oddly shaped beards, hair so sleek it seemed combed with honey. Women dangled under spires of curls and ringlets. Abstracted and disdainful, these ladies paid more attention to their ruffled hems hovering over the slime than to the constant brawls around them. On a threshold, by a wagon, under a billboard, at a counter, someone was being yelled at, shoved, punched, or kicked. Some fights were broken up; others were encouraged by loose circles of onlookers. Luxurious carriages drove by, pulled by teams of four and even six horses. Floating on their subtle springs and braces, the ornate cabs seemed to be bobbing on placid waters instead of rolling through the muck—at least until they got to a street corner, where, invariably, there was another carriage or wagon wanting to cross or turn, resulting in a turbulence of horses nervously neighing and huffing while the coachmen screamed and cracked their whips in the air. Inside, the women, with calculated indifference, looked ahead. Would the lady who had held Håkan captive still be alive? Where was her inn? He looked right and left, trying to find that single block with no opposing sidewalk that had been the beginning of Clangston, but there were so many buildings and so many streets. All constructions, from stables to taverns, looked new but also worn by constant activity. There were many elaborate houses, some of which reminded him of the ornate dresser he had found in the desert years ago. Almost every building was some sort of shop. Many sold goods, while others were simply full of rows and rows of desks at which groomed clerks in shirtsleeves toiled away on large sheets of paper. Despite stillness reigning in these places, it was plain that the anxiety and the strain of those scriveners bent over their ledgers exceeded that of any man yelling or fighting on a corner. All the stores were busy. In bright, hectic showrooms, customers examined each piece of merchandise with expert eyes, gravely compared different items presented by aproned salesmen, haggled, bought things by the dozen. Sacks, casks, and boxes were brought out from backrooms and placed on shelves and counters. Fabric was rolled up into soft pillars. Wires and ropes of different kinds were spooled into massive wheels. Bundles were opened, their contents displayed, inspected, and sealed up again. Confections and fruits glistened in their glass cabinets and domes. Scores upon scores of packages were ceaselessly being wrapped in brown paper and tied with sisal string. Money changed hands. Gold in different forms—coins, small ingots, nuggets, dust. There was also some paper money. The commercial frenzy overflowed the confines of the stores and poured out on the streets in the form of stalls and stands with wares of every sort. And beyond these makeshift displays thrived yet another, smaller, form of trade. With shrill, hoarse cries, peddlers, street traders, and merchants with boxes strapped to their torsos walked around advertising their products. The ones without boxes were preachers, and there was a great profusion of them.

Noticing that the sun had set but that the streets had not darkened, Håkan realized that they were lit by lamps whose blue-and-yellow flames were distorted and multiplied by wavy glass panels. Together with the glow coming from stores, bars, and offices, the streetlamps created a constant twilight. Håkan found this nightlessness disturbing. He was also getting tired and could not imagine where he would be able to sleep. Men and women in rags lay in foul alleyways, but even if the reek and the proximity of other bodies had not repelled him, he could not leave his horse unattended. There was also the risk of being recognized and captured in his sleep. Turning back, however, was unthinkable, so Håkan decided to traverse the city and rest once he could pitch camp out in the wilderness. Under a streetlamp, a man with a harnessed wheelbarrow (which reminded Håkan of the contraption he had designed and pulled for the Brennans) was setting up shop. He put a cloth with some words sewn onto it over the pushcart and then proceeded to line up a long series of bottles and jars.

"Ladies and gentlemen, ladies and gentlemen!" he cried. "A physic for every condition, a tonic for each malady. Every distemper has its cure, ladies and gentlemen. And I have all the remedies right here. Blisters, blemishes, blackheads? This unguent here will soothe your skin while eradicating the most inveterate corruptions. Catarrh, cough, congestion? This syrup here removes all manner of disorders from your air passages. Complaints of the stomach? Is it, perhaps, your fluids or your bowels? Dropsy, dyspepsia, diarrhea? My apologies, ladies. Forgive my language, but the flesh is a vile thing. Is it, more gallantly put, your digestion? You will never believe what marvels two or three drops of this powerful patent preparation here can work. Instant relief! Weak, weary, wan? You can't go on. You've had enough. Waking up is a struggle. The smallest chore is a tiring titanic travail. Even pleasure is a burden. Here. Here is the cure. In this bottle. The rejuvenator! The one, the only, the original rejuvenator. A cordial made of herbs gathered by an Indian doctor, combined with the latest discoveries made by European chemical practitioners. Contains critical corporal nutriments and vital essences that impart to all humors their restorative principle. Life! Feel it return! The vitality, the vim, the vigor! And even if you're healthy, try my specific for that extra zing, zip, and zest!"

A small group of people had gathered around the wheelbarrow. Håkan was enraptured. For years, he had wondered what sort of progress the medical sciences might have made. Had anatomy and physiology discovered new relations between organs and their functions? Had Lorimer's theories been proven correct and spread throughout the world? Could new findings have surpassed them?

"Bone setters, ladies and gentlemen, are creatures of the past. Stiff joints? Beset by bothersome backaches? Do you feel the weather in your hips? Magnetism," he whispered as he produced a metal rod the size of his palm. "A Frenchman has discovered how to use this invigorating magnetic cylinder here to reverse the flow of energy and turn pain into well-being, and sickness into health. And it is made of iron, the single, solitary source of all vitalizing substances."

This was the third man of science Håkan had met in his life. With Lorimer, truth had been an immediate, clear feeling. Reason came later and validated it, but at first, it had been an almost physical experience, like waking up from a vivid dream. His second encounter with science had been through the short-haired Indian. Here, again, the evidence of his talent left no room for doubt. His understanding of the human body and how to mend it, his reliable drugs and salves, his almost infallible method of preventing infections, and even his soft and caring touch gave him an authority matched only by the power of nature. But this man, at his pushcart, with his tonics and magnets, was a fool and a liar. This was as clear to Håkan as the genius of the other two men had been.

"But why talk of iron when we can talk about gold? Yes, gold, ladies and gentlemen. We all want it. We all do. But when you get it (for you will, yes sir, you will), how will you know that what you got is, in fact, gold? Eh? Not all that glitters, ladies and gentlemen. Fake gold is everywhere. A plague! The cure? This detecting liquid here. Watch this matchless miraculous mixture react to the fake stuff."

Håkan turned away and left.

Shops were closing down, and people now congregated in taverns and inns. The throngs were so thick that it was almost impossible to see what was going on inside each establishment. The music had become livelier. In some places, the patrons sang along. At the door of a saloon or at the entrance to a hotel, the multitude opened to swallow or expel powdered women in shimmering dresses and their long-tailed, top-hatted escorts. The scent of unfamiliar dishes sometimes managed to overpower the stench wafting up from the mud.

As his draft horse plodded along, dragging his shaggy hooves in the mire, the lights grew dimmer and the fights louder. No carriages rolled through this part of town. Eventually, the streetlamps disappeared, replaced by sporadic fires on the side of the road. Houses and taverns no longer glowed with chandeliers but were only spotted with the tawny glimmer of oil lamps hanging here and there. In the quivering darkness, there was drinking, gambling, singing, and quarreling. The report of not-so-distant guns was disregarded. Nobody seemed to care about what happened beyond their narrow circle of light. As Håkan made his way down the street, each one of these illuminated stains revealed an isolated scene—miners with faces ravaged by dust and defeat; Chinese laborers smoking from thin, sweet pipes; broken women, sad in their seduction; black men trying to remain unseen while enjoying their modest pleasures; a little boy bent over a box, blowing on a pair of dice in his cupped hand; drunks reduced to heaps on stoops, under wagons, in the filth. The eye could reach only a few feet into the dubious gloom, but the ear got a sense of the depth of the city from the distant layers of laughter and brawls. One of these fights sounded so violent that Håkan felt compelled to ride in that direction. He heard women scream. It was a sound he had heard only once before in his life. Was someone helping them? He finally got to the thick crowd that had assembled around the scene and looked over their heads.

Years before, when he feared that he had traveled around the world and was trapped in those vast plains framed by two equally vast deserts, he thought that he was losing his mind—that he was brainsick, adrift in his illness. The light-headed terror he experienced at that time was nothing compared to what he felt now, looking beyond all those heads. Madness would have been a benign justification. Death. That was the only explanation he could find for what he was seeing. At some point, he thought, he must have died. And now he was watching from the other side of life. For a brief moment, that was the only answer he could find.

Over flat-crowned hats, wide brims, bonnets, and towering hairdressings, by a bonfire, Håkan saw a gigantic man wearing a lion skin, his head invisible under the beast's head, holding a gun and a bloody knife.

At his feet lie two slain women in bloodstained dresses. The man is even taller than Håkan. He is panting. Everyone looks on. Nobody intervenes. The giant stands there, facing them, his body still tense with violence. His face is lost in the shade of the hood, but it must have a savage expression. From some indeterminate place, a sheriff and two deputies come in. Shots are fired. No one is hit. Somehow, the sheriff and his men prevail. The giant in the lion skin is captured and dragged out into the darkness.

Out of nowhere, a couple of men rolled out two screens and hid the two women from sight. A man in a bright red suit followed them and, standing in front of the screen, addressed the onlookers.

"We'll be back in an eye blink, my friends. Don't leave your spots. We'll be ready in half a jiffy. How will the Hawk get out of this predicament? A warning: not for the faint of heart. Stay right where you are for the next act. We'll be coming around for contributions."

Håkan shrunk in his saddle and gently touched his horse. As he rode behind the screens, he saw the women changing out of their bloodied clothes, giggling. A youth was putting up a tall wooden cactus made of angular planks painted in a green that was actually blue. The giant sat on a crate drinking from a flask. His lion fur was a grotesque fake, made of patched-up rodent skins and wool. He was wearing stilts.

What Håkan had seen was beyond his understanding. But it was clear that he was far better known than he had ever imagined, and that, rather than muting his story, time had amplified it. His only consolation was that, despite his unwanted notoriety, nobody had recognized him. He was safe in his aged body.

From what he remembered, it would not take him more than three days to get to the mine. The gold, San Francisco, and the sea were not far away. He turned off the road and bivouacked in some discreet spot, building a meager fire.

The following morning, Håkan discovered that Clangston never really ended. Buildings grew more scattered, and there were fewer people walking down the road, but dry goods stores, bars, and other mysterious establishments could still be found here and there, and the traffic in and out of the city was constant.

Just like Clangston never really ended, the mine never really started. At some point, Håkan noticed that almost every flatbed wagon was packed with gangs of chalky men leaning on their pickaxes and shovels. The ground itched with the rumbling of distant explosions. Cracks and holes, many of them framed and supported by beams, interrupted the ochre monotony of the land. Out of nowhere, the heavy heads of iron tools would emerge from the ground in different points only to dive back in immediately. Every blow on the rock was followed by a short, dry echo. When the road turned, it was to follow a narrow river. Håkan could not remember that stream from the Brennan days. Soon it was revealed to be a man-made canal—it flowed in an inflexibly straight course, and some stretches were faced with slabs and boulders. Every few hundred steps, there were open sluice gates guarded by armed sentries. On the other side of the watercourse ran a pair of parallel lines of wooden bars resting on thick planks placed at regular intervals. Håkan was wondering what purpose this construction could serve when a flat-bed wagon, its four grooved wheels fitting perfectly on the wooden bars, whizzed by, powered by two men pushing a beam on a pivot up and down like a seesaw or a pump. Shortly after noon, Håkan saw the end of the road, the stream, and the lines of bars.

Vast, frantic, intricate, terraced, roaring, twisting, the quarry was an insane city for an unknown species. Through this maze ran roads on which debris-filled carts tottered behind miserable beasts. Those pump cars on wooden bars rolled in and out of tunnels with rocks, tools, and men. The sound of metal on stone, like hard raindrops, filled the air. Clouds of smoke blossomed here and there, followed by the roll of an explosion. Under the malignant sun, dusty men walked back and forth along narrow ledges, climbed up and down ladders, and crawled in and out of caves, carrying gear and boulders. Some of them gestured and screamed out their instructions, but no voice was heard beneath the tumult. Armed guards everywhere. At almost all times, there was a minor avalanche somewhere that sent handfuls of little miners running in every direction. This inhuman place, with its filthy pits, abrupt walls, and tiered plateaus descending into the broken earth like a gigantic staircase, extended beyond the reach of the eye. Wherever Brennan's hoard was, it had been swept away like dust.

24.

Nothing left behind in the wilderness could ever be retrieved. Every encounter was final. Nobody came back from beyond the horizon. It was impossible to return to anything or anyone. Whatever was out of sight was forever lost.

The initial disappointment swelled into despair but soon ebbed away, leaving behind a sense of relief. Håkan had never owned anything. Pingo, the only horse that had been rightfully his, had died shortly after being given to him. The tin box with medical instruments, the compass, and the lion coat—those were his sole belongings. What would he have done with the gold? How was gold even used? How much did one give and what could one expect for it? He had handled money only a few times in his life and conducted just a small number of modest commercial transactions ages ago, back when he was on the trail. His heart pounded with anxiety at the mere thought of being involved in the complicated exchanges his plan would have required. Much better, he thought, to end this journey as it had started—with nothing.

He kept traveling west, toward the sea, across the steppe, into the forest, over the mountains, down the valleys, across fields, avoiding roads, shunning travelers and herdsmen, steering clear of the many towns that had popped up everywhere, trapping when he could, eating what he found, and feeling, for the most part, secure, hunching and shrinking on his big horse.

During the following weeks, a sense of exhaustion overcame him, as if his body were catching up with the old man it had been impersonating.

He would nod off on his horse and wake up without knowing how much time had elapsed. On occasion, he would open his eyes to find that he was headed for a barn or a house and had to turn around with a sudden jerk of the reins. More often, the horse would just stop, and it was the stillness that awoke him. Once, he was startled out of his slumber to discover that the horse was standing in front of a pair of lines on wooden blocks, similar to the ones he had seen at the mine. But these bars were made of metal, and they stretched out of sight. He waited for one of those pump wagons to come by. Nothing. Before crossing the lines, Håkan thought the construction looked like a helpless, maimed bridge.

He passed a yellow church, the first he had seen in years. It was run down—maybe even derelict—but it was easy to see from the moldings, carvings, and statues that it had once aspired to grandeur. Not too far from the church, at the foot of a hill, he ran into a strange orchard of sorts. What at first appeared to be little trees turned out to be small but stern-looking bushes whose main branches were contorted into tortured positions around sticks, to which they were tied with strings. In the shade of their own leaves, each one of these stunted bushes bore clusters of a fleshy kind of berry Håkan had never seen before. Hundreds of these shrubs were planted at regular intervals, rather close to one another, in straight lines separated by the exact same distance. There was something punitive and angry about this method. As he rode on, down where the rows of shrubs presumably ended, a large house with turrets took shape. A few smaller buildings surrounded it. It was Håkan's idea of a castle. Not too far away, he spotted some laborers working on the bushes. He was about to turn away, as he always did at the first sight of people, when he heard a child crying. His first thought, a mere flash, was that it was, in fact, a lion cub wailing. Another kitten, he thought. Immediately, common sense rectified this impression, and he started looking for the child. He found it a few rows down, muddy with dirt and snot, bawling in a somewhat abstracted fashion while staring at the string of its own saliva driveling onto the ground. When the child saw the orange horse and the rider, its crying subsided, yielding to curiosity. Håkan did not know whether it was a boy or a girl.

"Are you lost?"

The child stared up at him, with those hiccups that often follow weeping. Håkan looked around. The workers had not seen him—or had ignored him.

"Do you live in the big house?"

Håkan thought the child nodded. Either way, the castle with its adjacent buildings was the only house around. Perhaps he could leave the girl (without knowing why, he had decided that it was a girl) with one of the workers and be on his way. He dismounted and very gently picked up the child and sat her on the saddle. To keep her distracted, he gave her a stuffed fox paw, which she found endlessly fascinating. Slowly, he walked the horse toward the house. As he got closer, the laborers dropped whatever they were doing and stared at him, the horse, and the child. Håkan, in turn, noticed that they were Indians. They wore only white clothes, which were, in every case, spotless, even if they were all working with shovels, pruning shears, and hoes, and handling those dark berries. He locked eyes with a young woman. He stopped the horse and then nodded toward the child and the house. The woman nodded yes. With a gesture, Håkan conveyed that he was going to pick up the girl and hand her over to the woman. She recoiled and looked down. Håkan turned to the rest of the workers, who also dropped their heads and avoided all contact. The little girl played with her fox paw. He would leave her in some safe spot, close to the house, from which she would surely be seen, and turn around without having to engage with any of its occupants.

As he reached the front garden, full of vibrant, strange flowers and hedges pruned into straight walls, a lady in a lavender dress came running out of the house, screaming in a language Håkan did not recognize. She rushed toward the girl, picked her up, gently scolded her, wiped her face clean with a handkerchief she produced from her sleeve, and covered her with kisses. Noticing the fox paw, she asked the girl something. She pointed at Håkan.

"Oh dear. Pardon me," she said with a thick foreign accent. "The excitement. You found her, yes?"

Håkan nodded.

"Thank you, sir. She always does this. You don't look and poof, she's gone. All the time. Terrible when the night comes. Ay, ay, ay, ay!" she said, pinching the girl's cheek and kissing her again.

Håkan looked down and raised his hand to indicate he was leaving.

"No, no, no, no," she remonstrated. "We must thank you. Please."

"No, thank you."

"But you look so tired."

"No, thank you."

"Yes, sir. Food and drink."

Just then, a stately man, impeccably dressed in tails and with a perfectly groomed white beard that looked very much like the surrounding garden, walked out the door, down the steps, and toward them. Håkan found it strange that they were probably the same age. Before he was halfway there, the lady had explained to him, in her language, pointing at the girl, the fields, and Håkan, everything that had happened. The man arrived with an outstretched hand.

"Many thanks, sir, for finding my adventurous daughter and bringing her back to safety."

He noticed the fox paw, took it from his daughter's hand, examined it while she whined, and then gave it back to her.

"You made this?"

"Yes."

"Do you like wine?"

"I don't know."

"Well, sir, you're about to find out."

"Edith, please make sure the gentleman gets a glass of claret," the man told the lady as he started to turn back to the house.

"Yes, Captain."

"And some meat," he added, briskly walking away.

"Thank you. I'm leaving," said Håkan. "I must go."

The captain stopped, paused, as if suddenly remembering something, and then turned around.

"Where are you from?" he asked.

Håkan hesitated. Did people know that the Hawk was Swedish? Even if they did, he was unable to lie. He knew nothing about other countries.

"Sweden."

"Ha!" The captain, excited, tapped himself on the forehead and walked back to Håkan. "Jo men visst! Självklart!" he exclaimed, holding Håkan warmly by the shoulders. "Ert å lät så utomordentligt svenskt, förstår ni: I must gå. Ingen här, i Amerika, kan uttala gå just på det viset. Kapten Altenbaum. En ära."

"Håkan." He paused. "Söderström."

"Får jag visa herr Söderström runt på godset? Och jag skulle bli väldigt glad om jag fick bjuda på ett glas vin."

Captain Altenbaum was from Finland but, like most wealthy men in that country, had been raised in Swedish. He gave Edith some instructions and told one of the Indians to feed Håkan's horse. Before it was taken away, Håkan took the bundle with his belongings from the saddle.

"You can leave your things. They'll be safe."

Håkan looked down and clutched his rolled-up lion coat that contained his few possessions. The captain nodded and led him toward a building a few hundred paces away from the main house.

The grounds around the castle were like nothing he had ever seen. The triumph of man over nature was complete. Every plant had been forced into some artificial shape; every animal had been domesticated; every body of water had been contained and redirected. And all around, Indians in white made sure that each blade of grass stayed in place. Captain Altenbaum pointed out every detail. He spoke in Swedish and used many words Håkan did not know. Having heard Swedish only in his head since he had lost Linus—being its only speaker and modeling it after his own thoughts—Håkan found it almost impossible to reconcile those words with the captain's voice and to believe that they could mean anything to anyone other than himself. An additional surprise was that he, Håkan, did not feel more confident or safer speaking in his native tongue. He discovered, now, that his shyness, his vacillation, his preference for silence had nothing to do with language. He was the same in Swedish. This quiet, hesitant being was simply who he was or had become.

As they moved away from the main house, the greenery regained some of its wildness, and the place gradually started looking like an ordinary working farm. Still, there were few animals (probably just enough to support the household), and most activities had to do with the long rows of tormented shrubs.

"My vines," the captain said, sweeping the fields with his upturned palm. "But more about that later. First you. Tell me, please, Mr. Söderström, what are you doing so far away from home? Gold?"

Håkan shook his head. A long pause. He had never told his story in Swedish.

"I was going to New York. I got on the wrong boat. I lost my brother. Since then." Håkan finished the sentence by gesturing toward the world around them. "I've been. I've been."

During the ensuing silence, as he considered Håkan's few words and the restrained despair that leaked through the silence between them, the captain's brow darkened, affected by his visitor's plight.

"I must leave," Håkan said at last.

"But you just got here."

"No. This country. I must go away."

"Well, Mr. Söderström, I may just be able to help. But not if you refuse my claret again."

They went into the most unassuming building on the premises. The structure was revealed to be the entrance to a long staircase. With each step down, the temperature and the light decreased. At the end of the stairwell, a corridor led them to a vast, dim cellar—the biggest indoor space Håkan had ever seen. It was full of barrels lying horizontally on wooden cradles in neat rows that faded into the dark. The walls were covered with labeled bottles. They sat at a table in a corner. Captain Altenbaum uncorked one of the barrels and, with an oversized pipette, drew some of the black content, which he poured into two stemmed glasses.

"Your first glass of wine, then."

Håkan nodded.

"I am honored that it is my wine and that I am the one pouring it for you. I hope you like it."

They looked into their glasses. The black liquid dawned into light crimson toward the surface. Håkan took a small sip. It made his tongue dry and harsh, like a cat's. It tasted of unknown fruit, salt, wood, and warmth.

"What do you think?"

Håkan nodded.

"Oh, wonderful. I'm glad."

The captain swirled the wine into a vortex, stuck his nose into his glass, closed his eyes, inhaled deeply, and then took a sip, which he held in his mouth for a while, moving it around like a bite of scalding food, and then swallowed. He opened his eyes, and his face, relaxed with pleasure as he was drinking, wrinkled into a thoughtful expression.

"How long have you been in America?"

"I don't know."

From under his brow, Håkan looked at the barrels and then back down. He wanted to look at the ceiling. Instead, his eyes fell on his hands, which appeared to him like articles someone else had placed on the table. He put them on his lap, out of sight. Now that he had tasted the wine, he could smell its sugary presence all over the cellar.

"A long time?" the captain insisted gently.

"Almost all my life. I was a boy when I left."

"You lost your brother. Do you have any other family here? Friends?"

Håkan shook his head.

"Where in America have you been?"

"I don't know."

"You don't know?"

"I arrived in San Francisco. I've been to Clangston. Twice. Then another city. But that was just for a few days. All these years, I've been traveling. The desert, mountains, the plains. I don't know what those places are called."

"How did you live? What kind of work have you done here?"

"I've been. Traveling east, to find my brother. I couldn't. Then I stopped."

The captain repeated the swirling, the sniffing, and the sipping.

"Trouble?"

Håkan nodded.

The captain nodded.

"Well, whatever it was, it must have been a long time ago. We're both old, after all."

Both men stared at the table.

"I make this wine now. The best in America," Captain Altenbaum said, addressing the wine in his glass more than Håkan. "But I used to be a fur trader. That's how I paid for all of this. Furs." After a pause, the captain looked up and across the table. "That paw you gave Sarah. Remarkable. I took a quick look, but I noticed that you stretched it open to tan it. Exceptional tanning, by the way. The soft yet lifelike feel. I wonder how you did it. Very rare. Then you stuffed it and stitched it back. With sinew! Visible only to an expert eye. Extraordinary. Extraordinary work."

Håkan looked down.

"With your talent, I could find you work. Quiet work. You could even live here, if you like. We'd be neighbors of a sort."

Hoping the captain would be staring into his glass, Håkan looked up, but as he met the fur trader's kind eyes, he lowered his head.

"May I look at that rolled-up fur you have there?" the captain asked.

Håkan looked at the bundle next to his chair but did not move.

"Please. I noticed how many kinds of skin you've used. It seems so unusual. Just to satisfy the curiosity of a fellow trapper. Please."

Slowly, Håkan got off of his chair, crouched down next to it, undid some leather straps, removed the tin box and the few other things kept inside the bundle, and then, little by little, as he let the coat unfurl, gave up his humped and bowed posture and drew himself up to his full height.

The captain stood up, leaving his fingertips on the table, as if that slight contact with a familiar object could keep him anchored to reality, while he stared ahead, gaping in disbelief. His eyes trembled as they traveled over the coat and then up to Håkan's face.

They stood there, in silence.

Captain Altenbaum finally sat down and filled his glass. Håkan's had remained untouched since his first sip.

"I can see how much you learned through the years. You've become a master. And all those animals. From everywhere. Of every kind. Even reptiles." A brief silence. "And that lion."

What Håkan saw in the captain's eyes as he uttered those last words made him roll up the coat and glance toward the staircase.

"Please sit down. Please."

Hesitating, Håkan sat down on the edge of the chair. He was about to shrivel back into his decrepit pose but stopped himself.

"Are those your instruments?"

Håkan nodded.

"May I?"

Håkan slid the box across the table, and the captain, gently, with the utmost respect, opened it and looked in without touching anything.

"Incredible." He paused, passed the box back, and drank—this time, without ceremony. He sighed and seemed to be absorbed by a stain on the table that he was scratching off with his fingernail. "I have a child," he said at last. His voice was serious but very calm—even sweet.

Håkan got up.

"Wait. Please. Whatever happened to you." The captain failed to find the right words. "Whatever you've done, I can tell that your life has been hard enough already. I've heard all the stories, but I don't know what the truth is. You may have been a bad man once. I don't know. But what I see now is a tired old man who has been traveling without rest and needs to end his journey in peace."

Håkan could not look at him.

"Like I said," the captain resumed in a more composed tone. "I used to be a fur trader. My shipping company now has a vast fleet. Have you heard of Alaska?"

Håkan did not respond.

"It's a new territory. Not new to me—that's where I made my fortune. But it's a new territory for the Union. You would like it there.
Nobody around. Good trapping. It can look like Sweden. I can get you
there safely."

Later, in the main house, the captain showed Håkan Alaska on a globe.
He pointed out the different stations and outposts his company had
along the coast and discussed the virtues of each one of them.

"I have fur trading posts here." The captain showed him three or
four patches of coast. "Some salteries and canneries here and here. Small
mines here. And we get ice from here and here. Whichever spot you
choose, you can be sure that you will be left alone. And that game will
be abundant."

Then, in passing, the captain pointed out how close Alaska was to
Russia, how the two lands were separated by a narrow strait, and traced
a line with his finger across that immense country that went straight to
Finland and then Sweden.

"Just the place for you," Captain Altenbaum said, bringing his finger back to Alaska.

Håkan, who had never seen a globe before, walked around it, trying
to track his long journey and seeing how all those lands came together
in a circle.

A bleak glow was washing away the stars. The black sky and the white expanse hesitated for a moment before merging into one boundless gray space. Now and again, the groan of the icebound hull, the snap of slack canvas, or the crack of a fracturing floe revealed the scale of the silence.

They had kept the fire going through most of the night but had run out of fuel some time ago. Even so, none of those who were still gathered around the dimming embers had moved. The fringes of their circle were littered with oily tins, food scraps, burned tobacco, and empty bottles. Nobody looked up, except for the boy, whose eyes were fixed on Håkan's face.

Throughout the long night that was now coming to an end, Håkan had spoken in his soft, vacillating voice. No one had interrupted him; no one had asked questions. He had often made long pauses. Sometimes he had seemed to nod off. During these prolonged silences, the men would exchange confused looks, wondering if the story had concluded. A few prospectors and sailors even got up and left. But no matter how absent Håkan was during these pauses—however long they were—after opening his eyes and stroking his beard, he always continued, in his hesitant way but as if he had never stopped, with his narrative. This time, however, after telling how he had traveled to San Francisco with Captain Altenbaum's help and then boarded the Impeccable, one of the many ships in his fleet, Håkan stood up. His listeners pretended to arrange their coats and their few belongings scattered around them. The boy kept staring at him.

There was activity below and on deck. Someone shouted brief orders across the ship; a few seamen rushed by with poles, sledgehammers, pickaxes, hooks, and coils of rope. When it became clear that they were getting ready to climb off the schooner, several passengers and the rest of the crew clustered on the starboard rail to watch.

Almost tiptoeing, as if somehow that would make them lighter, five men made their way on the ice with their gear. The snow soaked up every sound. They seemed to be trudging through a dream. Some fifty yards out, the frozen surface cracked under one of the sailors, and he vanished in a turmoil of black and white water. The screams attracted more spectators to the railings. The sailor's unconscious body was hooked out of the hole and hoisted on board with a rope.

Moments later, a bell rang. Flanked by his officers, Captain Whistler stood by the foremast, holding a speaking trumpet. This device amplified his voice but also his irresolution. He announced that the ice was breaking up and that they might be able to resume their course soon. They could speed up their release by blowing up the thickest section, a hundred yards or so away from the bow of the ship. He called for volunteers. The captain looked at the sky and fidgeted with his watch during the ensuing stillness. Håkan broke away from the rest of the men and took a few steps forward, in the direction of the foremast. The boy joined him. So did the officers and, lastly, the captain himself.

It took them most of the day to prepare for their short expedition. After the earlier incident, Captain Whistler took every precaution. He equipped the company with life preservers, planks, and cables so they could set up small stations at regular intervals, and he rigged a pulley system on the deck to drag all the men out at once, should the ice completely collapse. One of the aft rowboats was lowered halfway.

In the afternoon, the small party walked out to set the charges. The men were roped to one another for the march—and all of them were tied to the pulley on the ship. Håkan led the way. From afar, they looked like a group of children on a walk with their father.

Soon, they were at work with their tools. Everyone deferred to Håkan when it came to dealing with the ice—where it was safe to stand, where the explosives would be more effective, how to plan their return. They drilled holes for the charges, and one of the officers readied the fuse. The detonation was a mere cough in the void. The ice, however, cracked in every direction around each blast, and the men had to make their way back to the ship jumping from floe to floe.

Once aboard, Whistler proclaimed, with an unusually steady voice, that the expedition had been a success. He could not make any promises, but they might be able to push through the loose sheets of ice and be on their way as soon as the wind picked up.

There was a festive mood on the Impeccable. As they went through their equipment, which they expected to be using soon, the prospectors shared their plans and hopes with one another. On the bridge, the captain and his men laughed over steaming mugs. For the first time, the man from the San Francisco Cooling Company condescended to mingle with trappers and ordinary seamen. As the day drew to an end, right before the early sunset, the sky cleared up.

For most of the afternoon, the boy, enjoying the new status he had acquired after volunteering for the blasting team, was carried away by the cheery atmosphere and his shipmates' tales of imminent wealth and fame. When he suddenly remembered Håkan, he could not find him. He thought that he might be taking an ice bath and spent a good while scanning the new breaks and holes in the ice in front of the ship. In the end, the boy found him in a nook below deck, squatting over his few effects. Like everyone else, he seemed to be getting ready to land. He got up when he noticed he was being watched.

"Can I come with you?" the boy asked. "When we anchor in Alaska, can I come with you?"

"I am not going to Alaska," Håkan said, as he brushed by the boy and got out on deck.

The sun was low and red. Unlike the previous evening, land and sky were now split by the horizon. The men had started drinking. They were playing dice within a circle they had formed, crouching down around some chips and coins. Expectant silences were followed by loud cheers. Standing outside the ring, the officers looked on, smiling.

Håkan walked toward the quarterdeck, away from the gamblers. The boy caught up with him. They were alone in that part of the ship. Håkan felt the boy's presence behind him, paused, glanced over his shoulder, and then kept walking sternward, all the way to the last port-side cleat. Once he got there, he threw his bundle overboard.

"Wait," the boy cried. "Where are you going?"

"West," said Håkan.

The boy looked confused.

"What west?"

"Now, I may be able to walk over the sea. Otherwise, next winter. Then, a straight line west. To Sweden."

Perplexed, the boy turned to the solitary expanse. He seemed disoriented by the horizontal vastness—indefinite and bare, like another sky under the sky. When he looked back, Håkan was already straddling the ice-lacquered railing. The boy approached him, wanting to say something. Without pausing or looking back, Håkan started his descent.

A moment later, the boy, leaning over the deck, saw the colossal man pick up his bundle and stare at the icy extension ahead. Spindrift smudged the horizon. Although the wind had not reached him yet, Håkan fitted the lion hood over his head. The sky purpled behind plumes of snow blown up from the ground. He looked at his feet, then up again, and set off into the whiteness, toward the sinking sun.

© Jason Fulford

Hernan Diaz is the Pulitzer Prize–winning and *New York Times* best-selling author of *Trust*. His first novel, *In the Distance*, was a finalist for the Pulitzer Prize and the PEN/Faulkner Award for Fiction, and it won the William Saroyan International Prize for Writing. *Trust* was translated into more than thirty languages, received the Kirkus Prize, was longlisted for the Booker Prize, and was named one of the 10 Best Books of the Year by *The New York Times*, *The Washington Post*, NPR, and *Time* magazine, and it was one of *The New Yorker*'s 12 Essential Reads of the Year and one of Barack Obama's favorite books of the year. His work has appeared in *The Paris Review*, *Granta*, *The Atlantic*, *Harper's Magazine*, McSweeney's, and elsewhere. He has received the John Updike Award from the American Academy of Arts and Letters, a Guggenheim Fellowship, a Whiting Award, and a fellowship from the New York Public Library's Cullman Center for Scholars and Writers.

Winner of the Pulitzer Prize for Fiction

A *NEW YORK TIMES* BESTSELLER

#1 NATIONAL BESTSELLER

THE NEW YORK TIMES
10 BEST BOOKS OF THE YEAR

THE WASHINGTON POST
10 BEST BOOKS OF THE YEAR

BARACK OBAMA'S
FAVORITE BOOKS OF THE YEAR

THE NEW YORKER
12 ESSENTIAL READS OF THE YEAR

TIME
10 BEST BOOKS OF THE YEAR

WINNER OF THE
KIRKUS PRIZE

LONGLISTED FOR THE
BOOKER PRIZE